Also by Portia MacIntosh

Off The Record
Love On Tour
Always the Bridesmaid
Truth or Date
It's Not You, It's Them
The Accidental Honeymoon
Never the Bride
Here Comes the Ex

Marram Bay series
Falling For You
Snow Love Lost
Met Your Match

Praise for Portia MacIntosh

'Smart, funny and always brilliantly entertaining, every book from Portia becomes my new favourite rom-com.'
Shari Low

'I laughed, I cried – I loved it.'
Holly Martin

'The queen of rom-com!'
Rebecca Raisin

'This book made me laugh and kept me turning the pages.'
Mandy Baggot

'A fun, fabulous 5-star rom-com!'
Sandy Barker

'Loved the book, it's everything you expect from the force that is Portia! A must read.'
Rachel Dove

'Fun and witty. Pure escapism!'
Laura Carter

'A heartwarming, fun story, perfect for several hours of pure escapism.'
Jessica Redland

PORTIA MACINTOSH is the bestselling author of over 30 romantic comedy novels. From disastrous dates to destination weddings, Portia's rom-coms are the perfect way to escape from day-to-day life, visiting sunny beaches in the summer and snowy villages at Christmas time. Whether it's southern Italy or the Yorkshire coast, Portia's stories are the holiday you're craving, conveniently packed in between the pages.

Formerly a journalist, Portia has left the city, swapping the music biz for the moors, to live the (not so) quiet life with her husband and her dog in Yorkshire.

Find out more at portiamacintosh.com

Drive Me Crazy

PORTIA MACINTOSH

ONE PLACE. MANY STORIES

HQ
An imprint of HarperCollins*Publishers* Ltd
1 London Bridge Street
London SE1 9GF

www.harpercollins.co.uk

HarperCollins*Publishers*
Macken House, 39/40 Mayor Street Upper,
Dublin 1 D01 C9W8
This edition 2026

1

First published in Great Britain by HQ,
an imprint of HarperCollinsPublishers Ltd 2015

Copyright © Portia MacIntosh 2015

Portia MacIntosh asserts the moral right to be identified as the author of this work.
A catalogue record for this book is available from the British Library.

ISBN: 9780008818852

This novel is entirely a work of fiction. The names, characters and incidents
portrayed in it are the work of the author's imagination. Any resemblance to
actual persons, living or dead, events or localities is entirely coincidental.

All rights reserved. No part of this publication may be reproduced, stored
in a retrieval system, or transmitted, in any form or by any means,
electronic, mechanical, photocopying, recording or otherwise,
without the prior written permission of the publishers.

Without limiting the exclusive rights of any author, contributor or the publisher of this
publication, any unauthorized use of this publication to train
generative artificial intelligence (AI) technologies is expressly prohibited.
HarperCollins also exercise their rights under Article
4(3) of the Digital Single Market Directive 2019/790 and expressly reserve this
publication from the text and data mining exception.

Printed and bound in the UK using 100% Renewable
Electricity by CPI Group (UK) Ltd

For my family

Chapter 1

'We should get up.'

'Just five more minutes,' I plead as I snuggle closer.

'Two more minutes,' he negotiates. 'Someone will be round with the post any minute. Do you want them to see us like this?'

'Let them see,' I gasp. 'I'm too happy to care.'

Of course I'm joking, and Will knows this.

For two peaceful minutes we just cuddle up, naked, in perfect silence. I have my head resting on Will's chest, gazing down at his bare stomach. He's starting to get a bit of a belly, the one a lot of men seem to develop as they approach the big 4-0. Will can't be blamed for 'letting himself go' a little, though. As the managing director of his family's massive haulage company, he works tirelessly to keep the business running smoothly.

I use a finger to trace lines on his body, of where his six-pack used to be. His heart is pounding, but the gentle rise and fall of his chest relaxes me, quickly returning my own heart rate to normal.

I wonder what he's thinking right now. I often wonder what's going through his mind, and how often he thinks about me when we're not together.

'I'm starving,' I say out loud, although I'm pretty sure I only meant to think it.

'You're always starving.' He laughs. 'Sticking to the diet though?'

'Of course,' I lie. I mean, I am sticking to it for the most part, but it's so hard when you have to pass a branch of Millie's Cookies on the way home from work – that temptress still manages to seduce me every now and then.

Conscious of the tummy he's developing, Will is on a health kick at the moment, and knowing how much I love my junk food, he suggested I might like to join him. I suppose I was a few pounds overweight – and maybe this was his tactful way of telling me – so I agreed to do the same. Oh, how I wish I hadn't now.

'OK, fine, I'm getting up,' I say, although I make no attempt to move whatsoever. 'Can I get you a coffee?'

'Please,' he replies, also remaining in position. 'This thing wreaks havoc on my back. It's not very comfortable, is it?'

'Well, it's a desk, not a bed,' I say as I pull myself upright. 'It's not supposed to be comfortable.'

'Maybe we should get a bed for in here. Well, not a bed, that would seem odd.' He laughs as he glances around his office, as though trying to figure out where one could go. 'Maybe a sofa bed?'

'Yeah, maybe,' I reply, unable to fake even a little enthusiasm. He makes it sound like we're a married couple, picking out furniture for our home.

A few more seconds of silence together, me alone with my thoughts and him with his – that is until a knock on the door breaks us from our thoughts. We know the drill.

'Damn,' Will says quietly as he wrestles on his trousers before calling to whoever is behind the door: 'One minute, please.'

'It's locked, right?' I ask as I hurry on my underwear, then my dress.

'Yes, it's locked, but that still makes us look bad.'

This isn't our first moment like this; you think we'd be better at it by now.

'No rush, Mr Starr.' It's Caroline, his secretary. 'Except I've got the post for you, and it's quite heavy.'

'She's not going anywhere,' he whispers to me, panic in his voice.

I exhale deeply. Being romantically involved with your boss

is not all it's cracked up to be, especially when you have to keep your relationship a secret.

Will and his wife, Stephanie, were in love, once upon a time. They got married, had a couple of kids but then, as Will moved through the ranks of the company, eventually reaching the top spot when his dad retired, they just fell out of love and decided to call it a day. The thing is, Will is very much the face of the family business, and despite the company being huge, they really play up the family angle. Now that Will is in charge, they paint him as a good guy, a family man, so leaving his wife and two young kids simply because he didn't want to be with his wife any more would not have painted a pretty picture. And in a way Will was lucky that Stephanie agreed to pretend they were still together, to keep up appearances, and to keep Will's/the firm's wholesome reputation intact. So, despite Will and Stephanie's understanding, divorce isn't on the cards any time soon, and if Will were to be caught sleeping with his assistant, it would ruin him. So it isn't exactly unusual for us to sneak around and keep our relationship a secret.

'You're going to have to hide,' he snaps at me in a whisper – like this is *my* fault.

'Hide?' I ask in disbelief. I've never had to hide before. 'Where?'

'Under the desk,' he instructs, pushing me under the large, oak desk in the centre of his office.

'You're effing kidding me?' I ask, and Will shoots me a look – I know that he doesn't approve of swearing, but I thought that might be OK given the circumstances. I can tell from the look in his eyes that he is dead serious. 'Fine.'

Down I go, underneath his desk. I watch as Will straightens up his tie before brushing his suit down, exhaling deeply as he heads for the door. I am just about to tuck myself away when I realise that I forgot to put my stockings back on. I spy one of them on the floor, and it's within arm's reach so I grab it. No sign of the other one, but there's nothing I can do. Will is opening the door.

'Good morning, Caroline,' he says breathlessly. 'I thought you were at the doctor's this morning?'

'I was,' she replies. 'I've been, all is well. I know I took the morning off, but I thought there's no sense in waiting until the afternoon to come in – may as well make myself useful. I see Candice is running late.' Caroline sighs. 'Ah well, best she has a lie-in. I think that one is getting a lot of late nights at the moment.'

I can only see Caroline's feet, but I feel my eyes narrow as I shoot them a death stare.

Sweet Caroline (that's what I call her – because she isn't) may just be an evil genius, and were I not the target of her evil master plan to oust me from the company, I might actually be impressed by the way she operates. You see, Sweet Caroline is nothing but sweetness and light to me – in front of other people. Sometimes, I even hear her saying nice things about me to other people, making caring excuses for any mistakes I might make, or excusing my lateness for me like she did today (by making it sound like I'm out partying every night). This means that, to everyone else at the firm, Caroline *is* Sweet Caroline, but when it's just me and her she is horrible to me, and because I know her niceness is an act I cannot be nice back to her, or be nice about her to others. This leaves everyone else wondering why I don't like Caroline, because she's just *so* nice to everyone, and speaks *so* highly of me… I'm telling you, she's an evil genius.

There aren't too many female employees here, but Caroline is certainly the queen bee. As female employees come and go, she takes them all under her wing (everyone but me, who she took an instant disliking to) and I'm guessing she drips poison in the ears of them all, because none of the women seem to like me. Thankfully, I always have Will on my side.

'You look warm,' she observes, not suspiciously as far as I can tell, just curiously.

'Yeah, I was just getting a bit of exercise in,' he tells her, before laughing it off. 'Getting a bit portly in my old age.'

Oh, that was fast thinking. I'd probably be impressed were I not so incredibly mortified right now.

'I just bumped into Stephanie,' I hear Caroline say.

'What, she's here?' Will replies.

'No, no. I saw her at the doctor's – how is she doing? She looked a little peaky.'

'She's fine, she's fine,' Will babbles, instantly arousing my curiosity. I get that Will is sticking around for his kids, and because it's a smart business move, but it never occurred to me that he might be staying around for other reasons – is his wife ill? I mentally pinch myself as Will and Caroline chat about work stuff. It's this silly situation; it makes me paranoid and needy and feel just plain bad about myself. I know that we're not doing anything wrong and that it's only a matter of time before we can be together properly – Will assures me every day – but on days like today, when I'm hiding underneath a desk clutching one of my stockings, it doesn't feel like I'm not doing anything wrong. I feel very much like the 'other woman' that I am most certainly not.

As Will and Sweet Caroline chat, I watch them from my hiding place – well, I watch them from the knees down, like the opening sequence of *The Bill* circa 1985. That's when I notice my other stocking, caught on the heel of Caroline's shoe.

I slowly peep out from under the desk, in an attempt to quickly grab the offending hosiery before it can be spotted. I pull it, but it's not budging. It's well and truly caught on her heel. I give it a hard yank and it finally comes loose, but Will spots me out of the corner of his eye.

'Come here,' Will instructs Caroline, pulling her close for a hug. 'I'm glad you got on OK at the doctor's.'

'Oh, thank you,' Caroline replies brightly. I quickly crawl back underneath the desk and Will finally releases her and she leaves.

With the door closed, Will locks it before leaning back against the wall and breathing a sigh of relief so huge, I practically feel my hair blow in the breeze.

'That was a close one,' Will says.

'Yep,' I reply, scooching out from underneath the desk. I feel deflated at having to hide, but I do my best to remain positive.

'You want to be careful hugging Caroline like that.' I laugh brightly. 'She'll have you for sexual harassment.'

'Candice, that's not funny,' my lover ticks me off. 'That was too close. Way too close. And when she mentioned Steph, I thought she might be here.'

'Is Stephanie OK?' I ask, curiosity getting the better of me.

'Yes,' Will replies quickly, 'why do you ask?'

'Just that Caroline said she'd seen her at the doctor's… I was just checking.'

I smile sweetly, hoping that if my face looks happy then my mood will follow. The truth is, I'm starting to grow tired of our situation. I mentioned this to Will recently and he promised to do something about it.

'Your stomach is looking a little…full today,' Will observes, changing the subject.

'What?' I run my hands over my tummy self-consciously. 'Oh, I ate a bagel yesterday – wheat makes me a bit bloated,' I explain.

'Wheat isn't great for the body,' he reminds me. I know that he's just trying to help me keep healthy and in good shape, but sometimes it feels like criticism and it makes me feel self-conscious.

Will walks over to me and helps me up from the floor.

'Don't be grumpy,' he says, pinching my cheek between two of his fingers as he flashes me a smile. I am weak for him; I wish I wasn't, but I am. 'Everything will be better next week, when we have our little holiday from the world.'

I feel myself defrost almost immediately and my forced smile blends seamlessly into a real one. I cannot wait for my holiday with Will. It's going to be an entire week, just the two of us. We won't need to sneak around or hide, no sex on uncomfortable desks, we can hold hands in public and go out for dinner together – all the little things that couples take for granted. It's going to be pure bliss, and the mere mention of it appeases any doubts I may be having about our relationship. I just want things to be normal, and this holiday is going to be a glimpse of that. Depending on how it goes, I think this will be make or break for us, which just makes me all the more determined to make sure things are perfect.

I examine my stockings before I put them on and realise that the one I yanked from Caroline's shoe is laddered. I toss them in the bin. It'll have to be bare legs today. Thankfully I keep on top of waxing them, or I'd have been in big trouble.

'So, how about that coffee?' he reminds me as he starts tapping away on his laptop. 'And, Candice, maybe put those in a bin somewhere else. And make sure no one sees you leave.'

'Sure,' I reply, grabbing them from the bin before heading for the door. He isn't exactly in my good books after making me hide under his desk, but that combined with the fact he now expects me to reach into the bin…! If we were a normal couple I'd be able to tell him to get his own fucking coffee. I've no choice today, though. He is my boss, after all.

Chapter 2

There are certain things that we, as women, learn not to do. One should not, for example, become romantically involved with any of the following types of men: married men, bosses, control freaks and egomaniacs. We know this. It is instilled in us by every failed relationship we've ever seen play out, every cruel-to-be-kind piece of advice our best friend has offered us, every romcom storyline we've ever watched and every magazine article we've ever read on 'types of men to avoid'.

Despite all of this knowledge, my fella ticks every box on the list. Well, I say 'my fella' but he's not my fella at all, he's his wife's fella. He's *my* boss.

I worked in the sales and marketing department at Starr Haul for a year before Will even noticed me, and our first conversation actually took place when he called me into his office to fire me. The truth was that not only did I hate working for the sales team (haulage, warehousing and distribution – yawn) but I wasn't particularly good at it either, and I think those two factors only made each other worse. Combined with the fact that I was often late, employee of the month I was not, and if I were Will, I probably would've fired me too.

I could tell from the look on his face when he called me into his office that he was going to let me go, but with everyone always banging on about what a kind, generous family man he was, I thought I'd try and appeal to his better nature. I told him about losing my parents, about being alone in the world and barely having enough money to live on. Suddenly, Will started talking to me about his problems too. About how things weren't working with his wife, telling me they were separated but pretending to still be together to save face. It was nice to have someone to talk to and our long chat comforting each other about the state of our lives eventually turned into a kiss, which quickly turned into sex on his desk – the first time of many.

After that first time, as I buttoned up my white shirt (as best I could considering he'd ripped a few buttons off) and watched Will thoughtfully rub his stubbly chin (probably pondering whether or not it would be wise to fire me so soon after fucking me), I swore to myself that it wouldn't happen again. Separated from his wife or not, I didn't want to get involved.

Unsurprisingly, Will decided not to fire me, taking me out of the sales department so that I could work under him (yes, I did just say that). As we started spending more and more time together, we started getting closer and closer and here we are. Nearly a year together and still sneaking around.

I push my key in the door to my flat and let out a sigh before letting myself in.

'Honey, I'm home,' I call out as I ditch my handbag on the sideboard. No, I'm not so lonely that I've resorted to cracking witty jokes to myself about my situation – Honey is my cat. So not so lonely that I've started talking to myself, but lonely enough to talk to my cat, it would seem.

'Well, it's about time,' a voice calls back and, despite being a familiar one, it is unexpected and causes me to jump out of my skin.

'Gosh,' I exclaim. 'Don't do that to me, Aims.'

'I told you I was going to be here. You must be missing me if you're talking to that thing.'

My soon-to-be ex-flatmate nods towards Honey, who hisses back at her.

'You two still not getting on?' I laugh.

'Let's just say it makes me feel less bad about hardly ever being here, and the fact that in just over a week I will be officially moved out helps too. Nice use of "gosh" by the way. I take it your old bloke doesn't appreciate you blaspheming, as well as swearing.'

Amy wanders into the kitchen. It's only now that I notice the smell of food drifting through the house.

'There's nothing wrong with being more ladylike,' I call after her. 'I can't believe you're getting married and moving out like a grown-up.'

Amy returns, spoon in hand, and points at me with it as she speaks.

'And I can't believe you're wearing that disgusting dress,' she says harshly. 'Or what you've done with this place. Or that you have a cat. Or that you have nothing but vegetables, chicken and milk made from fucking almonds in your fucking fridge – thank *God* I brought shopping.'

My friend puts extra emphasis on the word 'God' and she reels off her list of things that she can't believe about the new me. Well, the *new* new me.

As Amy stands there, still brandishing her spoon in an attacking position, she waits for me to justify all of the above. I don't see her as much as I'd like to these days, and I guess I must be changing a lot.

Amy Kelly is my best friend, and she came into my life when things were the most difficult for me. By the time I was twenty-four I had lost both my parents. With no grandparents, siblings or even so much as a distant aunt I could turn to, when my dad passed away I became an orphan. Both my mum and dad were very ill in the years before they passed, so as soon as I finished sixth form, rather than going to university or travelling like the rest of my friends, I stayed at home to take care of them. I was happy to do it, and if I had the time again, I wouldn't do things even a little differently, but it had a huge impact on my life. I stopped seeing my friends; I had no social life, no love life. When my mum passed, it just made my dad and me even closer. As he got worse, he had to go into a home and that's where I met Amy – she was one of the carers who looked after him. When my dad died I was left with pretty much nothing. That's when Amy told me she was looking for a new flatmate. Growing up so shy combined with my lack of a social life as an adult had turned me into this quiet little mouse, and Amy saved me from that. It took a year of my life to get there, but I was happy. Truly happy.

Growing up, I was not a tidy child. I would take out a toy, play with it for a while, and then take out another, leaving the previous one on the floor. I never made my own bed, and any clothing I took off would wind up inside out on my bedroom floor. My mum would be constantly telling me to tidy my room, and every now and then she would offer me something in exchange for cleaning up and I would do it, and for a day or so my room would be tidy…until it wasn't again. I wish my mum were still around to see my Manchester city centre apartment, because she wouldn't believe just how tidy it was.

When I first moved in with Amy, our place was everything you would expect of the home of two twenty-something chicks. We had fairy lights almost everywhere, fluffy cushions, lots of weird and wonderful ornaments and pictures on the wall. We had so much pink shit, it would make even Barbie herself dizzy and, my gosh, was it messy! No matter which room you were in, the chance of you being able to see a wine glass (clean, dirty or decorative) was very high. The place was full of smells too: hairspray, coffee, a cocktail of perfumes, the unmistakable whiff of chocolate from that one time we tried to use a chocolate fountain and it malfunctioned epically, spraying chocolate everywhere. I remember that night so well, and yet when I think about it, it feels like it didn't really happen, like it's something I saw in a movie once.

It was a particularly cold December, not long after I'd started working at Starr Haul – before I got with Will, in fact. I don't even think he'd given me a second glance at that stage. Both Amy and I were skint, and we were stuck in a battle with our landlord over who should pay for our broken central heating, because he thought it was our fault it had broken down. I was young, I didn't have my parents to support me and things were so bad I couldn't even afford to take the bus to work – I had to walk. One evening we decided we needed to do something to try and keep us warm and it just so happened that for Amy's birthday someone had bought her a chocolate fountain and bars of the stuff to use with it. So for dinner that night, melted chocolate was on the menu, but without any wooden skewers to stab our Poundland marshmallows with, we resorted to using forks, and when Amy dropped her fork into the fountain it jammed it and the result was us, our furniture and our living room being lashed with chocolate.

As well as smelling delicious, the place had bags of personality. Amy is very hippy-chic. She's into all this weird and wonderful stuff that I don't understand, like crystals and dream catchers, and I've no idea what they do, but they definitely made the flat look cool. As she started spending less time here and more time at her fiancé's place, she started taking all the stuff away. And as it started disappearing I realised that although the flat had bags of personality, none of it was mine.

My friend stares at me, waiting for an explanation.

'What's wrong with my dress? It's not that bad,' I protest, glancing down at the black pencil dress I wore to work.

'Yeah, not that bad if you're going to a funeral,' my friend (who is wearing a white cheesecloth gypsy top *as a dress,* might I add) says harshly, 'or you're still trying to turn yourself into a weird clone of your boss's wife.'

I stare at my friend for a moment. She hasn't been back to the flat for a while, and she's been so busy with wedding stuff that we haven't spent much time together – not to have a proper chat – but it's clear that she still doesn't approve of my situation with Will. She can't even say his name.

'This isn't for anyone's benefit, I just like dressing a bit smarter,' I lie. 'And maybe I have made this place a bit more neutral, but if Will is going to move in here with me eventually then it needs to be less girly.'

'Ergh, listen to yourself.' Amy rolls her eyes theatrically. 'All you go on about is him. You dress for him. You decorate for him. What does he do for you? He won't even be with you publicly.'

I feel my face fall, and my friend reacts.

'Candice, I'm sorry, it just upsets me to see him treat you like this. You deserve better.'

Amy carelessly places the dirty spoon down on the chest of drawers next to her and grabs me for a hug.

'I know I deserve better,' I tell her honestly. 'But that's what this week away is all about. It's going to be our first anniversary so we're just going to concentrate on being normal together, seeing how it goes and then working out what we're going to do about our future.'

'Remind me again how we're spinning this little holiday-slash-business trip?' Amy asks, pulling a face.

'As managing director, Will needs to visit all branches of the company. He'll make sure things are running smoothly and put in a bit of face time with the other employees. It's good for his image.'

'It's good for an excuse to nail you in a hotel bed instead of a supply cupboard,' she tells me.

'That was one time.' I laugh.

'And this explains why you're away for the weekend too, because…'

'There's always someone working day and night, seven days a week, to keep things moving,' I tell her. 'Haulage never sleeps.'

'That might be the saddest thing I've ever heard.' Amy laughs.

Before I met Amy, I was so *so* shy. Somehow, she brought me out of myself and for that brief moment between meeting Aims and meeting Will, I felt like a whole new person, like a normal girl in her early twenties. I will admit that since I started seeing Will, I have gone back into my shell a little. I worry about keeping in shape. I worry about coming across as the scrappy, foul-mouthed, party girl I turned into when it was just Amy and me against the world. I know that Will wouldn't be into that kind of girl, and I hid her from him well until I got out of those bad habits. Will is a smart, educated, well-respected man. He comes from a good family. He's so well-spoken his accent is almost neutral, despite being born and raised in Manchester. Guys like that don't wind up with girls like the one I had become, so I cleaned up my act. I know that Amy holds Will responsible for this regression in personality (that's what she calls it) but I do feel like a better person for being with him.

'Right, go get your comfies on,' Amy insists. 'Dinner will be ready in ten. I've made steaks, chips and my own special secret sauce,' she sings. 'I know you've been missing it so you better be off your silly diet.'

As I head for the bathroom, a sick feeling washes over me. I don't know what exactly is in Amy's special sauce, but I know that it's full of calories. As are steaks and chips. The thing about being on a diet is that as soon as you have a little slip-up, it undoes your progress for the past few days and it feels like it was all for nothing. And if that bagel yesterday made my tummy blow up like a balloon today, then tomorrow, after Amy's cooking, I'll look like I'm expecting one hell of a food baby, and that will have Will worried.

I close the bathroom door behind me, slip off my dress (and my underwear, because an underwired bra will easily add one pound to my weight), pull out the scales from behind the sink as quietly as possible and place them on the bathroom floor. As I am about to step on them, a bang on the bathroom door causes me to jump out of my skin.

'Bitch, are you weighing yourself?' my friend yells through the closed door. 'Seriously, you've gotta stop with this shit. You are a perfectly normal and healthy weight. Stop trying to change *for a man* and come and get some chips into you.'

'I'm not weighing myself,' I lie, although it's pointless. Amy knows I'm on a quest to lose a bit more weight, but I'm just trying to get healthier with Will, that's all. 'I'll be out in a minute.'

I flush the toilet before returning the scales as quietly as possible. I slip on a pair of joggers and a vest top and open the door to find Amy waiting for me.

'Stop weighing yourself,' she ticks me off, hitting me on the nose with a CD.

'Stop leaving the pans unattended,' I tell her off in return.

'OK, I was just bringing you this.'

Amy presents me with a CD called 'Anything you want is yours'.

'Cool, what genre do they play?' I ask, knowing full well it isn't music.

'Very funny. It's that cosmic ordering I was telling you about. This one teams it with meditation; it's bound to sort your life out.'

'Oh, thanks,' I reply, unsure what to say to that. 'I'll put it in my room.'

As Amy heads back to the kitchen, which hopefully isn't on fire, I frisbee the CD into my bedroom. I'll need to be pretty desperate before I resort to asking thin air to fix my problems for me.

Chapter 3

I tap the step counter on my wrist to check my progress for the day. After inputting my calories consumed into my health app, I can see that my usual target of a calorie deficit is unsurprisingly a calorie surplus after my epic dinner (and too much wine) with Amy, but after her catching me out with the scales, I felt like I had to clear my plate to prove a point.

With just ten minutes to go until midnight, I walk laps around my bedroom to try and get my steps up for the day, because more steps equals more calories burned. The fact that I am tipsy from all the wine is only making this more difficult, but that's all the more reason for me to do it. I don't have much floor space in my room, which makes this even trickier, but Amy had decided to stay the night and she just doesn't get why I want to lose weight. That's because she's so happy in her skin. If she caught me exercising at this time, she'd flip.

I pace back and forth a few more times before stumbling over nothing – possible the thick fumes of alcohol in the air – and hit the deck. Unhurt (or just too tipsy to feel it) I laugh at myself. That's when I notice the CD Amy gave me and curiosity gets the better of me. I pop it in my CD player before hitting play (making sure the volume is low enough not to be heard) and getting in bed.

As I listen to what the voice on the CD has to say, I frown. This is silly. I'm supposed to just repeat a few chants and tell the universe what I want and it will just hand it over? If only life were that simple.

The voice talks about deciding what you want, and asserting yourself.

'Repeat after me,' the voice instructs. 'I am in charge of my own destiny, and I deserve a better life.'

'I am in charge of my own destiny, and I deserve a better life,' I replying, mockingly.

'It doesn't work if you take the piss,' I hear a voice say softly from behind the door. 'Can I come in?'

'Sure,' I reply, embarrassed, although I'm not sure why – at first because she caught me listening to it, but then because I was taking the piss just a bit. The thing is, after the shitty cards life has dealt me, it annoys me that the voice on the CD is implying that all I had to do was ask it not to.

Amy turns off the CD player before climbing in my bed next to me.

'So, what are you asking for?' Amy enquires.

'Hmm, let's see… How about that I fall in love with Mr Right, ASAP?'

'Beats the Mr Wrong you're with now,' she teases, before changing her tone to a more serious, concerned one. 'You're not yourself, babe.'

'I'm fine, just a bad day,' I tell her and leave it at that. I won't tell her about Will pushing me underneath a desk because she'd hit the ceiling.

'Not just today – generally. You're like a different person. He quashes your spirit.'

I laugh it off. 'Just a bad day,' I tell her again, but I feel my eyes filling up. Stupid alcohol, letting my emotions get the better of me. Suddenly, it's all flowing out.

'My life is passing me by,' I admit. 'With each second that ticks by, my death gets that little bit closer. I watch the seconds turn into minutes, then hours, days, weeks, months and eventually years. I see the so-called "best years of my life" vanishing before my eyes. And I hate my job so frigging much.'

'So quit,' Amy suggests.

'I can't, because I need the money, and it's the only time I get to see Will. But it's just so boring, and all the women in the office hate me – I don't know if it's because they have suspicions about Will and me, but it only pushes me closer to him, because he's the only person there who cares about me, which only fuels their suspicions,' I babble. 'Argh, I am miserable.'

And drunk, apparently.

'So do something about it,' Amy insists, wrapping her arm around me.

'I am,' I sob. 'That's why Will is taking me away, so we can sort out what we're going to do. I don't want to lose him, but I told him that I can't go on like this. He says we'll figure it out.'

'Well, there you go,' Amy replies, although she sounds unconvinced.

Despite telling Will that I cannot go on like this, the truth is that I would rather go on like this than call it a day. Sometimes I worry that he's only organised this trip to appease me, and then when we return things will just go back to normal, except it will be worse because I will have had a taste of what life would be like as a proper couple. It has appeased me, whether it was intended to or not. The mere suggestion of us spending a few days alone together was enough to drag my mood from my impending death to filling me with hope that one day we will be a proper couple, when he can finally go public about the fact he's separated from his wife. But with enough alcohol in my bloodstream to kill an elephant, all my worries are at the forefront of my mind. If all goes well I'll feel on top of the world, but if not then it's back to reality, back to our hopeless situation.

'Look, you know that I think you can do much better, but if you want him to get serious then you need to show him that you're not just this thing that will wait around until he's ready to love you.'

'Tried that before – remember?' I remind her.

'I'm not saying you should get with someone else, but show him that other people do want you. Is that Geordie guy at work still bugging you for a date?'

'He asked me out during his first day on the job last week. That was when Will saw and told him off. Since then he hasn't asked again. He does sit on my desk every day and chat to me though.'

'Good. Let your boss see.'

I nod thoughtfully, but the truth is I couldn't do that to Will. In fact, despite the new guy being nothing but friendly with me (and ridiculously gorgeous – probably way out of my league), I am borderline rude to him. The thing is, I don't want Will to be upset by seeing the two of us together, and the new guy just won't take the hint and leave me alone.

'Try and get some sleep,' Amy insists, climbing out of my bed. 'Things won't seem so bad in the morning.'

'Thanks for everything. Dinner was great,' I call after her.

'You're welcome,' she calls back. 'I'll be listening out for you throwing it back up.'

Chapter 4

Megan McLaughlin isn't just my childhood best friend. Despite us not really keeping in touch, she means so much more to me now. Megan is an idea, a gauge that shows me just how far off track my life is, a living example of what my life should probably be like right now, as I approach the big 3-0 (just six short years away).

Thanks to Megan, I am fast realising that my life isn't taking the same route as the chicks I grew up with. School is like a massive competition where everyone – your friends especially – are your competitors, your life rivals. Who got the best Christmas present this year? Who has the best trainers? Who can get the hottest boyfriend? Who is doing the best in English? And you think that you'll turn sixteen, grab your GCSE certificates and leg it into adulthood, and that all of that crap will be behind you. While that might have been true once upon a time, we millennials have things so much tougher now that social networks are a thing. Everyone from your school days is going to want to keep in touch with you on Facebook – even the bullies, bizarrely – and we all know that Facebook is nothing but a platform for boasting. So now these childhood rivals follow you into your grown-up years, and serve as a reminder of how badly you're doing at life compared to them.

Take my secondary school bestie, Megan, for example. Megan and I met in nursery and our lives pretty much mirrored one another until one day, suddenly, they didn't. We both lived on pretty little cul-de-sacs with our happily married parents, we were both into the same hobbies and the same music, and we were even both on the chubby side all the way through school.

Both tomboys through middle school before going all-out punk in secondary school. Both ash blondes. We were one and the same until sometime during sixth form when Megan got her first boyfriend. She'd had boyfriends throughout her teens but this was different because Megan's new boyfriend was older – much older – we were seventeen and he was about to turn thirty. He had a job, his own house and the social life of a grown-up. When Megan started going out with him, not only did she abandon being my fun friend, but it aged her like a fifty-a-day smoking habit too – which is incidentally a habit she took up because he did. Over the past ten years I have watched my friend fly through the motions of growing up, not unlike the way I do when I get bored playing The Sims while I'm trying to kill time on the computer at work. Megan left school, moved in with him, got engaged, got married and had a couple of kids.

So Megan isn't just my former bestie, she is symbolic of the life goals someone at some point decided that we, as women, are supposed to be achieving as adults. Find a man, settle down, put whatever kind of career you have on hold and pop out some babies. I am doing terribly on all counts, and there Megan is, every time I log on to Facebook, posting photos of her newest smiling baby or the latest addition to the work she's having done to her kitchen that never seems to be finished. She's like an alternative reality version of myself, if I'd made different (better?) life choices. I don't own my own home; I am in the weird position of both having never been in a traditional serious relationship while at the same time not being truly single. And as for kids, well, in the presence of the truly annoying ones you often find splashing in puddles next to you while you're wearing a white dress or yelling in your ear on a train, if you listen carefully, you can sometimes hear my tubes attempting to tie themselves.

My work day today has so far consisted of aimlessly scrolling through Facebook – breaking only to answer the occasional phone call while Caroline is away from her desk – looking at everyone post all their stupid shit. Photos from nights out, their kids doing cute stuff, discussing their wedding plans and even taking those stupid quizzes – you know the ones: Which *Friends* character would you be? What's your spirit animal? Are you probably going to die single and alone? I don't need to take a silly quiz to answer those questions for me. I'd be perennially single, early series Chandler, with nothing but my sense of humour to keep me warm at night. My spirit animal would be a mouse, a timid, lonely, little mouse. And the mood I'm in today, I can confidently predict that I will in fact die alone. Still, without all the fun life events to populate my profile, a few annoying quiz result posts would at least remind people that I'm alive. My online presence is fading, fast.

'Do you need a licence to ride a forklift, Candy?'

I am snapped from my increasingly depressive thoughts by a Geordie accent.

'Do you need a licence to *drive* a forklift?' I correct him as I repeat his question in an attempt to remind him that a forklift isn't in fact a ride he can put 20p in to 'have a go' on. 'I'd imagine you need some kind of certificate of competency before they'll let you zip around the warehouse on one.'

'Crap. That's what Rick said,' he replies with a disappointed sigh.

Rick is the warehouse manager. The new guy is here working in the IT department; there's no need for him to even be in the warehouse, let alone 'riding' one of the forklifts.

I avert my eyes, look back at my screen and begin typing an email that I won't in fact send to anyone, but I want Geordie Shore here to think that I am hard at work and leave me alone. He's only been here a little over a week, and on his very first day he actually asked me out on a date. He's *that* sure of himself, because he's gorgeous and he knows it. So far he's managed to make time to sit on my desk and annoy me every single day. I try to ignore him, the way the school swot blocks out the annoying antics of the class clown, and I'm not doing too badly. To be honest, I couldn't even tell you his name – in my head, I've been calling him Geordie Shore. Everyone gets an unflattering nickname in my head. I do try to keep all of this stuff locked away in my head, though, never to be uttered out loud.

When I met Will's wife, Stephanie, for the first time, I was blown away by how perfect she was. She was effortlessly classy, ladylike, and she always looked flawless. I decided then that I needed to be more like her so I made a real effort to be as close to perfection as possible. This only fuels the need for my eternal diet, my religious exercise routine and the real effort I make to be this wonderfully behaved, reserved little lady – because clearly that's Will's type – and I've even managed to master keeping a lid on the casual swearing habit that I'd picked up from Amy. Even when no one is watching, I strive to be as ladylike as possible, in the hope that one day it will truly be second nature. I do still feel like I'm forcing it – just a little. Inside my head is a different story, however. Even my thoughts are peppered with expletives, and some of the terrible things I think about people are far from ladylike.

I wouldn't say that Stephanie had let herself go – Will would, though. After having a couple of kids, Stephanie has put a little bit of weight on. She's still classy and beautiful, but when I hear Will talking about her like she's a mess, it makes me even more careful to keep in good shape.

The new guy is still standing in front of me, his hands in his pockets, squirming and twisting his ankles like a fidgety child who has been called to see the headmaster.

'Did you want something?' I ask in an attempt to make him go away quicker.

'I had a message to pop up, something about some changes to the...' he begins to explain before stopping abruptly. Perhaps the look on my face is representative of how boring that sounded.

'That wasn't me, it'll have been Sweet Caroline,' I tell him. 'She's just gone for her lunch.'

'Why do you call her Sweet Caroline?' He laughs.

Oh shit, did I say that out loud? That's never happened to me before.

'Erm, because she isn't,' I admit truthfully, my mind blank of any other logical explanation.

New guy cracks up laughing.

'I thought it might because she puts those doughnuts out in the staffroom every morning,' he replies.

'Yes, that would have been a better explanation, wouldn't it?' I reply, almost for my own benefit.

'Do you mind if I wait around for her?'

'Knock yourself out,' I reply.

He takes a seat at her desk and twirls in her chair.

I continue to type nothing in particular so he doesn't speak to me, and so that I can get on with all my non-existent work.

I try not to give it too much thought, because I don't want to admit it, not even to myself, but it sometimes feels like the only reason Will didn't fire me was because he wanted to keep me around. On paper I am his assistant. The thing is, he already has Caroline working as his secretary, and she seems to tick all the boxes an assistant would too. I think Caroline thinks I am useless to the company and massively overpaid for the work I do. Caroline is probably right in thinking this. Still, that's no reason for her to be as rude to me as she is. Sometimes I think it's because she knows about Will and me. I suppose that, if she is wrongly under the impression that he and his wife are still together – like everyone else is – then it's no wonder she dislikes me.

'So, Candy – ' new guy starts, but I cut him off.

'Candice,' I correct him. 'I hate being called Candy.'

I instantly feel bad for correcting him. Come to think of it, I don't think I've been very nice to him since the day he started. On his very first day he just breezed in here, all fun and freelance and I couldn't believe it when he asked me out, in front of Will, before we'd even exchanged pleasantries, before Will had even shown him to his office. His confidence left me dumbstruck, but before I had a chance to say anything I clocked the unimpressed look on Will's face. He couldn't hide his jealousy, and gave Geordie Shore a telling-off for flirting with me.

I would have been mortified but the new guy just laughed it off, like it was no big deal. I'd have been in tears in the toilets, just like I am every time Sweet Caroline gives me a dressing-down, but not new guy; he still comes and sits on my desk, chatting to me like we're old friends, even though I give nothing back. Well, I don't want to upset Will, do I? So I figure if I'm not too pally with the new guy then maybe he'll stop trying to be my friend. The thing is, it's like the more I try to ignore him, the harder he tries with me. This really winds me up.

'You need to lighten up,' he tells me. 'All the cool kids shorten their names.'

I shrug my shoulders.

'Candice just takes so much longer to say,' he persists, and I'm not sure if he's kidding or not.

'Well you could take it up with my parents, but they're dead,' I tell him harshly, in an attempt to shut the conversation down.

'Rough,' he replies, and I don't know if he's referring to my orphan status or my manner.

Before I got involved with Will – when I was young, sweet and approachable – I didn't attract much attention from guys. As a shy and unremarkable teen with only female friends, I had no confidence to talk to boys and in turn they had no desire to talk to me. I think that's why I was so blown away when a handsome, grown man like Will wanted anything to do with me. Now that I'm happy (ish) with Will, the last thing I want is men coming on to me, but now that I'm not interested in anyone else, I seem to have my pick of the fine, eligible bachelors of Manchester. Why yes, I am being sarcastic. Catcallers in the street, drunks in bars, well-travelled IT freelancers – the harder I try to seem uninterested, the more people seem to try. It's weird.

When Geordie Shore first asked me out, I didn't get a chance to reject him before Will intervened, but after that I made sure he knew I wasn't interested. Could I have been interested were it not for my relationship with Will? I'm not certain, but what I am certain of now is that he has become this huge pain in my arse. I'd be lying if I said I wasn't flattered when he showed interest in me, because he's undeniably gorgeous, but he upsets Will when he hits on me, he stops me getting my (admittedly near non-existent) work done, but worst of all he just irks me in a way that I can't even explain.

There's something about the way he looks at me that I just don't like. I'm a very closed book; I keep myself to myself, but with the new guy it's like that doesn't matter. I feel like he looks through me, like he can see all my secrets and there's nothing I can do about it.

'I might go grab a doughnut,' the new guys announces to fill the silence. 'Can I get you one?'

'No, thank you,' I reply, my eyes fixed firmly on my screen.

'Don't tell me you don't like doughnuts?' he gasps, faux dramatically for effect.

'I don't really eat junk,' I tell him. It is technically true that I am trying not to eat junk. It's not fun at all and sometimes, when I'm having a rough day, I'd love nothing more than to work my way through a baker's dozen, but I don't. OK, I maybe sneak one now and then, but after last night, I need to behave today.

'Healthy eater?' he asks, nodding towards my body. 'Well, you look good for it.'

'Thank you.' I look up at him, and smile briefly.

He smiles back before dashing out of the room. The staff

room isn't far and soon enough he's back with four doughnuts on a plate, each a different flavour, but all absolutely delicious-looking. At least two of them clearly involve chocolate and I feel my breathing quicken as I eyeball them longingly. I try not to make eye contact with delicious food, lest I fall off the wagon and eat everything that crosses my path on my way to the ground. I know that as soon as I hit the floor – like when Will makes any kind of remark about my weight – it will hurt so much, and no food is worth that, right? What is it they say? Nothing tastes as good as thin feels. Whoever came up with that phrase has obviously never tasted a chocolate and peanut butter doughnut.

'Right, two each and you can have first pick,' new guy says as he pulls up Caroline's chair, placing the plate on my desk and pushing it towards me. Oh God, what the hell is wrong with me? Why am I so weak for food? My mind is telling me no, but my stomach is telling me hell yes.

'Just one,' I say, convincing neither myself nor the new guy that I'll stop after just one. I mean, look at them! I grab the chocolate and peanut butter one and start delicately nibbling away at it, instead of trying to stuff it in my mouth whole like my instincts are telling me to.

'I'll take the raspberry ripple one,' he says, stabbing it with his finger before eating it off like a lollipop. 'Your move,' he says, his mouth full of food.

I make sure to empty my mouth before I speak.

'It's going to have to be the pink, glittery glazed one,' I sigh.

'I knew it,' he says, clapping victoriously, absentmindedly forgetting the doughnut in this hand. He laughs and licks jam from his hands like a messy little boy. 'I knew you'd go chocolate and then sparkly.'

I shrug my shoulders.

'Have you ever been to Thailand?' he asks.

'No,' I reply, my instincts telling me not to get into conversation with him, to just eat my doughnut, feel ashamed of my lack of willpower and get on with pretending to work.

'I went last year, amazing place,' he tells me. 'There's this thing they eat, it's high-protein and low-fat – you might like it. They're pregnant crickets.'

I snap my head upright, taking my eyes off my blank screen to look at him in disbelief. I swallow hard to empty my mouth.

'Excuse me, they're what?'

'Yeah, they're crickets that are full of eggs. Apparently they raise them on a farm, feed them well so it makes for a yummier cricket.'

'That's disgusting,' I squeak. It annoys me that I find him so interesting when I try so hard to ignore him. 'Did you eat one?'

'Of course,' he tells me as he spins around in Sweet Caroline's desk chair. 'YOLO – that's what the kids say, right? Also, when in Thailand… It was just one of many culinary delights they have over there.'

Unfazed by his disgusting story, I grab my second doughnut and start munching away.

'Do I want to know?' I ask, unsure if I do or I don't.

'Oh, you'd be amazed what you can eat if you travel – even just outside Manchester.'

I no sooner crack up laughing when we are interrupted by someone joining us. It's Will.

He stands in the doorway, looking at me, then Geordie Shore, then me again.

'Well, it looks like you two are having fun,' Will says. 'Remind me, do I pay you two to work or to sit around eating and laughing together?'

'It's my fault,' the new guy says, still twirling in his chair like he couldn't give a fuck, whereas my body has gone rigid with fear. Not for my job, but because I'm terrified of upsetting Will. 'Caroline called for me. I'm just waiting for her to get back.'

'Tell you what, you get back to work and I'll have Candice

call you when Caroline gets back. And you,' he points at me, 'my office, now.'

Will storms into his office and slams the door behind him.

'Ah shit, I'm sorry,' new guy says to me softly. 'Didn't mean to land you in it. You're going to get a ticking off now, aren't you?'

'Yes,' I reply. 'But I'm used to it.'

Chapter 5

I sit down in the chair opposite Will's desk and anxiously nibble a fingernail, terrified of his reaction. With each second that ticks away, the anticipation of what he might say fills me with more and more fear, and I can feel my doughnuts doing somersaults in my stomach – minus the half of the pink one that is still in my hand, because I panicked and brought it with me. At least I think that's what happened, unless I subconsciously just really, really want it.

Will glances towards it, a disapproving look on his face.

'I only had the one,' I say defensively.

'Candice, you have chocolate on your face, and that is not a chocolate doughnut in your hand,' he says with a sigh. 'Why are you lying to me?'

'OK, so I had two, but I'm going to the gym later and – '

'What else are you lying to me about?' he asks, interrupting me.

'What? Nothing!' I insist, almost offended. I try so hard to be the perfect girlfriend for him, no matter how tough things get. I can't believe he's so upset about a few hundred calories.

'It's not the doughnut,' he insists. 'The new kid's not going to be a problem for us, is he?' Will asks.

'The new guy?'

'Yes. I see the two of you talking a lot, laughing and joking together...'

Will struggles to hide his jealously, but like a good girlfriend, I do my best to put his mind at rest. He really doesn't have anything to worry about, and I'm not about to pretend he does to try and force his hand into going public before he's ready.

'Of course not. It's always him talking to me – usually talking at me. I hardly give him the time of day.'

Will narrows his brown eyes at me thoughtfully.

'I could get rid of him.'

I can't help but giggle, because that almost sounded sinister. Of course, this is Will we're talking about, and in his voice it couldn't be clearer that he's talking about sacking him, and not having him bumped off.

'Don't be silly, it's not worth the trouble,' I tell him, grabbing his hand.

Will squeezes my hand and gives me a smile.

'Well he's only working for us on an ad hoc basis, on the new network and website. We spoke about more work after that, but he didn't seem keen. From the look of his CV, he doesn't stay anywhere long but he's good at what he does. Great, in fact. He's quite the colourful character.'

I've picked up on as much from the stories he's told me, and the things I've heard him telling others. He's certainly an interesting one.

Safely in the privacy of his office – except I don't feel that safe in here, nor does it feel that private any more – Will walks around the desk and massages my shoulders. But not before taking the remainder of my doughnut and throwing it in the bin. I watch solemnly as it lands with a thud, and as I momentarily consider if it might still be edible, I realise that I need to up my diet game, because that is a disgusting thing to think.

'Look, I understand that you're upset because I made you hide under the desk and I'm sorry,' my lover finally apologises to me for the events of the previous day, like it's some silly man crime he's committed. Not noticing a new haircut, keeping his socks on during sex, leaving the toilet seat up, oh, and having you hide under the desk while his secretary is in the room. Standard stuff.

Despite Will's instructions, the new guy didn't seem anxious to get back to his department in a hurry, as Caroline was expecting him. He explained this again to a furious Will when he came back out to summon me into his office. I suspected that Will was only so angry with the new guy because he was flirting with me again, and not because IT productivity would be down. I worry that he might be able to hear our conversation if he's still outside and lower my voice.

'It's fine,' I tell him, finally taking my eyes off the bin.

'Not long until our holiday from the world,' Will says brightly. 'I'll just pop my head around the door at each office, and then the days and nights are ours. I've got us booked into some beautiful hotels, and I've got some romantic surprises set up. It's going to be great.'

'It is.' I sigh.

'I love you, Candice Hart,' Will tells me, before he kisses me. And just like that, I am his again. Any little doubts in my mind or worries that he might not be worth it are wiped out as soon as he shows me any affection. With one kiss, he is out of my bad books.

'You too,' I tell him when our lips finally part.

Will pinches my cheek like he always does. I've never understood why people do that as a sign of affection because, if anything, it's kind of uncomfortable – borderline painful – but I've come to associate the feeling with Will and what he means when he does it and it makes me feel great.

Our moment only lasts a few seconds.

'Oh, before I forget, I've got Charlie's leaving card here. I need you to sign it, and get the few remaining people who haven't done so to do the same. It's just Rick and the IT team, so if you could get that done ASAP.'

He walks over to his tidy desk and locates the card without much searching, then he hands it to me, before adjusting my outfit a little for me, making sure I'm tidy too. Will kisses me on the forehead before the ringing of his phone drags him back to his desk.

'Hello, Caroline,' he answers, so she must be back at her desk, which means hopefully the new guy will have cleared off. 'OK, send her in.'

'I've called for a meeting with Julie, you know the girl who cleans the offices?'

I nod, uninterested. I don't know much about Julie, other than the fact that she's my age, Sweet Caroline's right-hand woman, and just as horrible as Caroline is. She once would have certainly lost me my job, were it not for my relationship with Will. She was tidying my desk as I was working, and I was panicking to get an email sent before the end of the day. I had two piles of invoices on my desk, one of which needed shredding. She was going on at me to clear them, so I told her which pile needed destroying. Anyway, she shredded the wrong one, and Will hit the roof. I was so certain I carefully told her which pile was for the shredder, but she wouldn't have it. She started crying and Will fell soft, because he's useless around emotional women, and the whole situation was just quietly forgotten about. But I know that somewhere there's a HR record of the events, probably saying it's all my fault.

'Well, she's doing an awful job. Look at this.'

Will runs a finger across a framed photo that sits on his desk. I glance at his finger, which looks absolutely fine to me, but he does have a reputation for being a perfectionist.

'I'm going to have to have a word,' he insists.

As I head for the door, Julie walks inside, squeezing past me.

'Candice,' she says, acknowledging my existence without a hint of pleasantness.

'Julie,' I reply as I go to pass her in the doorway.

'Breathe in,' she says with a sweet little giggle as I squeeze past her. Well if she'd just move, I wouldn't need to.

I close Will's office door behind me, pissed off at Julie but satisfied with another successful interaction with Will. It's hard spending so much time around him at work, always so close, but never being able to touch – only when we can squeeze in these brief moments together. That's all they are though: moments. Now it's back to work.

Chapter 6

'Honey, I'm home,' I call out, as I do every night, and my dutiful little cat runs up to me and shows me affection, like she always does when I get home. It was Will's idea that I get a pet, so that I had some company when Amy finally moved out. I would've preferred a puppy, but a kitten was less work. Cats are much more independent, and don't take much looking after. They're capable of showing affection, but they don't need to. They're happy on their own, doing their own thing – the perfect pet for me then.

As much as I love Honey, sometimes I look at her, and feel like she's the first step to my never-ending spinsterhood, a reminder that I'm going to be forever alone. Deep down, at the back of my mind, I do worry that I'm going to live here at the top of my tower until someone comes to rescue me from a life where I have more cats than I do husbands. Even if I don't get more cats like the crazy cat lady I imagine I'll turn into, one cat still makes that a fact. Unless, of course, we're counting other people's husbands, but that's merely a technicality, isn't it?

The first thing I do is head for my wardrobe, where I hang up my clothes, before taking a seat at my dressing table. I let my hair down – immediately scraping it into a bun and removing my make-up. Despite it being June there's a chilly breeze tonight, so I put on a pair of pink flannel pyjamas, which, despite being purchased from Victoria's Secret, are sexy by no stretch of the imagination. Then I head for the kitchen, throw some diced chicken into a pan and cook it, before throwing in a packet of stir-fry sauce. It's not that there's anything wrong with having this for dinner, it's just that it's this kind of healthy, low-fat, low-calorie, low-fun stuff that I live on to make sure my new dresses keep fitting me. I am bored of it, but I toss it around in the pan with the wrist action of a professional chef, breaking only to pop out onto the balcony to water my plants.

I never really thought I had a problem with my weight, until that first time Will pointed out that I was making unhealthy lifestyle choices. I wouldn't say he was keeping tabs on my weight, but he started making helpful suggestions about how I could drop those extra few pounds I've been carrying around. At first, I was good at it. It was simple maths, just eat less and move more and those few pounds melt right off. But then, when I wanted to go back to eating 'normally' Will explained to me that I would pile it all back on – and more. The diet was OK for a few months, but I miss food so much. Eating steak just reminded me how much I love it, and I miss chocolate more than anything, which is probably why I'm powerless to resist when someone literally offers it to me on a plate. I'm healthier though, right? I'll live a longer life, even if it will be a joyless one without big bars of Cadbury's chocolate to keep me happy.

After sitting at the dining table to eat, all alone, I make myself a cup of tea, grab a SkinnyKwik chocolate cereal bar (a poor excuse for the real thing) and get comfortable on the sofa, ready for another night in, all alone.

Netflix has become my best friend. I recently started binge-watching *Breaking Bad* of a night and, I have to say, I am hooked. It's a huge shift in genre from the last thing I watched, which was *Gossip Girl*, but as much as I loved that, *Breaking Bad* is just something else. Watching the journey Walter embarks on is eye-opening to say the least, and as much as it is reminding me that life can be short, it is also showing me just how much you can change your life. In a way, I relate. No, I'm not embarking on a career cooking meth – even stir-fry is a stretch for my culinary skills. Walter is trying to be this Heisenberg persona to fit in with his new world, just like I am trying so hard to fit into Will's world. I'll be interested to see how it plays out for him – and me. It's hard to imagine anyone can keep up the act of pretending to be something they're not, not without someone figuring out that they're a fraud, or them turning into the person they're pretending to be and losing their identity for ever.

As I sit here on the sofa, alone, cuddled up in the dark, with my new favourite show on the TV, I realise something: my relationship with TV is a lot like my relationship with Will. It takes me on an emotional roller coaster. It can make me so happy and then leave me so crushed in so much as a scene. A happy ending can lift my mood, just like a plot twist can distract me from my thoughts all day, or a sad scene can leave me feeling devastated. A character death leaves me feeling like I've actually lost someone. I mourn them. I think about them, about what the show would be like if they were still in it, just like I wonder what my life would be like if I'd made different choices. TV never lets me down, though. It keeps me entertained on these lonely nights. It excites me... I've just realised I'm living vicariously through Walter White.

It's a particularly tense moment of the show, and as I await the fate of a main character, I feel my fists clench and my nails dig into the palms of my hands. The TV is silent, I am silent and just as tension is building my phone comes to life on the table in front of me, lighting up and vibrating with a message, causing me to jump out of my skin. As my heart finally stops pounding, I narrow my eyes, giving my phone a suspicious glance. Who is texting me? People hardly ever text me. Not since I got involved with an unavailable man and alienated all my friends.

I pause my show and grab my phone. It's Will! That's so weird; he very rarely texts me. I don't give myself a chance to worry. I grab my phone and open it.

Will: Hi.

Me: Hey, you OK? xx

Will: I'm good. Steph out. I'm babysitting. What are you up to?

Oh, so that's why he can text me, because he's alone tonight. Not that I'm complaining – it's nice to hear from him.

I'm not quite sure where to place it, but there seems to be a line – a generational gap – where people above a certain age seem to be bad at texting. Perhaps it's because they were just that little bit too old to get caught up in MySpace and, for some reason, they just never signed up to Facebook like everyone else did. At the moment it's around the forty mark. Messages are blunt, to the point and without kisses or emoji. Occasionally you'll see a 'LOL' but it's ten years too late. That's when I notice the age gap, when he LOLs, when I realise that he's never going to find a message containing nothing but a banana emoji funny. I remind myself that I shouldn't find that funny either, because I'm a grown-ass lady.

Me: Just reading a book in bed. You?

Liar. But I'm not about to tell him I'm over-emotionally investing in a TV drama about the drug trade. It hardly screams 'wife material' does it?

Will: Just in bed. Thinking of you. What are you wearing?

Oh no he didn't. In all our time together, sexting has never been a part of our thing – hell, regular texting is hardly a part of our thing. Will always said it was too risky. It's when he says stuff like that, that this feels wrong, like I'm a dirty little secret. I remind myself that I know the score, but there's always this little niggling feeling somewhere at the back of my mind that this is wrong.

I glance down at my pink flannel PJs.

Me: Pink lace bra and pink French knickers.

Another lie, and one that no female would ever believe because we all know how uncomfortable going to bed in a bra is, especially an underwired one.

Will: Send me a photo.

As I read this, I feel my eyebrows jump up and my eyes widen. He's never said anything like that to me before. I think for a moment. It's weird and I know it, but one thing that has always served me well is to wonder: 'What would Stephanie do?' when it comes to Will. So not to make any mistakes, I always consider my actions and whether they make me worthy of Will, and I am fairly certain that swapping sexy photos is not something Stephanie would do – and that's Will's type – but he's asking for it. It's not like I'm sending him one out of the blue. I don't think it's the kind of thing the type of lady Will goes for – the type I have painstakingly forged myself into – would do, and there's a voice in my head telling me that it's not the kind of thing I would do anyway, so…

Me: Nice try ;)

Will: Come on. I'm alone and I'm fantasising about you. Need a visual and I miss you.

Me: You'll be seeing me tomorrow. Surely you can wait until then? Hehe.

When Will talks to me and interacts with me like I am a human being, it's the greatest feeling in the world. Not the business-related stuff he says at work or the blunt texts he sends me to try and keep me sweet, but when he says things in a way that makes me feel like he'd probably be a bit bothered if I died. Those are the moments I live for.

On the flip side, when he doesn't text me back, it hurts like hell. Being able to see that he's read my message, but hasn't replied; it doesn't feel good and it makes me do stupid things. I try and think of reasons to talk to him, to coerce him into replying to me, just to get a message from him, just to have a moment where I know he remembers that I'm alive. On the occasions I don't hear back from him, I'll double-text him. I know it's a needy thing to do, but I can't help it. Our conversations that end with a goodbye and a kiss leave me feeling on top of the world – another successful interaction – but when he doesn't reply, I can drive myself crazy wondering why not. Is he with his wife? Playing with his kids? Does he really think that much about me when he isn't with me? Because I think about him a lot. I often wonder how his day is going: if he's feeling OK, if he's happy or sad, if he's having fun. I see things in shops and think that he'd love them, or it will occur to me to forward silly internet memes to him, because he might find them funny (even though I usually decide that he won't find them funny and don't bother), but does he feel that way about me?

Even if it is because he's fantasising about me, the fact he says he misses me means the world to me. What's interesting is that, although I often fantasise about Will, it's rarely sexual. I imagine what it would be like to cuddle up on the sofa and watch TV with him, to walk down the street holding his hand and to be able to take him along to parties with me as my plus one.

Amy's wedding is coming up and I'm dreading it. I hardly ever get invited to these things, but it would be nice to have someone to go with. Someone to support me, someone to complain about the food with and dance with until the small hours. Someone to get drunk with, go home with and have them take care of me and make me breakfast the next morning. That's the kind of thing I fantasise about.

> Will: OK. Will see you tomorrow bright and early.
>
> Me: Sweet dreams. Love you xxx
>
> Will: You too.

I place my phone back down on the table, ecstatic about hearing from Will outside of work hours. In a way, I'm lucky that Will has such a busy job. It means he spends more time at work than he does at home, but it's always nice to hear from him during time that is not ours.

I grab the remote and hit play. Now, where was I…

Chapter 7

As if it wasn't bad enough that I'm a little bit late for work today, I have just sat down at my desk and there is Charlie's leaving card staring me in the face, the one I was supposed to have everyone sign yesterday – the one that is for her leaving party at lunchtime today, which, thanks to my lateness, is not that far off.

I sit down at my desk, without so much as a 'good morning' from Sweet Caroline, and stare at the card thoughtfully, wracking my brains for who Will said was left to sign it. Rick in the warehouse and the IT department – I'm pretty sure that was it.

As I sip the cup of tea that I picked up on my way into work, I catch Caroline's attention. She spies the drink that obviously made me that bit more late than I already was, and narrows her eyes over the tops of her tiny spectacles at me. Caroline is in her late sixties, and is pretty much a permanent fixture here at the firm. She's known Will since he was young, and as such they have a mutual level of respect. When she was his dad's secretary, Will told me she would always be nice to him when he would visit the office, so as soon as he started working here and moved up in the company, he never stopped respecting her as one of his elders, like the well-mannered man he is. This means that he finds it very difficult to boss her around, and when he wants to shout at her (in that way bosses with stressful jobs do when things aren't going right) you can see him suppress it, almost to the point of discomfort – a skill he seems to lack when it comes to me, his girlfriend. I guess he just doesn't have the sweet spot for me that he does for Sweet Caroline.

Caroline's look is interesting. Her short, auburn hair is always flicked out at the sides, with the tips highlighted bright red, which I don't like. I've never been a fan of unnatural hair colours. It's not that I'm against having hair coloured as a thing, but if you can tell that it's not natural then it's not for me. Caroline always dresses like a *Loose Women* panellist, that is until there is work do, then she really goes to town and goes all Truly Scrumptious on us.

As Caroline stands up and walks around her desk, I see this as my opportunity to shift a little of my already light workload onto her.

'You on the move, Caroline?' I ask.

'Yes, why?' she replies curtly.

'Oh, it's just Wi- Mr Starr,' I stop myself from calling Will by his first name, because this 'display of disrespect' always seems to irk her, 'asked that Rick and the IT boys sign Charlie's card.'

As I say the words I remember the other person who I was supposed to have sign the card: me. I grab a pen and quickly scribble something inside.

'Did he ask *you* to do it, Candice?'

'He just said *it* needed doing. He didn't say that he needed *me* specifically to do it.'

Caroline carries on walking.

'You know what they say,' she lectures me. 'If you want something done right, do it yourself.'

'I don't care if it's done wrong,' I call after her hopefully, but she's gone. Crap. I'll just have to do it myself.

I drain the last of my tea before exhaling deeply. It's not that I don't want to do any work, it's just that I can't face the 'banter' of the warehouse, nor the weirdness of the IT department.

I stand up and smooth out my dress before grabbing the card and a pen, and making my way along the corridor towards the warehouse. The nauseating yellow corridor walls seem especially harsh on the eyes today. Yellow is very much the colour of the company, and it's clear that a variety of marketing experts over the years have really abused the fact the company name is Starr. Queue lots of space puns to do with storage and light speed in relation to deliveries. The logo is a little yellow shooting star, going round in a circle, which is OK, but the idea of having yellow walls to match is just too much. They would've been better having dark walls, with little twinkling lights in the ceiling to look like stars in the night sky – but I was removed from the marketing department, so what do I know?

'...and you know how hard bloodstains are to remove.'

As I walk into the warehouse office, I catch the end of whatever Tommy is telling Rick, and it doesn't sound great, does it?

As I enter the room, they both pause and stare at me for a second.

I try to be well mannered at work, well, with everyone except Caroline and now the new guy, I guess, but with everyone else I do quite well. I keep myself to myself, but most of all, I keep my bitchy comments to myself. That said, if someone were to put a gun to my head and force me to break character by asking me what I thought of the warehouse staff, then I'd most likely admit that I thought they were all probably serial killers, with a couple of sex offenders thrown into the mix for diversity. OK, maybe the term sex offender is a little harsh, but only because charges were never filed. Matt, one of the warehouse minions, has been spotted touching himself on several occasions and everyone here at the flagship Manchester branch knows it. I, personally, have never seen him at it, and Will tells me it's an urban legend, but I'm not so sure. I just passed him on my walk through the warehouse – he always looks so shifty.

If anyone were going to put a gun to my head and force me to do something, it would be Tommy. Tommy is truly terrifying, and I always seem to catch little snippets of his conversations that make him sound like his hobbies involve strangling women before chopping them up and dumping them in the canal. Tommy is Scottish, and a retired semi-pro rugby player. He's very tall and broad with big arms, perfect for choking the life out of women. Thanks to his bald head, bulging eyes and big ears, he looks like a pale version of Shrek, and thanks to his accent he sounds like him as well. Apart from being bald too, Rick is Tommy's polar opposite. He's short with very little muscle, but he doesn't have to do the heavy lifting Tommy does. Rick is the manager down here so he mostly just tells people what to do and 'rides' the forklift. He always has a helmet on, making him look like an old, Mancunian Bob the Builder.

With no one prepared to explain the blood remark to me, I decide it's best to get the card signed and get out of here before I end up in pieces, in a crate headed for the seabed.

'Rick, I need you to sign Charlie's card, please.'

He beckons me over with his hand and takes the card from me. Rick is the very serious, silent type around women. I have witnessed him laughing and joking but it's very much a with-the-lads kind of thing. Around women, he just clams up. Not Tommy, though. No one is safe from his banter.

'How's tricks at the top of the banana with the boss?' he asks me.

The banana is what we call the yellow spiral staircase and subsequent corridor up to Will's office. Were it not for the fact everyone calls it that, I might wonder what he meant by it.

'Fine, thanks,' I reply. 'How's…' I glance around, taking in my surroundings. Even though we have a lovely canteen and staffroom here, this place doubles up as both Rick's office and a sort of man cave for the warehouse workers. The walls are covered with posters and pictures, and the only 'piece of art' that doesn't involve a naked lady or a car is a framed photo of the warehouse team doing Movember last year. They're all standing huddled together, clutching the massive cheque that shows just how much money they made for the cause, and it was a lot, in spite of the fact most of them have moustaches all year round anyway.

Other than Rick's messy desk, there are two tables. The first is in the centre of the room, surrounded by chairs. This is where Tommy and Rick are sitting, with both playing cards and dominos laid out in front of them. There's a work surface at the side of the room that looks a bit like a pop-up amateur meth lab (or maybe I've just been watching too much *Breaking Bad*) where they have all their protein powders and bars and all the various bottles and mixers and tools they need to remain 'hench' and 'make gains' and all the other stuff I hear them say before going back to my desk to google what the fuck it all means.

'How's...this?' I ask, unsure what word to use.

'All good. Just killing time before the meeting with the pricks from HR,' Tommy tells me. 'There's been a few complaints.'

I decide not to ask, nor tell him that he probably shouldn't refer to the HR team as 'pricks'.

Rick hands me back the card so I thank him and head for the door. As I close it behind me I hear Tommy resume their conversation.

'So I'm scrubbing at this bloodstain with that meat tenderiser powder shit that Sharon cooks with, because I read online that it helps...'

I decide not to stick around and listen to the rest of their conversation, lest I become an accessory to something unsavoury – and I'm not talking about whatever it is Sharon cooks with her 'meat tenderiser', whatever the fuck that is.

Next up I head for the IT department, which, unlike Rick's office with its big windows that look out over the warehouse, has no windows at all. I knock on the door before stepping inside. All six of them are gathered together as Garth, who is head of IT, animatedly tells them a story.

'...and I looked down at my chest, and this sword was sticking through it, blood everywhere! I look up, and there's an army of them in front of me as well as behind me, and I desperately need an adrenalin shot to get my health up...'

Garth pauses as I enter the room but, unlike Tommy the serial killer, he feels he should probably explain himself to me.

'This must sound well weird.' He laughs. 'We talking about the Oculus Rift,' he tells me, like that makes things crystal clear and this not seem weird. I remind myself to google that as soon as I get back to my desk.

'Cool,' I reply, only managing to fake enough sincerity to make me sound super sarcastic. 'I won't keep you long, I just need you all to sign Charlie's leaving card before the party this afternoon. You guys are the last ones.'

The new guy is staring at me and smiling. It's a friendly smile, but I still feel awkward about yesterday, just in case he could hear Will and me.

'Roger that,' Garth replies, taking the card from me. 'I'll pass this around if you do me a favour – have a play around on this.' He plonks a silver MacBook on the desk in front of me. 'We've had some complaints that the UI is affecting the UX.'

With that, Garth leaves me to it. I stare at the screen in front of me and scrunch up my face as I try and work out what the fuck that could possibly mean. I look left then right, like the answers might be on the walls amongst all the design plans, code and posters for things I am too 'cool' to get. As I look right I see the new guy still smiling at me. He pushes off the desk next to him, which sends him flying across the room to me on his desk chair. That's the kind of thing that, if I did it, would see me crashing through a third-storey window, but Geordie Shore makes it seem cool and effortless.

'That's just his pretentious way of saying that people think how it looks affects how it works,' he explains to me, and put like that it sounds simple.

'Oh,' I reply. 'Thank you. Well, yeah, the yellow is too much.'

'Ever since I got here, I have been telling them to go easy on the yellow crap,' he tells me, relieved at least one other person shares his views. 'I keep telling them that clean and minimalistic is on-trend right now, but they're pushing the stars. We get it, the company is called Starr, but enough of the pretty little yellow things with five points – that's not what a star looks like. A star is a big ball of exploding gas. They're orange or, if they're really hot, they're blue. Although I suppose a big ball of exploding gas might not be the best option for branding considering our guys drive around in trucks all day.' He laughs.

I chuckle. 'I guess not.'

There's silence for a few seconds before Garth hands the card to new guy to sign.

'What did you think?' he asks me.

'Mate, she said same as me – too much yellow,' new guy answers on my behalf.

'Candice has been here long enough to know that this company and yellow go together like Jaime and Cersei Lannister.' Garth laughs, taking his laptop and returning to his desk.

'Yeah.' I laugh, before turning to the new guy and staring blankly. He looks up from signing Charlie's card and sees my puzzled, expectant look.

'Oh, so I'm your dork translator now, am I?' He laughs.

'Something like that,' I reply sweetly.

'They're characters from *Game of Thrones*,' he informs me.

'Oh, I see. I'm guessing they've been married a long time then,' I reason.

'Not quite,' he replies. 'So, will I be seeing you at Charlie's leaving party?'

'Maybe,' I reply. I always seem to clam up a little when we start getting on, an involuntary reaction, I think, probably because I worry what Will would think if he saw us together.

'Maybe?' he gasps. 'Candy, it's Charlie's leaving do; you can't swerve it!'

'First of all, my name is *Candice*,' I correct him, as always. 'Second of all, you've been here five minutes; you don't even know Charlie.'

'How dare you,' he gasps dramatically again. 'Charlie is one of the nicest blokes you could hope to meet. He's been great with me while I've been here – even if it's only been five minutes.'

I purse my lips and nod my head. It was a nice try, but I'm not buying it. 'Charlie is one of the *ladies* who works in the canteen.' I laugh.

'Oh,' he replies. 'Oh! It might seem weird that I wrote "good luck, pal" in the card.'

'Yeah, you might want to change that.'

'Well you said we were the last, so I sealed the card.' He laughs as he scratches his head. As I watched him sign his name, it had occurred to me to maybe have a peep, to see what his name was. I didn't really listen when he introduced himself, and no one ever seems to say his name. It seems rude to ask him now and I don't want to make myself look like a bitch.

I hate to stereotype, but everyone in the IT department looks exactly as you would expect an IT department employee to look – not the new guy, though.

I'm not sure if I have a type, but I don't think the new guy is it. Well, he's nothing like Will, that's for sure. That said, Geordie Shore is a very attractive man. I doubt he has any trouble getting girls, which is what makes me wonder why he tries so hard with me. I'd guess he's about my age, he's tall and thin. Not skinny though – he's very well toned and it shows underneath the fitted V-neck T-shirt he's wearing. God, I hate that I'm looking. He has tanned skin, big, deep brown eyes and brown hair, making him fit the tall, dark and handsome bill that most go for. He's got one of those short, neat beards – not the dirty, overgrown hipster type, but the kind that's almost just like long stubble, and his longish dark hair is twisted up into one of those topknot things that are so popular at the moment. He wears thick-rimmed, black glasses, which only add to his cool look. He doesn't look like an IT nerd; he looks like a Topman model.

The most striking thing about him isn't even the way he looks, but the way he carries himself. He's that guy all the warm-blooded females in the office have a crush on, the kind who flirts with everyone because he can. He doesn't come across as smarmy though, not with those baby-faced dimples. He's got the kind of face that could get away with murder.

'So, which one is Charlie?' he asks, snapping me from my thoughts and dragging my gaze from his muscular arms back up to his eyes.

'Erm…blonde, curly hair. Early forties. Short,' I say.

'I don't think she's had the pleasure of meeting me yet,' he jokes.

'Unlucky for her,' I reply with a smile. 'Well, I'd better get back to work.'

It's strange, but I kind of don't want to go. Perhaps it's because there's such a nice atmosphere in here, even if I don't know what anyone is talking about most of the time.

'Well, I'll see you at Charlie's leaving do then,' he tells me.

I can't help but leave the IT department with a big smile on my face, grinning to myself all the way back through the banana. For once, I'm actually looking forward to a work thing.

Chapter 8

'What kind of party is this?' the new guy asks as he sidles up to me, disappointment in his voice. 'There's no booze.'

New guy. Again. I can't get rid of him! The truth is, though, that I'm glad he's here because until he came to stand next to me, I was just hanging around in the canteen on my own and it would have certainly stayed that way. I did catch the attention of my female fan club when I entered the room – minus Caroline who isn't here – but her minions made me feel suitably unwelcome. You'd think Julie would show me a little solidarity considering we're the only two young female employees, but I've been able to feel her burning a hole in the back of my head with her death stare since I arrived.

'It's lunchtime and we're at work,' I remind him. 'Anyway, this lot don't do well with drink.'

From where we're standing in the corner of the canteen, we have a clear view of everyone. Well, everyone but Caroline – and Will, who is stuck in a meeting, so I decide it's safe to tell the new guy a little bit about everyone.

'That's Charlie, the guest of honour,' I say as I point her out.

'Okay, got that,' he confirms.

'You see that guy.' I subtly point at a young, skinny blonde lad who is entertaining the gaggle of female staff members. 'That's Craig. He's the main reason we have dry office parties now. Last Christmas we had the bash at a hotel in town. The bosses went all-out. It was amazing.'

Well, the party was amazing, but it wasn't amazing for me. Stephanie was supposed to be away with the kids, staying with family, so Will and I had a room booked at the hotel. I spent so much money on my outfit, I had my hair done and I spent ages getting ready. Then I turned up at the party and there was Stephanie on Will's arm. She'd spent even more money on her outfit and looked like she'd spent even longer getting ready. She looked perfect. She knew that Will was staying at the hotel so, to keep up appearances as always, she stayed with him. Will and I had a big row that night. It's the closest we've ever come to ending things.

'So what did Craig do?' the new guy asks, snapping me from my thoughts.

'He thought he'd try and steal a bottle of champagne from the bar, reached over and somehow managed to catch his arm on something sharp. I've never seen a cut like it – or so much blood! It was all you could smell; it filled the air. He had to be rushed to hospital for an operation!'

The new guy shakes his head with despair, and that's just the tip of the iceberg of Craig's behaviour.

'Man, I love a drop of champers, but that's insane.'

'It's completely insane,' I agree. 'Especially considering the fact it was a free bar.'

The new guy laughs. 'So who else do I have to blame for enduring this sober?'

I glance around the room and spot a red-headed fifty-something lady wearing a navy blue twinset. She's delicately sipping from her plastic cup, occasionally pinching crisps from the plate of the person next to her as she chats away.

'That's Cindy. See how prim and proper she seems? She turned up to a party with her husband – such a nice man! Very small and bald though, makes him look a bit like a turtle because he wears his suits too big for some reason. Anyway, Cindy had a bit too much to drink, made her way to the dance floor and started trying to grind on the men – then the women. Poor hubby just stood at the side of the room, watching, without a hint of any kind of emotion.'

'That dirty devil.' New guy laughs. 'Who's that twat?'

I look over in the direction he's pointing and spot Karl. He's simultaneously picking his nose and drooling over Charlie as she eats her sausage roll.

'That's Karl. He's from Liverpool. He's one of the drivers, and an office party repeat offender. He's actually the reason there's now a "three strikes, you're out" behavioural policy.'

'This I need to hear. Shall we sit down?' new guy asks. 'I'll grab us a couple of lemonades.'

I smile and nod.

I take a seat at one of the canteen booths and shortly after the new guy joins me. He doesn't take a seat opposite me like I expected him to, he sits next to me and scooches up close so we can continue our conversation without anyone hearing.

'Do you know what this is?' he asks, flashing me his key ring.

'Of course,' I reply, almost offended. 'Just because I didn't know what the Ocu- Ocul—'

'Oculus,' he interrupts me, putting me out of my misery. 'It's virtual reality gaming – even I'm not nerdy enough for that, don't sweat it.'

'Oh. Well, I know what that is – it's a flash drive.'

New guy wiggles his eyebrows before popping the top off it and pouring its crystal-clear contents out into our drinks, half in each lemonade.

'What is that?' I squeak.

'Vodka,' he says coolly. 'For emergencies.'

'What kind of emergency requires vodka?'

'Dull parties.' He laughs. 'Now tell me about Karl and his previous.'

I'm not much of a big drinker these days, but I sip my drink gratefully.

'His first strike was not long after I started working for the company and the party was at Wi- Mr Starr's massive house,' I begin, correcting myself as I go along. 'It was a Friday night and Karl got so wasted he had to go and throw up in one of the bathrooms. Anyway, he must have passed out. The party ended, everyone went home...'

'But not Karl?' new guy guesses.

'Not Karl. Karl woke up on the floor the next morning and was too scared to leave. As the story goes he had planned to try and sneak out, but the opportunity never arose. He stayed in the bathroom until Saturday evening when the cleaner found him – and the toilet he'd blocked with his vomit.'

'Nice.' New guy nods, almost impressed by Karl's antics. 'What was his second strike?'

'That took place in this very room last Halloween – we had a costume party,' I explain, widening my eyes, pre-empting his disbelief.

'This lot in fancy dress?' He laughs. 'It's mostly middle-aged women and old truckers.'

'Yes, a superhero costume party,' I continue, and he finds this even funnier.

'Who were you?' he asks, quick as a flash.

'I was – of course – Wonder Woman,' I tell him, modestly.

'This I need to see pictures of!' New guy looks visibly surprised as he says this. 'I've never seen you in anything but your office Stepford get-up. I bet you were a hit with the fellas.'

I flash the new guy an unimpressed side glance.

The truth is that my outfit was actually a big hit with the drivers, who were also only used to seeing me in my office attire – although back then it wasn't quite as Stepford as it is now. With my big, brunette curled wig, my boobs pushed up underneath my chin and the red thigh-high boots I had to visit a sex shop specifically just to find, I actually felt like I looked pretty cool. Will didn't agree, and he took me to one side to tell me as much. He thought that it was far too revealing, and not really me. I remember the exact words he used: 'not right for my body'. I glanced over at Stephanie in her red-belted mac and her red fedora, that he was obviously fine for her to leave the house in. I had accidentally whipped Will with my lasso of truth, and that's when I realised he didn't want a thigh-flashing Wonder Woman with her cleavage on show, he wanted Carmen Sandiego, in her figure-hiding clothes and with her educational agenda. That's when I realised I needed a Wonder Woman makeover circa 1950s, when they took away her whip to get rid of any bondage overtones, and made her more traditional and Christian. I'd already been watching my mouth and behaviour, but that's when I started dressing more appropriately.

'Karl came dressed as Mr Incredible and at some point in the evening, the Flash decided to tell him a superhero-themed joke.'

'Dare I ask what the joke was?'

'I believe it was something along the lines of: "What's the difference between Batman and a Scouser?"'

New guy widens his eyes.

'I know the one.'

'Well Karl didn't, and when he heard the punchline…he got a bit punchy himself. He launched at The Flash, the two of them crashed through the buffet table and they had to be pulled apart. If you look over at the table, you can see where the leg was repaired. The best part of the tale is that no one actually knows who The Flash was. So not only did he not get into trouble, but Karl doesn't feel like he properly avenged Liverpool. He swears he'll find out who it was, one day.'

As I realise how quickly I'm getting through my drink, I puff air out of my cheeks and I examine my glass.

'Gosh, what is this?' I ask. 'It's…powerful.'

'Just a little something I picked up while travelling Europe. Balkan vodka – there are thirteen health warnings on the bottle,' he announces proudly. 'I was in Serbia and there was this rugby team from Yorkshire on a stag party. One of them thought he could knock back neat shots. You should've seen the paramedics trying to get him onto the stretcher. You don't drive, right? Probably don't drive today.'

'I don't drive,' I assure him. 'Do you?'

'Yes, but not today, babe.' He laughs. 'Maybe not tomorrow if you come back to mine after work and have a drink with me.'

We are interrupted by a loud, exaggerated cough. For a moment, Will just hovers near our table, staring at us, before walking over to grab a glass of orange juice and taking his position in the centre of the room to make a speech.

'Think the boss thinks we're up to no good,' the new guy whispers to me, giving me a pally nudge that Will definitely notices. As he gives his speech, he can't take his eyes off us.

'We're a family here at Starr Haul, and it's always sad to say goodbye to a much-loved member of the team. But I, for one, am proud of Charlie for leaving to open her own café,' Will says, trying to direct his words at Charlie, but his eyes keep darting back to me and the new guy. 'If Charlie ever needs any support, I'm sure you'll all join me in extending a hand.'

Danny hiccups. He's clearly underestimated the strength of his vodka. I'm definitely feeling tipsy, and new guy is definitely acting it.

I place a hand on his arm, as if to shush him. Will, who seems to have one eye constantly on us, notices this too.

'Charlie truly was, er, the bread and butter of the…the canteen,' Will babbles, the distraction clearly ruining his perfectly planned speech. 'Basically, we'll miss you,' he adds, clumsily, wrapping things up. 'To Charlie.'

We all raise our glasses.

'So, drink, after work?' new guy starts again once we all go back to chatting amongst ourselves.

'I'm just…I'm not really interested,' I tell him, unsure how best to get out of this one, but panicking as I spot Will approaching us. If I tell him I have a boyfriend he might start asking me questions – questions that I won't be able to answer.

'You're clearly interested in drinking – you just made short work of eighty-eight per cent vodka.' He laughs, and I widen my eyes at the alcohol content. No wonder I'm feeling it.

'I'm not actually much of a drinker,' I tell him.

'So we'll drink tea and play video games. Your nerd knowledge clearly needs a bit of expanding.'

With Will nearly at our table, I need to do something to defuse the situation.

'Is it so hard to believe not every single girl finds you attractive?' I ask harshly.

'Shit, Candy…' new guy laughs '…it's an invitation to play few games of Battlefield not a blow job.'

And, of course, this is the part of the conversation that Will catches. He stares at us, like maybe he's expecting an explanation but neither of us offer one up.

'Well, this is about as awkward as a Tinder date.' New guy laughs again.

'Sorry to drag you away from the party, Candice, but I've got something urgent I need you to take care of.'

The new guy raises his eyebrows but takes the hint. He scribbles something down on a piece of paper and hands me it.

'If you change your mind,' he says before wandering off.

Will stares at me for a second, so I theatrically screw the new guy's number into a ball, making it clear I have no intention of using it. Will gestures with a nod of his head for me to follow him, before we make our way to his office in silence.

Caroline is sitting by her desk, manning the phone.

'You get off to the party,' Will tells her. 'Candice will answer the phone for a while.'

'Thank you, Mr Starr,' she says with a smile, before subtly narrowing her eyes at me.

As soon as she has gone we step inside Will's office. He closes the door behind him, unbuttons his suit jacket and takes a seat behind his desk. I hover in front of him like a naughty child hauled before the head teacher.

'You know how difficult it was to organise this trip, don't you?' Will asks. 'Squaring it with all the appropriate people, booking hotels, getting the car ready for the journey, making it seem like it was absolutely vital that someone stop by each branch of the firm to make sure that everyone was happy this week, and that that person be me specifically?'

'Yes, yes, yes, yes, yes,' I reply, giving him an answer to each of his questions. I am never usually so cheeky with Will, and my behaviour doesn't go unnoticed. That'll be the vodka.

'So you know that I am doing all of this because I don't want to lose you.'

I nod my head.

'So why do I feel like I need to worry about you and the new lad in IT?' he asks. 'You're always together, laughing and joking – having inappropriate conversations.'

'That's all him. And no, I don't want you to fire him,' I say before Will has a chance to suggest it. 'He's just being friendly.'

'Candice, take it from a man – he is interested in you. All you would need to do is say the word and he'd be all over you. Do you know how that makes me feel?'

'But I'm only interested in you,' I tell him as I walk around his desk and take a seat on his lap. 'We were just having a chat and a drink at the party, that's all.'

I lean forward and give Will a reassuring kiss while we have a moment alone together. It's a slow, sexy kiss. The kind that would usually lead to other things, except…

'You've been drinking,' Will says accusingly. 'The two of you have been getting drunk at work. I could fire you both for this.'

'It was one tiny, little drink,' I tell him, suddenly aware of how tipsy I sound, but equally aware of the fact that, the harder I try to disguise it, the more tipsy I seem. 'To toast Carly leaving.'

'You mean Charlie?' he asks angrily.

Isn't that what I said?

I place my hands on either side of Will's face and look him in the eye.

'Look, it was daft. I'm sorry. But nothing is going on between the new guy and me – I don't even want to be his friend. You know I'm head-over-heels in love with you.'

Will softens a little. 'It's just…I worry. You know why I worry.'

'I know why you worry,' I tell him. 'But it's fine. This trip means everything to me – to us. This is our chance to see how we function as a proper couple, to figure out our future.'

Will nods thoughtfully. 'Good.' He pinches my cheek. 'OK, we'll figure all this out while we're away.'

'What's the plan for Friday then?' I ask.

'Well, we'll need to set off nice and early. Caroline has made all the arrangements – apart from the hotels, obviously. I sorted that so she wouldn't pick up on the fact we're sharing a room. I'll swing by your place, pick up your lovely self and your luggage and get straight off for the ferry to The Isle of Man, and a week of bliss.'

'I can't wait,' I tell him honestly.

'Can you do me a favour, please?' he asks.

'Anything,' I reply.

'I know we're going to figure everything out while we're away but, in the meantime, can you keep clear of the IT department?' he asks. He must be really worried, to be trying to keep me separate from the new guy.

'Sure,' I reply. Anything to keep him happy and to show him that I'm serious about this.

'Right, get back to work, you lush,' he teases, slapping my arse playfully as I stand up.

'Yes, boss,' I giggle, unable to hide my excitement. This trip really will be make or break for us, but I just can't imagine it going any way other than perfectly. We love each other, we get on so well, the thought of me flirting with other guys drives him crazy – you don't get much better than that, do you?

Chapter 9

Moments after leaving Will's office and sitting back at my desk, the new guy turned up with a slice of cake for me. With Will just in his office, I panicked. As amazing as the cake looked…

'I told you,' I don't eat junk, I reminded him.

'I can vividly recall the speed at which you made two doughnuts disappear this week,' he reminded me in turn, 'which proves you do.'

'That was a one-off from my usual diet,' I replied, but that wasn't enough of an explanation for the new guy.

'Who told you that you need to lose weight?' he asked. 'Because if you really are doing this for yourself, someone needs to have a word with you, and if someone has told you that you need to, then I'll be having two words with them and the second one is "off".'

I could have been almost touched by the new guy's concern for me, but I was just so worried about Will walking out and catching us fraternising that I panicked, snapped at him and insisted that I was definitely doing this for myself and that my willpower was flawless. Now I've had to make a mental note to never eat junk in front of him again, because I just know he'll be all smug about it.

Despite my afternoon getting off to a rocky start, it's not enough to take the spring out of my step as I climb the stairs to my flat. I feel on top of the world right now, so much so I can't help but sing to myself as I unlock the door. I walk through the door as I get to a part of Huey Lewis and the News's 'The Power of Love' that my limited vocal range just cannot pull off, only to be greeted by Amy and her gaggle of bridesmaids. Everyone laughs at me.

'Sorry, just really happy today,' I say by way of an explanation.

'Why, have you finally met someone?' Amy's nosey younger cousin Jackie asks. That's the thing about secret relationships, to everyone else I seem like I'm eternally single.

I smile widely.

'Oh my God, you have,' Jackie squeaks, sounding delighted for me. I like Jackie; she's like a fun, energetic little springer spaniel. The same cannot be said for Amy's friend Lea who is, to put it bluntly, a fucking awful person. We've never really got on, and the amount I'm having to see her for wedding-related stuff is really bugging me. It's only as I'm standing here in the living room with Amy and the other bridesmaids that I realise we've got one final dress fitting this evening, just to make sure everyone's dress still fits nicely.

'So you'll be bringing a plus one to the wedding?' Lea asks in disbelief.

'Yep,' I reply confidently. I see Amy pull a face, but I'm confident. My week with Will is going to be perfect, we're going to work everything out and I just know he'll come to the wedding with me. He's really going out of his way to make this work. I'm sure he'll understand that I need him to do this.

'Well I'll pencil it in,' Lea says, making a note in Amy's wedding planner.

'Use a pen,' I tell her, full of confidence. 'In fact, I'll get you one.'

Before I have a chance to start launching stationery at Lea, Amy grabs my dress and steers me towards my bedroom to try it on. I completely forgot we were all meeting here, so I stopped at the shops on the way home to get a few bits for Friday, just in case I didn't have time tomorrow. Everyone has tried her dress on except me.

As Amy closes my bedroom door behind us, I notice the parcels on my bed.

'It's a good job I was in,' Amy starts, 'there was a delivery for you.'

I tear open the larger box like a child on Christmas morning. Inside is a Louis Vuitton suitcase and a holdall, and a note that reads: 'New luggage for the start of a new journey. Love Will.'

'From your fancy man?' Amy asks, and I nod. 'They look expensive.'

I open the second box to find a garment bag with a note attached that reads: 'Not to be opened until day seven.'

'Well, these are going to make my present seem shit,' Amy sighs.

'You got me a present?' I smile. 'Why?'

Amy hands my a little piece of card with a silver bracelet attached. The card reads: 'good luck' and the bracelet has a little silver horseshoe charm hanging from it. I love it!

'Aims, that is beautiful,' I tell her honestly as I remove it from the card to put it on.

'Just a little something to wish you all the best on your little life-changing trip,' she says pulling a face, but I know that she cares about me and it means a lot.

'One thing though,' I start. 'I thought you didn't believe in luck? I thought we were all fully in charge of our own destinies?'

'Oh, we are,' she admits. 'But you need all the help you can get.'

I laugh.

'Right, let's get this dress on and off so I can get you guys out of here, get to bed and get on with the first day of the rest of my life,' I squeak excitedly.

I chat as Amy helps me into my dress. It's baby blue, and one of those multi-way bridesmaid dresses that you can wear several different styles, depending on how you fasten it. It's actually a really beautiful dress, which surprises me. Not because I don't think my friend has good taste, but because I was expecting something hippy-chic to match her usual style. Her wedding dress isn't as hippy-esque as I'd feared it would be, but I'm yet to see what her fiancé, Ted, will be wearing. He's a beardy, plaid-shirt-wearing hipster, so you know it's going to be something cool.

'Thank you for looking after Honey while I'm away,' I tell her as she bandages me into my dress. I know she's not a cat person anyway, but she and Honey really don't like each other.

'Never mind that,' Amy says. 'You've lost more weight!'

'I don't think I have,' I say innocently.

'Oh, "I don't think I have"?' Amy says, mocking my voice. 'You don't notice the number going down when you weigh yourself sixteen times a fucking day?'

'I'm just losing a little body fat,' I tell her.

'You're losing your shape,' she tells me. 'This dress doesn't fit you anymore.'

I examine my body in the mirror, running my hands down my front to smooth my dress out.

'Make sure you eat right while you're away,' Amy insists.

'OK,' I reply with a smile. Maybe I can relax my diet once Will and I have sorted things out. I only panic so much about perfection because I don't want to lose him. So I work out a bit more, eat a bit less, watch my language and dress more appropriately. It's all worth it because I am in love, and when you're in love that's what you do: you make sacrifices.

'And don't forget tomorrow night,' she reminds me.

'Tomorrow night?'

'You forgot tonight, you've forgotten tomorrow night – girl you are forgetting what's important in life and that is my wedding.' She laughs. 'We're meeting here for drinks – my last as a single woman. Remember, it was supposed to be nearer the wedding but you're doing a bunk on me.'

'Oh yeah, of course. I'll be here,' I tell her. I mean, of course I'll be here, I live here, but I'll endure it. It's safe to say that Amy's friends are not my friends, so you can imagine how little I enjoyed her hen party a few weeks ago. Thankfully I survived it, but only by spending it wasted. No chance I can do that tomorrow night though. I can't meet Will in the morning to hit the road with a hangover – he doesn't like it when I drink too much.

I smile at myself in the mirror. Not long to go now. This time on Friday I'll probably be out to dinner with Will. Then we'll be heading to the hotel for a night in a luscious king-size bed. As much as I love Honey, it'll be nice to get a break from her hogging my double bed and waking me up whenever she feels like it because she's hungry.

Nope, not long to go now. From Friday, everything will be different.

Chapter 10

'Oops.'

I feel my eyes dart from left to right, covering every inch of the screen in front of me as I try to work out what the fuck I just did.

'That doesn't sound good,' Caroline observes, looking at me over the top of her glasses. 'What have you done now?'

She makes it sounds like I'm always making mistakes, when really – most of the time – we just differ on what is the most practical way to do things. Sweet Caroline and I often have different opinions. What she will brand 'laziness', I will call 'selective participation' – as a way to better manage my time, of course.

The truth is that I have no idea what I've just done. I've only been at work twenty minutes and already I'm making mistakes. I was going through Will's emails, highlighting the high-priority ones when, suddenly, my screen flipped 180 degrees. Everything is upside down now.

'Erm, everything is upside down now,' I tell her, with no better way to explain my predicament springing to mind.

'Don't be silly, that's not possible,' she tuts.

'No, really.'

I twist my screen around so she can see it.

'How on earth have you done that?' she asks.

'I didn't do anything,' I say defensively. Well, I don't think I did. I was just tapping away on the keyboard and it flipped. This is what happens when you try to get on with work while you're pondering what you'll be ordering from room service in each hotel.

Caroline exhales deeply. 'I'll call IT.'

'There's no need to do that,' I say quickly.

'What are you going to do?' She laughs. 'Stand on your head?'

'Of course not.'

But she's given me an idea. I take a large blob of Blu Tack from my top drawer and fix it firmly on the top of my flat screen monitor, and then I turn it upside down and secure it to my desk.

'Why on earth have you done that?' Caroline asks.

'I don't want to bother IT with it. It's fine, I can work like this,' I insist.

Caroline doesn't have a response to this. She simply picks up her phone. 'Hello,' she says to someone at the other end. 'Candice has had a little accident with her computer – lots on her mind,' she explains. 'Can you send someone up to help? Thank you so much.'

She hangs up the phone before getting back on with her work.

'Someone from IT is on the way. Don't touch anything.'

'Great,' I reply, hoping it's anyone but the new guy. Will is currently in his office working. He just sent me a copy of the itinerary for the week and I couldn't be more excited – that's why I started looking at hotel restaurant menus and getting distracted. The last thing I need is the new guy coming up, talking to me and pissing Will off so close to our trip. I can't think of anything that would better mess up our plans!

I take a piece of hair that isn't wrapped up in my usual, sensible side plait and twirl it with my fingers as I stare at the ceiling. The Isle of Man is the first stop on our trip and while it isn't exactly a trip abroad, I've never actually left Lancashire before. We'll be taking the ferry, which I'm weirdly excited about because I've never been on so much as a pedal boat. That said, my only knowledge of big boats I picked up from two movies: *Titanic*, a movie that everyone has seen (if not during its maiden voyage in 1997, then certainly at least once since) and something called

Ghost Ship that I stumbled upon by accident after getting lost in a dark corner of Netflix one evening. Neither of these films paints a particularly pretty picture when it comes to hitting the open waters, but I'm looking forward to it none the less.

The phone on Caroline's desk is ringing, but she's gone to use the photocopier. I know that I should answer it, but as I approach it I can see from the caller ID who it is: Stephanie, Will's wife. I hesitate for a moment too long and the call goes through to voicemail. No message is left.

I start walking back towards my desk when the phone starts ringing again. I turn around and stare at it, too scared to check if it's Stephanie again. If she's calling for a second time she must really need to speak to Will, but why?

Deep in thought, I don't even notice Caroline re-enter the room. She darts for the phone to answer it.

'Good afternoon, Starr Haulage,' she chirps.

I slink back over to my desk and take a seat behind my upside-down screen. It looks absolutely ridiculous, but it was a fast and effective solution – so long as I remember to move the mouse in the opposite direction, of course.

I look up at Caroline who has gone awfully quiet. I watch as the colour drains from her face, before she quickly dashes into Will's office, closing the door behind her. Now I wish I'd taken the call, or at least looked to see who it was the second time. My mind has gone into overdrive.

'Morning,' I hear a cheeky Geordie accent in the room, snapping me from my thoughts.

'You,' I can't help but say out loud.

'Yes, me,' he replies, confused. 'You have an IT problem, I work in IT – who were you expecting?'

'Never mind,' I reply. 'It's my screen.'

The new guy stares at it thoughtfully for a moment, rubbing his chin as he assesses the issue.

'Right, yes, I see the problem here… *Your monitor is upside down*,' he says patronisingly, raising his voice and enunciating each word.

'*I know that,*' I reply in a similar tone. 'It was the only way I could use it – everything is upside down. I don't know what could've possibly caused it.'

'I do,' he tells me as he returns the monitor to its rightful position. He hits a couple of keys and in an instant everything is the right way up again.

'You probably knocked a keyboard shortcut that rotates your screen without you needing to go into the graphics control panel,' he explains, but I'm not really listening. I'm just staring at Will's office door, wondering what's going on inside.

'You'd be surprised how many people knock it. Candy…Candy!'

'What?' I snap.

'I said you'd be surprised how many people do it by accident. It's probably that Monday morning feeling.'

'It's Thursday,' I remind him.

'Yeah, but any time I'm at work, it feels like a Monday, you know?'

'Right, well, cheers,' I say, hoping he'll clear off. If Will comes out and sees him, he won't be happy.

The new guy takes a seat on my desk.

'So, what you doing tonight?' he asks.

'Packing. I'm working away for a week from tomorrow,' I tell him. Actually I'm already packed but he doesn't need to know that. 'Will is visiting the other branches of the company, making sure everything is in order. I'm his assistant so, I'm assisting.'

'Nice gig, Candy, who did you have to sleep with to get that?' he jokes.

I don't get a chance to correct him getting my name wrong again. I go to open my mouth just as Will's office door opens.

Both Will and Caroline walk out of his office, Will hurrying on his jacket.

'Candice, I'm going to need to postpone the visits to the other offices,' he tells me in that cold, forced professional tone that he uses with me in front of other people so as not to arouse suspicion. Unluckily for Will, I've been so looking forward to this trip that I temporarily forget to adopt a similar tone.

'But you said it was important,' I reply.

'Some things are more important,' Caroline replies.

'But I had to plan my life around this week,' I say to Will directly, hoping he'll take the hint. What I mean is that we arranged this for a reason and it's important. He can't back out now, not the day before we're due to leave. I don't understand.

'You're absolutely right,' he tells me as he pats his pockets, eventually locating his keys. 'Listen, you're right, I know it's affected your plans. Everything is in place – take the trip. Treat it as a sort of working holiday,' he babbles. 'Take one of the girls from the sales department if you like. Have some fun. You've earned it.'

'That's most generous,' Caroline can't help but say.

I look at him, puzzled. If he thinks a week off work staying in hotels with one of the ditzy sales team who he knows I'm not that friendly with is going to make up for him letting me down, he's crazy.

'But you said it was important,' I say again with my voice, but with my eyes I'm pleading with him to reconsider.

'Candice, take Mr Starr's more than generous offer,' Caroline insists. 'He's got a lot on his plate.'

Will heads for the door.

'But – ' I start, but Caroline cuts me off.

'Candice,' Caroline snaps. 'Mr Starr has to get to the hospital right away. His wife has gone into labour much earlier than is safe for the baby.'

Will halts by the door and turns around and looks at me for a moment.

'What?' I ask quietly. I can't have heard that right.

'Hopefully everything will be OK,' he tells me, and I'm not sure if he's talking about the baby or our situation.

For a moment, we just stare at each other. It's probably only a few seconds, but it feels like an eternity. The realisation crashes over me like a huge wave on a beach and it takes my breath away. Will's wife is having a baby – *his* baby – and I don't need to be a mathematician to work out that it was definitely conceived after Will and I started seeing each other. All this time I've felt like an 'other woman' – that's because I was one.

'Well, I'd best get back to work,' the new guy says, making his excuses to get out of this awkward situation.

I'd forgotten he was still in the room, but in a moment of madness and anger I realise how I can hurt Will, even if it's just a bit.

'I want the new guy to come with me,' I tell them. Everyone stares at me. 'On the business trip – I'll take the new guy.'

'You…you can't do that,' Will stutters.

'Why not?' I ask. 'I can show him the company, see if we can't get him to stick around full-time. That's what you want, isn't it?'

'That's a great idea,' Caroline says. She's certainly not immune to the new guy's charm – few women are.

'He has work to do,' Will insists.

'Actually,' new guy speaks up, 'I'm front-end. There's nothing for me to do until some back-end stuff is finished. That's why I'm getting the rubbish jobs, like rotating screens.'

None of us has the remotest idea what this means. The new guy winks at me, and I see Will's face flush with anger like I've never seen before.

'See. And he drives, so travel problem solved.'

'Well, that's all sorted. You get off, Mr Starr,' Caroline insists. 'Know that you don't need to worry about this. I'm sure Candice is more than capable.'

'But – ' Will starts, but she cuts him off.

'Mr Starr, go see your wife. She needs you. I'll take care of everything here.'

I watch as Will leaves reluctantly. We hold eye contact for a second, and then he's gone.

With the new guy and Caroline still in the room, I know that I can't cry. To be honest, I don't think I could cry. I can't even think straight.

'My name is Danny.'

'What?' I ask.

'My name,' the new guy repeats. 'It's Danny. You don't know my name, do you, Candy?'

'Of course I know your name,' I snap. 'It's you who doesn't know my name. It's Candice. Not Candy.'

'Are you sure you want to go with *her*?' Caroline asks, amazed Danny is considering it.

'Happily,' he replies. 'It'll be a nice break from this place, and it sounds like she needs a ride.'

Danny nods towards me and I raise my eyebrows.

'Well, Mr Starr has taken care of hotels for the entire trip. I'll print you a copy of the travel itinerary, get you the money for fuel...'

As Caroline fills Danny in on everything he needs to know, I tune out for a moment. There's a loud ringing noise in my ears that is blocking out everything but my thoughts. How could he do this to me? He told me that he loved me, and yet he's been lying to me all this time. Like my screen, in an instant everything has been turned upside down except, with my life, there's no shortcut that's going to put things right again.

Chapter 11

I walk up the stairs to my flat without the same all-singing, all-dancing spring in my step that I had yesterday. I unlock my door, close it behind me and then slide down it until I am on the floor, hugging my knees. That's when the tears start. Tears of hurt, tears of shock, tears of anger. I am experiencing so many powerful emotions that I was not expecting, I don't know which one to process first. And just in case things weren't bad enough, I've gone and made things much, much worse for myself by signing myself up for this trip with Danny, the new guy.

For a split second, it felt amazing to see the look on Will's face when he realised I was taking Danny on our romantic getaway. Now that things are sinking in, I've realised what a terrible mistake I've made because it isn't just enjoying that look on Will's face for that moment – I actually have to spend an entire week with Danny. I'll admit that Danny can be fun, but in short bursts. He mostly just annoys me; it's his arrogant confidence. He's so sure of himself. He doesn't give a shit what people think and for some reason that annoys me too. The thing is, I can't back out now. If I do, Will has won. I want to teach him a lesson, I want him worrying about what's going on, but being powerless to know. If I don't go, he'll know that I'm still just hanging around, alone and miserable. He'll know that I'm upset, but I want him to think that I'm expressing my sadness by shagging the hot new guy, at the very least.

I can't believe that all this time he's still been with his wife.

Actually with his wife. Living with her, loving her, knocking her up! I feel so monumentally stupid for believing they weren't together any more.

Here I am, sitting on the floor crying my eyes out, all while he's at the hospital playing happy families. He has ruined my life, and I've let him.

I pull my handbag close to me and search around for the screwed-up piece of paper with Danny's phone number on, to text him my address so he can pick me up in the morning.

Soon after I send it, a text comes through from Amy.

> Amy: Be over with the girls in 20 mins. Xxx

I exhale deeply as I type my reply. There's just something about committing what has happened to a sentence that makes it all the more painful. I have to constantly blink away my tears just so I can read my phone screen.

> Me: OK. Will has backed out of our trip – his wife went into labour today. Xxx

> Amy: That ducking count! Xxx

> Amy: Soz! Autocorrect xxx

I can't help but laugh and it feels good to smile, even if it's only for a second. Then the wave washes over me again.

> Me: Thank you. I'm still going, did a stupid thing – invited Danny the new guy from work to piss Will off. I'll have to back out, there's no way I can handle that. Xxx

> Amy: We'll talk tonight. Xxx

I head into my bedroom, only to be greeted by the luggage that Will bought me. Lying on top of the suitcase is the garment bag, the one with the note telling me not to open it until day seven. I unzip it and look inside to find a floor-length black dinner dress that looks awfully expensive but I couldn't care less. I wonder what to do with it. I could throw it out the window, I could set it on fire… I could write a little love story about my relationship with Will on it and then send it to his wife. Nope, that's not my style. I wish it were. I wish I could hurt him and ruin his life, but I'm too conscious of the other lives I'd be ruining in the process – his wife and kids don't deserve the fallout.

There's a note fixed to it, which I cannot resist reading.

'For a special girl on a special night.'

I screw up the note and toss it in the direction of the bin before hanging the dress in my wardrobe. Maybe I can find a way to subtly return it to him once I'm back, in a scenario where I'm less likely to stuff it in his stupid, lying mouth. I'd do the same with his stupid, expensive luggage too, were it not too late to unpack and repack. Anyway, I can't possibly go, can I? So I'll just sort it all tomorrow.

'Hello,' Amy calls out from the living room.

'I'm in here,' I call back, my voice cracking.

Amy walks into my bedroom and stares at me for a second.

'I know that you are too nice to even be thinking "I told you so" but you did tell me so. I'm such an idiot.'

Amy grabs me and hugs me tightly.

'You're not an idiot. You're not the first person to believe a lying, cheating bastard-man,' she assures me, but knowing that this has happened to other people doesn't make it any easier. 'Listen, the girls are through there setting up, popping corks, getting the cheesy chick music on so we can have a dance – just forget about it for now and we'll talk about it later, yeah?'

'OK, sure,' I reply, wiping my eyes and sucking it up a little before heading into the living room.

Unsurprisingly, Amy's hen party had not been my idea of fun. Things didn't get off to a great start when Jackie commented on the little bit of weight I'd lost. Lea obviously didn't like this, and she started making little comments. We all got talking about the bridesmaid dresses, which only come in two sizes: eight to eighteen and twenty to twenty-six. All of the bridesmaids fell into the smaller bracket, but when I mentioned that one particular way of wearing the multi-way dresses made me look a bit busty, Lea suggested I might like to wear the bigger size – the twenty to twenty-six. I mean, I know I'm taking Will's advice about getting into better shape, and I know that I have a fondness for baked goods, but I also know that I'm not even close to plus size and that Lea was only saying it to try and make me feel uncomfortable. But that didn't stop it upsetting me. Then she got on at me about being single, which is probably why the last time I saw her I was so quick to mention that Will would be coming to the wedding with me. Jesus Christ, what an idiot I was to think that would be an option. And now I'm definitely going to be going alone, and Lea is going to love it.

We all exchange hugs and hellos and as Amy's friend Sarah starts playing a CD called 'Chick Flick Classics', Amy shoves a glass of white wine in my hand. As I consider just how many calories are in wine, I knock it back quickly. Fuck the fucking calories.

'Easy now,' Amy instructs, topping up my glass while giving me a look that commands me to savour the next one.

'What's the matter?' Lea asks. 'Trouble in paradise?'

'Not at all,' I reply. 'I'm just getting the party started.'

Lea nods, although she seems unconvinced.

Jackie is pouring Maltesers into a bowl. The second she puts the bowl down on the coffee table, I scoop a handful and begin eating them two or three at a time, not even swallowing the previous mouthful before loading in the next. Because I'm hungry – so *so* hungry – and I'm angry. I'm hangry. I feel like every delicious thing I turned down to make Will happy was a mistake and I'm going to make up for it tonight.

'OK, something is wrong,' Lea insists. 'You're eating. I thought you stopped eating because you were getting a bit shapely.'

'All fine,' I tell her, ignoring her fat remark.

'Tell us about your bloke,' Jackie insists as she eats peanut M&Ms that I hadn't noticed were in the room, but that I'd much prefer to eat. Everyone looks at me expectantly. Amy looks anxious because she knows that I can't answer this. As I realise I've finished my second glass, I pour myself another and sit down next to Jackie as though I'm going to tell her all about my man, when really it's just so I can be closer to the chocolate.

'He's a guy from work,' I tell them. 'He's so cool and funny. I'm so lucky to have him.'

Jackie smiles and leaves it at that, but Lea persists.

'What's does he look like?' she asks.

It feels like an eternity in my head, but the lie comes quickly and naturally.

'Tall, dark and handsome,' I reply. It's a cliché, but it'll do. 'But he's so smart and funny too. I'm a really lucky girl.'

'All that matters is having a guy who makes you laugh,' Amy says, changing the subject.

'And it doesn't hurt that my bloke is rich,' Lea says smugly. Cash rich, but girlfriend poor, clearly.

I can't believe I'm doing this, making up stories to keep Lea off my back. But what else can I do? Tell the truth and watch as Lea revels in it? No, no, no. I guess I'll just pour myself another drink.

※※※

'Top night, girlies. Absolutely ace!' Jackie's screechy voice goes right through me. I rub my tired eyes, examining my black fingertips before realising I just rubbed eye make-up all over my face. I hold my glass up in front of my face and see that it is empty, but then I realise that the contents are all over my lap.

'What? We're calling it a night already?' I ask, trying to pull myself up from the sofa but rocking back onto my bum like a Weeble.

'It's two a.m., babe,' Amy says, like she's talking to a child who doesn't know when her bedtime is.

'Oh,' I reply. 'I think I've had too much to drink.'

'I think you have too.' She laughs. 'Let me show this lot out; we'll get you to bed.'

'OK,' I reply, resting my eyes for a moment.

I can hear Amy clattering around, tidying up before I feel her hands on my shoulders.

'Right, up we go,' she instructs. I do as I'm told.

'Are you leaving me?' I ask.

'So you can choke on your own vomit while you sleep? Nope.'

'You're such a good friend,' I tell her as I attempt to gently place a hand on her face. Instead, I poke her in the eye.

Amy pulls my clothes off me, sits me down on the toilet and begins wiping off my make-up with a wipe. We hold eye contact for a moment, but as Amy smiles at me I feel my eyes well up with tears. Suddenly, I'm wailing.

'Come on, don't cry. I know it might not seem like it now, but it's all going to be OK.'

'It's not though,' I insist. 'Everyone who I love leaves me. My parents are gone, you're leaving me and now Will is gone. And I still have to work for him because I'm too poor to just quit my job.'

Amy escorts me to the sink and places a toothbrush complete with toothpaste in my hand.

'Brush,' she demands, so I do as I'm told. 'Look, I might be getting married, but I'm always going to be here for you. And we can find you a new job that you love. And, OK, maybe you'll have to back down on a few things – like backing out of the trip and admitting that you've split from your boyfriend and going to the wedding solo – but people will get over it. Although you really sold Danny to Lea.'

'What do you mean?' I mumble through a mouth full of toothpaste.

'Spit,' Amy instructs.

'I said, what do you mean?'

'When Lea continued to quiz you about this boyfriend from work that you said you were seeing, I think you described Danny...'

'Why would you think that?'

'Erm, because you said his name was Danny and you described him like you did to me.'

'Oh God, what did I say?' I ask as Amy struggles my pyjamas onto my body.

'You said that he spent all day, every day hanging around your desk, trying to make you laugh.'

'I've said that to you before,' I remind her. 'I complain about that all the time.'

Amy pushes me in the direction of my bed.

'Yeah, but instead of saying it in your usual annoyed tone, you had this happy, upbeat voice going on. Just saying it in this positive way made what you usually think is a negative thing sound like a positive. Everyone though he sounded wonderful, especially when you described his looks – he sounds fit.'

Oh God, I know that I was lying, but I feel slightly pissed off at myself for giving Danny any kind of credit. It annoys me to speak positively about him out loud because if he knew, his ego would grow even bigger.

'Where's your phone?' Amy asks. 'I'll put it on charge for you.'

Probably where I was sitting in the living room.

From the comfort of my bed, I glance over at my packed bags. Unpacking them tomorrow is going to break my heart and I feel my eyes fill with tears again.

'Want to check it before bed?' Amy asks, tossing me my phone, which I do not catch.

I pick it up from where it landed and unlock it to see that my text thread with Will is open. Brilliant, I sent him six messages telling him how upset I am. I can see that as the night went on I was getting more drunk and more upset. My last message told him I 'feel dick', which I will imagine is AutoCorrect's take on 'feel sick'. Perfect. I'm not surprised he hasn't replied.

Amy puts my phone on charge and hops in bed next to me.

'I'll help you figure everything out in the morning, when you're sober, I promise. OK?'

I nod my head.

'And I'm sleeping in here with you tonight,' she insists. 'I'll keep an eye on you; just try to relax.'

'OK, thank you,' I reply soppily, snuggling up in my bed.

'I love you, babe.'

'I love you too,' I tell her, just as I feel my eyes getting heavy. I'll sleep this off and then in the morning, with a clear head, I'll be able to figure everything out.

Chapter 12

Amy places a strong coffee on my bedside table and prods me to make sure I'm awake.

'I don't drink coffee,' I tell her, just in case it might've slipped her mind.

'You do today.' She laughs.

As I pull myself upright, an epic headache hits me like a blow to the head.

'Ouch!'

'That's why.' She laughs again.

'Thank you for looking after me last night...' I start, but we're interrupted by someone ringing the doorbell to the tune of what I think is Bon Jovi's 'Livin' on a Prayer'.

'I'll get rid of whoever it is,' Amy says. 'Drink your coffee.'

As Amy dashes off, I pick up the cup and examine the jet-black contents. I hold the mug to my nose and inhale but the smell turns my stomach. I think I'll stick with the headache.

I grab my phone, only to see if I have any replies from Will, but I don't. Surprise surprise. That's when I hear Amy giggling with someone. My cool, tough, taken friend Amy is giggling like a teenage girl meeting One Direction.

I try to listen carefully but I can't make out what she's saying. Eventually she walks back into my room and closes the door behind her. She bites her lip theatrically.

'Danny is here,' she whispers.

'What? Oh, no. I never texted him to call off the trip.' I pull myself out of bed slowly. 'I'll go tell him now.'

'Don't you dare,' Amy says sternly. 'I think you should go.'

'Why on earth would I do that?'

'Because you deserve some time off, away from Will, and you might even have fun.'

'That sounds very unlikely…but I could do with the break from Will, I suppose.'

I can't stand the thought of having to face Will yet, and I can't quit my job without having another one to go to. And I know it will drive Will crazy to know that I'm away with Danny. Maybe the break will do me good, and Danny might not be so annoying outside the office.

'OK, go keep him distracted while I get ready.'

'Gladly,' Amy says with a wink.

I dash to the bathroom and take a long, hard look in the mirror. What a mess. And I'm not just talking about my situation, I'm talking about my appearance too.

I quickly pull my hair into a side plait and grab the outfit from the back of the door. It's the one I had ready for leaving with Will, but it's going to have to do – along with all of the other sensible clothing that I packed. I quickly apply my make-up with all the skill of a six-year-old who has found a way to reach her mummy's make-up drawer, before heading into the living room.

'Hey,' Danny says with a big smile.

'Hello,' I reply. I look over at Amy who is all giggly and gooey over Danny. With his fashionable stubble and his stupid topknot, I should've known he'd be just Amy's type.

'We all set?' he asks, and I nod. 'OK, well I'll take these to the car.'

Amy waits patiently for Danny to leave the room before squealing with joy.

'That's Danny,' she squeaks.

'You know it is,' I reply, awkwardly.

'Remind me why you turned down a date with him?'

'Not my type.'

'Not your type?' Amy gasps. 'He is fucking fit!'

Danny clears his throat in the doorway, alerting us to his presence before we can say anything else.

'Forgot my keys,' he says with a cheeky smile. He grabs them and then leaves again.

'Seriously,' Amy whispers. 'That wanker you were seeing – he was taken, he was old and he was boring. But this guy! He's young, he's hot, he's funny. Promise me you'll give him a chance.'

'Aims, it's a business trip. And I'm heartbroken! The last thing I want is another man!'

'Just think about it,' she insists. 'Anyway, you pretty much told Lea that Danny would be going to my wedding with you, so maybe if you get on well, he might come – even if it's just out of pity.'

'Wow, thanks.'

Amy laughs.

'Right, I'd better go.'

She grabs me for another big hug, kissing me on the cheek.

'Be careful, have fun – and try not to think about you-know-who. Just enjoy yourself.'

'I'll try,' I tell her, although I doubt that's going to be possible. 'Gosh, I won't see you until your wedding day. Sorry I won't be around to help get things ready.'

'So long as you're back in time, and you're happy. That's all I care about.'

My friend hugs me one last time before leaving, giving me just enough time to say goodbye to Honey before Danny walks back in.

'Of course you have a cat.' Danny laughs.

'What do you mean by that?' I ask defensively.

'I always find the kind of women who say no to dates with me have cats.'

'Meaning?'

'Just an observation.' He smiles. 'Nice place you got here,

very...' Danny visibly wracks his brains for the appropriate word '...clinical.'

'Clinical?' I squeak. 'What the heck does that mean?'

'Heck? Really?' Danny shakes his head. 'I just mean it's very tidy, babe. Clean. Like maybe you murdered someone and then cleaned up – like, really cleaned up. You know?'

'I really don't know,' I tell him. 'Good work offending me though. Twice. And in such a short amount of time.'

'You're welcome, Candy. Now, let's hit the road.'

Danny twirls his hands before pointing enthusiastically towards the door with both index fingers.

'Let's go,' I reply.

'Say goodbye to life as you know it,' he tells me. 'It's going to be a roller coaster.'

I laugh to myself. Danny doesn't know the half of it.

✳✳✳

'I thought you said you had a car,' I blurt out. We're currently standing outside my flat. There's a taxi bay, full of taxis as usual, but parked amongst them is what I can only describe as a clown car.

'I do,' he says proudly. 'Meet the Love Bug.'

He gestures towards the clown car with both hands, as if to say ta-da. Then he does actually say 'ta-da', catching the attention of one of the cabbies.

'Mate, this is drop off/pick up only,' the driver tells him angrily.

'I know. I'm picking her up.'

Danny nods towards me.

'For taxis only,' the driver adds angrily.

'All right, all right, we're going. Candy, get in.'

'If you think I'm going on a road trip in that, then you're out of your mind.'

'What's wrong with the Love Bug?' Danny asks, defensively.

'The name, for one. Also, it looks like Herbie.'

The taxi driver takes a brief moment from being angry to laugh at me, for teasing Danny over his car. The thing is though, I'm not joking. This thing looks like a death trap.

'Fair enough, they're both cream,' Danny starts. 'But Herbie is from the sixties. This car might share a name with the first Herbie movie, but that's where the resemblance ends. What you're looking at here is a fully restored 1978 VW Beetle 1300. It's a classic.'

'It's a relic,' the cabby laughs.

'Mind your own business,' Danny snaps at him, clearly offended on behalf of his precious car.

'This *is* my business,' the cabby yells. 'I can't get my fucking car out because you're blocking the fucking way.'

'I'm moving!' Danny yells back. 'Candy, get in the car.'

'No. We can't go in that. It won't make it.'

'Of course it will. I promise you, I've spent thousands doing it up.'

The cabby, who is back in his car, beeps his horn angrily.

'Please just get in the car,' Danny pleads. 'We'll drive around the block and see how you feel.'

'Oh, fine, fine. Can you put this in the boot, please?' I ask, heading for the back of the car with my holdall.

'The engine is in the boot,' he informs me. 'This goes under the bonnet.'

'Of course it does,' I reply, heading towards the passenger side. I pull on the handle but nothing happens, so I try again using a little more force this time.

'Whoa, gently, gently.' Danny winces as he places his hands on my shoulders and steers me towards the driver's side. 'That door doesn't work, so you've got to get in this side and climb over.'

'Death trap,' I mutter to myself quietly.

As I clamber over the driver's seat of Danny's car, or the Love Bug as he calls it, I notice it has a very distinctive smell that I cannot place. I'd imagine this was that 'new car smell' everyone talks about, were it not for the fact this car is so very, very old. To give Danny his due though, it does look like he's spent a lot of money doing the car up. The inside is all new and shiny, with a stereo system that looks like it's worth more than the car itself. It might look like a hunk of junk from the outside, but the inside has had a typical boy racer makeover.

As the cab drivers continue to honk their horns, Danny eventually hops in the driver's seat.

'And we're off,' he says as he pulls out. 'Well, babe, what do you think?'

I scoff. 'I don't know what's worse,' I tell him. 'When you call me Candy or when you call me babe.'

'Why do you hate being called Candy so much? I think it's cute.'

'My surname is Hart. Candy Hart – sounds like a name that a stripper would choose for herself,' I tell him. 'And I hate being called babe. Babe, love, doll, darling, beautiful – that's all I hear, all day long at work. They're all empty compliments.'

'Wow, that's depressing,' Danny says. 'Tell you what then, if you're sick of compliments, how about I call you bro? Nothing special, you're just one of the guys.'

'Oh, lovely, thank you,' I reply sarcastically.

'You're welcome, bro.'

I roll my eyes. Something I seem to do a lot around Danny.

Despite promising to drive me around the block, I can tell that Danny is definitely headed for Liverpool so that we can catch the ferry. I feel like a child who's being manipulated by her parents into doing something she doesn't want to do. I suppose Danny's car isn't that bad. I think the problem might just be that I don't want to go anywhere at all, and I'm looking for an excuse.

'So, we're all good to go in the Love Bug?' Danny asks, reading my mind.

'I suppose we'll have to be,' I tell him with a deep sigh. 'Why on earth do you call it the Love Bug?'

'Isn't it obvious?' he asks.

'Well, yeah, I guess – because it's a Beetle.'

'Let's just say that back seat has seen some things that, if it were a person, it would require a lot of therapy to sleep at night.'

'Ew! Remind me not to get in the back.'

'Hey, if you're squeamish about that stuff you're not going to want to sit there either.' He laughs. 'Or the driver's seat. Or the bonnet. I think something might have happened on the roof one time, but I was drunk so… Jesus, look at your face!'

'What's wrong with my face?'

'You're looking at me like you've never got wasted and had sex on a car before,' he says, like it's an everyday thing.

'And you're talking to me about this stuff like it's standard procedure.'

'How do you know it isn't?' he asks, side-glancing at me as he drives. 'Maybe you're just uptight.'

'I am not uptight,' I protest. 'You don't even know me so you can't make judgements like that.'

'You're right, I don't know you that well, but I'm a very perceptive person, and you are uptight.'

I shrug my shoulders.

'Do you not get tired of it?' he asks.

'Of what?'

'Being so perfect,' he tells me.

'Thank you.'

'Candy, that wasn't a compliment.' Danny pauses for a second, clearly battling with whether or not to continue sharing his opinion. 'It doesn't matter, I'll shut up.'

'Go on…'

'No, you'll get upset.'

'Do your worst,' I insist. 'I want to know what you think.'

'We're going on a road trip, and you're dressed like the prime minister's wife. You're sitting in a car with your legs crossed at the knees – who does that? In fact, whenever I see you sitting, you always have your legs crossed. Your posture is exhausting to look at. I just want you to slouch, even if it's just for a minute. You say things like "gosh" and "what on earth" and…even my nana dropped a few F-bombs now and then, you know what I mean?'

'Listen to yourself,' I start. 'If not swearing, not sitting with my legs open and keeping my back straight means I'm being perfect, then I'm happy to be perfect. What do you want me to do? Sit like a bloke with my hand down my pants and be like "eff this, eff that"?'

'But no one is perfect,' Danny insists, the debate getting more heated. 'That means you're pretending to be perfect and pretending to be perfect doesn't make you perfect, it makes you crazy.'

'Keep your eyes on the road,' I tell him. 'I don't feel safe in this thing as it is.'

'It's a great car and I'm an excellent driver, don't worry so much.'

'So, tell me, Danny, what do you suggest I do?' I ask curiously. Not that I give a shit what he thinks, but I'm fascinated to see where I'm going wrong. The thing he doesn't realise is that while I might not be the kind of girl he would go for, he isn't the kind of guy I would go for either. What he sees as crazy behaviour is the reason Will loves me. Well, said he loved me. He couldn't love me and hurt me so spectacularly, could he? I check my phone to see if he has replied to any of my texts but no such luck.

'I want to hear you swear. I want you to put your feet up on the dashboard so I can yell at you to get your fucking feet off my fucking dashboard. I want you to let your hair down for once.'

'I often let my hair down,' I insist.

'No, I mean literally let your hair down. You never seem relaxed.'

I can't help but laugh, but it's an infuriated laugh, the kind that is born of anger and not amusement.

'Well, thanks for that,' I tell him sarcastically. 'So rude.'

'I'm not rude,' he replies. 'I just have the balls to say what everyone else is too scared to. It isn't rude if it's true.'

I glance at my phone again. Still nothing from Will and I feel the anger surge up inside me again.

'Christ, you're in a mood today,' he observes. 'I mean, you're always grumpy, but you're especially grumpy today.'

I ignore him.

'Can we have the radio on or something, please?' I snap, unable to take a second more of his 'banter' – a term that I hate, because it's pretty much just a blanket excuse for being a wanker.

'Sure,' he replies, hitting a few buttons.

As his ridiculous stereo system booms some ridiculous dubstep tune, as much as I hate it, and as much as it's making my hangover worse, I realise the dreadful wub-wub-wub sound is preferable to Danny's character analysis of me. One thing is for certain, it's going to be a long week.

Chapter 13

The drive to Liverpool was a relatively peaceful one – probably because I pretended to fall asleep and then kept my eyes shut for most of the journey. I was very much awake though, fretting over Will not texting me back – and when we arrived at the ferry port, a little bit of that excitement came back. Yes, my world had fallen to pieces, but my first time on a ferry was still sparking a little something in me. We parked the Love Bug below deck and (after Danny spent the longest time making sure it would be OK down there by asking the steward a million questions) we headed up the stairs towards the passengers' lounge.

As we stepped out onto the open deck, I looked out to sea and couldn't get over how beautiful it was. It's a beautiful summer's day and the water looked so flat and calm. The world just seemed so open and full of possibilities. It wasn't like my world was everything that was in front of my face – I could see for miles, although it was impossible for me to tell how many. We could literally sail off into the sunset.

Danny popped inside to have a drink and relax but I wanted to stay outside. Partly to avoid spending time with him, but also because I wanted to take in the view as we left the shore. As we pulled away, I watched Liverpool getting smaller and smaller, and it felt great…until it didn't. You know that momentary feeling when you get off a fairground ride and your legs feel like jelly? You feel sick, dizzy and off your tits on adrenalin, but only for an instant. Well my brief longing for a life at sea – just aimlessly sailing towards the sunset – was exactly that, brief, because my body repels being on a boat like it does being in a proper relationship. Ever since we left the shore, I've felt like I have just stepped off a waltzer – after drinking twelve milkshakes and going on it three times forwards, then another three backwards – and it's been an hour now.

'You all right here, Elizabeth Swann? You're not looking too hot,' Danny says, strolling up to me on the deck.

'Thanks,' I reply, through gritted teeth. 'I'm just tired.'

'After that epic display of narcolepsy you displayed on the way here?'

I stare at him blankly.

'You one of those who sleeps through car journeys? Was a proper dull trek without company.'

I shrug my shoulders.

'You want to come inside for a bit? I'll get you a drink or something.'

The truth is, I don't think I could go inside if I wanted to. That just-off-a-waltzer feeling has my head spinning and the contents of my stomach feeling like they might be about to put in an appearance. I'm clutching the railing for dear life, and the thought of trying to put one foot in front of the other makes my head spin even faster.

'Seasickness?' he asks, and I nod gently. It doesn't feel good to move my head, but it feels worse to open my mouth. 'Thought you were looking a little green around the gills. Well, I could sing "Sailing" in the style of Rod Stewart and sway from side to side in front of you, or I could tell you what the mariner I met while I was travelling in – '

'Danny, I'm not in the mood for one of your stories right now. Can you just leave me alone, please?'

'Sure,' he says quietly, walking off.

For a second, I feel bad. Just because I'm feeling ill and upset over Will, there's no need for me to take it out on Danny, even if he does annoy me most of the time.

I lean over the side of the ferry and watch the choppy water lapping up against the side. I side-glance and see another girl leaning over the side. She's looking about as rough as I feel, and we exchange a sisterly glance of shared suffering. As I cautiously pull the corners of my mouth into a comforting smile, the girl leans over the railings and starts throwing up. Seasickness, it turns out, is like a cold in a primary school playground: contagious. Watching this girl being sick combined with the undulating movement of the boat is enough to push me over the edge, and we are sick in sync.

I slowly make my way to a nearby bench and sit down, exhaling as deeply as I can without being sick again. I hear a rustling noise, before I notice a little packet of ginger biscuits sliding towards me along the bench. I look up to see Danny, waving a white serviette at me.

'Been sick?' he asks.

'Yes,' I reply, quietly.

'Eat those, they'll help,' he tells me. 'And don't dangle over the side like that lass is doing – that's why she's throwing up. Focus on the horizon. It's the only thing that isn't moving.'

I do as he instructs, looking at the horizon as I nibble on one of the biscuits.

'I went on this fishing trip,' Danny tells me, sitting down next to me, leaning back with his hands behind his head. In his tight-fitting, muscle-hugging T-shirt, the bulging of his biceps temporarily catches my eye, but this is something I hopefully do subtly. 'We had this little stove below deck. It was my turn to make dinner, so I was heating up this tinned chilli – my culinary skills far surpass what I was capable of on the boat, just so you know.' He laughs. 'It was a particularly rough evening at sea – cold too – so I was down there cooking, shut in this little room, the boat bouncing around on the water like a beach ball, and then the smell of the food… It filled the room, filled my lungs. I hadn't suffered a second of seasickness until I caught a whiff of that food and I felt like I was going to die. I made my way to the deck to get some air, did exactly as the skipper told me, and it soon passed. I'll never forget that feeling through. Horrible.'

As I nibble my biscuits and alternate focusing on the horizon with focusing on Danny's arms/story, I realise that I don't feel quite so shocking any more. I don't feel great, but I don't feel like I want to throw myself overboard either.

'Thank you,' I tell him sincerely.

'You're welcome,' he replies. 'Anyway, we need to sort you out before you get back in the Love Bug. I can't have you throwing up in my woman.'

'Charming,' I reply.

Danny rummages around in his pocket and pulls out a folded-up piece of paper.

'Let's see what the boss's anal list dictates we do when we get off the boat,' he says. 'He a planner, our Mr Starr, isn't he?'

I nod. I suppose you have to be when you're living a secret double life. The devil is in the details, and it's the little discrepancies in your story that catch you out. Like, I don't know, how you can suddenly have a prematurely born baby with another woman when you've supposedly been in a committed relationship with someone for a year. You know, little things like that.

'First up, we check into the hotel,' he tells me. 'It's not too far from the depot, so we can clean you up a little then head straight over.'

Danny laughs at the state of me.

'Thanks,' I reply sarcastically.

'Are we not cutting it a bit fine?' Danny asks. 'It'll be close to closing time when we get there.'

'It won't take long,' I tell him. The truth is that we had no intention of calling in to the depot tonight. Will was going poke his head around the door in the morning, before we hit the road early to head to Newcastle. That way we could get settled and have some fun. That's the problem with pretending you're on a business trip – you have to pretend you're doing business.

'So, what exactly do you have to do when we visit these places, and why exactly did you think something so boring would convince me to stay with the firm full-time?' he asks.

Very difficult questions to answer without the truth, aren't they?

'Just look in, touch base, show everyone that the big boss thinks of them – that kind of thing.'

'So we can say hi and then go off and have fun?' he asks. 'Is that why you invited me? So we can use it as an excuse to slack off from work and have a laugh?'

'No,' I reply, a little too quickly.

'Didn't think that sounded like you,' he admits, like I'm the most boring person he's ever met. 'But you want to convince me to stick around?'

'No,' I reply, again, far too quickly. 'I didn't want to get stuck with one of the annoying women from marketing. I used to work in there, and all they talk about is what they bought from IKEA at the weekend and *The Undateables* and how to braise things. They are not my people.'

'And nerdy IT guys are?' He laughs.

'No, but you're preferable.'

'Preferable to chatting about lamps and meat – wow, Candy, you're killing me with kindness.'

I shrug my shoulders.

'Because you're a regular Prince Charming,' I reply.

'You're not going to be much fun this week, are you?'

I don't give him an answer; I just stare at the horizon.

'You never know,' he says, 'you might actually enjoy yourself if you let that hair down.'

I know that to Danny I probably seem more uptight than ever, but he has no idea what I'm going through. There's no way I can tell him though. I'll just have to suffer in silence.

Chapter 14

'And if you follow Samuel, he'll carry your bags to your room for you,' the receptionist chirps.

'Rooms?' Danny says.

'Sorry?' the receptionist is confused.

'You mean rooms, right?' he clarifies.

'No, room,' she repeats. 'The booking is for one double room.'

Danny and I look at each other for a moment. That's when it occurs to me that of course there's only one room booked. That's because Will booked them for the two of us and, wherever we go, there's only going to be one room booked. I try to think fast, but it probably takes me longer to come up with something than the instant it feels like in my head. If I can just explain away this one instance, I can get in touch with Will and have him sort it, so that tomorrow night there will be two rooms and it won't seem so obvious.

'There must have been some kind of error with the booking,' I reason casually. 'It's OK, I can just book another one.'

'I'm sorry, but we're full tonight,' the receptionist tells me, not sounding like she's going to lose any sleep over it.

Again, Danny and I look at each other, neither of us knowing what to say.

'Look, don't worry, we'll figure something out,' Danny assures me. 'Let's head up, get changed, show our faces at the office so you can do whatever it is you need to do, then we'll see what other options we have.'

'OK, sure,' I reply.

We step into the lift with Samuel, who takes our cases for us. It's an awkward journey, but a brief one thankfully. As we arrive at our room, Samuel takes us through where everything is. He flicks on the lamp next to the TV, illuminating the room. He gestures towards the double bed – which is neatly made up with floral print sheets – and the pine furniture. The fridge is tucked away, hidden behind a cupboard door under the desk, which Samuel lets us know by simply opening it. He isn't saying a word, just pointing out that there is indeed furniture in the room.

Samuel shows us into the bathroom, with its fluffy white robes and squeaky clean, brilliant white facilities. There's a selection of fancy-looking bath products sitting on the side, which I make plans for the second I clap eyes on them.

Samuel leaves and Danny pops into the bathroom to freshen up, leaving me alone. I check my phone. Still no word from Will, but I need to sort this hotel problem with him so I'll have to text him again.

Me: I need to talk to you. It's important.

With the message sent and Danny occupying the bathroom, there's not much to do but think. Rather than dwell on the epic fail that is my life right now, I take in my surroundings and conclude that hotels are weird.

It's uncanny, the way the room tries so desperately to be a 'home away from home', and yet that couldn't be further from the truth. Sure, there's the pretty furnishings, a TV and – of course, what every home needs – the kettle and teacups, but it's all a façade. Like anything, when you look closer, the cracks begin to show. There's the no smoking signs, the room service menu next to the phone and those anti-suicide locks on the windows that prevent you from opening them wide enough to even reach your hand outside to feel the air.

If I had come here with Will, I wonder what we'd be doing right now. If his wife hadn't gone into labour prematurely, I never would've known. We'd be here, playing house in this fake home, but our relationship would be just as false as the Monet on the wall above the bed. It might look like the real deal, but it's nothing but a copy, and a copy is worth nothing.

'Right, bro, I'm ready to go. Get a wriggle on,' Danny chirps, snapping me from my increasingly depressive thoughts.

'Must you call me that?' I ask.

'Must you call me that?' he repeats, mimicking my accent. 'The way you speak fascinates me.'

'The way *I* speak fascinates *you*, *pet*?'

'Playing the Geordie card – that's low,' he says, clearly feigning offence.

Despite his cheeky, 'lad culture' attitude and filthy mouth, I suspect Danny may be way smarter than he lets on sometimes and it scares me – like maybe he's onto me, knowing exactly what's going on, knowing everything I'm thinking before I've even thought it myself.

Danny grabs the remote and dives onto the bed, making himself at home.

I shoot him a look, which he immediately picks up on.

'I'm just getting comfortable while you're getting ready,' he explains. 'Had a quick look for another hotel while I was on the toilet – '

'Charming,' I interrupt, but he pays me no attention.

'Everywhere is booked up, so I'll just sleep in the Love Bug. That's one woman who never lets me down.' He laughs.

For a split second, I wonder whether I should tell him not to be so silly, and to just stay in here with me tonight. So many things occur to me though, like what Will might think if he knew (like that should matter) or that I might suffocate him with a pillow while he sleeps just to end this ordeal (well, he is annoying). He seems happy enough about sleeping in his car – maybe it's best we leave things that way.

I close the bathroom door behind me as Danny starts laughing loudly at an episode of *SpongeBob SquarePants*.

'Hey, Candy,' he calls loudly so that I can hear it through the door. 'SpongeBob and Patrick are on a road trip – they're just like us.'

The TV may have a volume cap, but there are no such restrictions on the volume of Danny's laugh, and he cackles wildly as he watches. Meanwhile, I sit on the bathroom floor and allow myself a little designated crying time while no one can see or hear.

Chapter 15

If the Isle of Man branch of Starr Haul makes one thing clear, it is that the yellow branding of the company is very much set in stone. This particular branch is the newest addition to the company, but things aren't just shiny and new, they're shiny and new and yellow – oh my!

Like the Manchester branch, this place also has a secretary called Caroline, although unlike Sweet Caroline, Isle of Man Caroline is young, fun and friendly. When she introduced herself to us, she insisted we call her Caz, which suits me just fine because, weirdly, if there is a person I don't like I have been known to inexplicably dislike others who go by the same name. She has bleached-blonde hair, although it looks like maybe she did it herself because she's a little orange in patches, and she's wearing a very stylish blue pencil skirt and white blouse, but she looks entirely uncomfortable in them.

Every word she says is accompanied by a hand action, like she's using a kind of sign language that only she understands, and as her arms move around her short sleeves keep revealing a glimpse of a tattoo at the top of her arm – something Danny notices during the rushed tour she is giving us of the warehouse before they shut up shop for the day. If there's one thing I'm noticing about how this branch of Starr Haul differs to the flagship branch, it's just how young the workforce is here. It's like head office is staffed with all the dinosaurs, the ones who were a part of the company when it first opened its doors. With branches like this one popping up, it's inevitable that when the Manchester lot become extinct, these guys will be taking their places.

'Cool ink,' Danny tells Caz. 'Let's see it properly.'

We're standing right in the middle of the warehouse, but Caz obligingly unbuttons her blouse enough to slip out her arm, fully revealing the tattoo that covers almost all of her upper arm and her shoulder. I look closely, trying to take in all of the detail because there's just so much going on. It's *Alice in Wonderland* themed – specifically the Tim Burton take on the classic tale – and I've never seen a tattoo with such vivid and beautiful colours. I don't have any tattoos, but I'm impressed by Caz's.

'Wow, that's beautiful work,' Danny admires. I glance around the warehouse, but no passers-by seem even remotely phased by the fact Caz is hanging out of her top. She couldn't do this if she worked in Manchester, not with Matt the warehouse wanker at large.

'Where did you get that done?' Danny asks. 'America?'

'No, right here! Just down the road, actually. There's a place – Sami, the guy who works there, is just amazing.'

'Got your tits out again?' a big, hairy, beardy man asks Caz, although he doesn't sound surprised.

'Only at the Christmas party – you know that,' she jokes. 'Just showing Danny here my ink. Show him yours, show him yours. This is Dowdy, by the way.'

As we introduce ourselves and exchange how-do-you-dos, Dowdy happily drops his trousers to his ankles, revealing his heavily inked legs. His legs are just the most beautiful showcase of different games: board games like Snakes and Ladders, Cluedo and Mouse Trap on one leg, and then the other has a Rubix Cube, Lego, a Slinky and countless little toy soldiers performing a variety of military manoeuvres across his skin.

'I got one on my cock as well – had it done in Amsterdam,' Dowdy tells us, although thankfully he doesn't show us that one.

'Mate, Amsterdam is awesome,' Danny enthuses. 'I went there

while I was travelling, and we'd heard about this coffee shop where they have a cat that is just permanently stoned...so, the first thing we do off the ferry, we go to check out this stoned cat, right? Anyway, turns out it'd died.'

'That's so sad,' Caz says, tipping her head to one side.

'I'm actually thinking of adding to my tattoos,' Danny says, whipping his shirt off. Suddenly I'm the only person fully clothed, and like a Jimmy Eat World video, *I* feel like the weird one. I only have a second to feel weird before I am captivated by the sight of Danny with his shirt off. Nerds don't have bodies like that. OK, maybe I expected him to have one impressive bicep on his dominant side (if y'know what I'm getting at) and maybe strong thumbs from playing too much Call of Duty, but he looks like he works out. A lot. With *very* heavy weights. If this were ancient Greece, they'd be making sculptures of him.

I know that I'm staring, but it's hard to look away. The only man I ever see without a shirt on is Will, and even when he was younger and fitter, I'm sure he wasn't this hot. I remind myself that, as sexy as Danny may seem, he is annoying and insulting and unstable. I try to focus on his various tattoos as he talks Caz through them. I don't know if he's shutting me out for this newer, shinier, blonder blonde, or if he just assumes I won't be interested, but I find myself moving closer to him, trying to prove to him that I am interested in his ink and not as boring as he thinks I am.

'This one, I had done in LA,' he says, pulling down the waistband of his boxer shorts. Across the bottom of his stomach is the line 'Put your drawers on, and take your gun off'. 'I lost a bet,' he explains. 'It's a quote from *The Good, The Bad and The Ugly* – my favourite film.'

'I love that,' Caz says, leaning in close for a look.

'Fantastic,' Dowdy agrees.

'My ribcage.' Danny lifts his arm and twists his body for us to see. This one is weird. It's like you can see his ribcage through his skin, but rather than the usual organs you would expect to see hiding behind the bones, there are all kinds of creatures that look like they're trying to break their way out. It is weirdly disgusting, but oddly captivating to stare at. 'A guy in London did that one for me. You wouldn't believe how many hours it took – easily the most painful. And my back.' Danny turns around and stretches out his arms to make a T shape, showing us his biggest tattoo: a pair of angel wings that start at the centre of his back and stretch out down the backs of his arms. It's something that I could never have imagined looking good, but across Danny's muscular back, it just suits.

'Protesting too much.' He turns around again and chuckles, his cheeky smile with those dreamy dimples lighting up the room.

'Wow,' I can't help but say. 'I wish I had the guts to have something like that done.' The three of them stare at me, none of them considering for a second that I might be being sincere. I realise that the cool kids are talking, and shut up.

'We're clocking off any minute, then we're having a work do tonight,' Caz tells us. 'We get pretty wild. You guys should come.'

I see Danny's eyes light up for a second, excited by the invitation of a wild night out with wild Caz and the wild team, but then his face falls.

'I don't think Candy will be up for it,' he says, visibly disappointed.

Caz and Dowdy stare at me.

'I'll get an early night, but you can go,' I tell him, and I mean it. To be honest, I'd much rather go back to my room, on my own, jump in the bath and then eat room service and watch TV. It would actually delight me to be shot of Danny for a few hours, especially if he's in one of his 'fun' moods.

'It's cool,' Danny tells her. 'Thanks for the invite though.'

There's a loud clatter from the far corner of the warehouse, so Caz excuses herself to go and see what's going on, closely followed by Dowdy.

'Think about it,' he yells to us as he dashes off.

'You should go,' I tell Danny as he puts his shirt back on. 'That's the kind of thing you were hoping to get out of this trip. I really don't mind if you go.'

'Why won't you come?' he asks me, raising his eyebrows expectantly, like I might be able to give him an answer that he'll accept. 'I find it enriches my life, to go Batman on a regular basis.'

I pull a face at him, letting him know I have no idea what he's talking about.

'Going Batman – taking care of business during the day, before taking on the nightlife at night.'

'Not my scene,' I tell him.

'Why isn't it your scene?'

'It just isn't,' I insist.

'But why?'

'You're like a child, you know that?'

'And you're like an old lady,' he tells me. 'What's the worst that could happen? It's like you're scared of letting your hair down.'

'I'm not scared. Just because I choose not to have wild nights out, doesn't mean I'm not capable of them.'

'Fine then, don't come,' he sings, and if this is reverse psychology, annoyingly, it's working.

'Fine. I'll go. But if I do this, you have to promise to get off my back for the rest of the week because you are like a broken flipping record with this.'

'Deal,' he says, jumping up and punching the air. 'I'll go find Caz and tell her. You won't regret this,' he calls back to me as he jogs off.

'I hope not,' I say quietly to myself.

Chapter 16

My body aches from head to toe. It's that kind of uncomfortable feeling you sometimes get, that can only be righted by moving… but I can't move.

Perhaps my balance is off – maybe something is wrong with my inner ear, my trip across the Irish Sea having messed with my head. This is definitely the worst headache I have ever had in my life, I know that for sure. So bad, I'm scared to open my eyes, let alone get out of bed. That's when I realise that I don't remember going to bed… Come to think of it, this doesn't feel much like a bed that I'm lying face down on. It's too hard.

I raise my head with great care before slowly opening my eyes. Not only am I in the back of the Love Bug, but I'm lying face down on top of Danny, cuddled up on his bare chest like we're replicating a black and white photo of a proud, handsome dad with his newborn. He's fast asleep, looking quite peaceful and comfortable, but I can't help freaking out the second I realise where I am, who is under me and just how little of the previous night I actually remember.

As I attempt to jump up, all I achieve is a bump on my head courtesy of the roof of the car, not only making my epic headache much worse, but also sending me back down towards Danny, my face stopping just inches from his as he wakes up. He doesn't seem as alarmed by our close proximity as I do, and as I freak out on top of him, he gently holds me still by my arms.

'Candy, calm down, you're flailing like a cat trapped in a ball pool,' Danny says as he tries to keep me still.

I pause for a moment. I have too many unanswered questions to calm down though, like how did we wind up sleeping in the back of Danny's little two-door car? Why am I on top of him? Why is he shirtless? I glance down at my own body. My skirt is rolled up and my shirt is unbuttoned and tied under my boobs, like a cross between Britney Spears in the 'Baby One More Time' video and a rebellious schoolgirl. Why the hell am I dressed like Britney circa 1999 and, worse still, behaving like Britney circa 2007?

None of these questions are the one I ask out loud though. Oh no, the question I ask Danny – while still sitting on top of him – is: 'My arse is killing me – what the fuck did we do last night?'

'Well we didn't do *that*,' he says with a cheeky laugh. 'I'd remember *that*.'

I stare at him in horror. 'I'm serious,' I insist. 'My skin is stinging and burning; I've never felt anything like it.'

Danny yawns a loud, exaggerated yawn. As he stretches his arms out as far as he can in such a confined space, he seems truly relaxed, like his night out did him good. I scoot off him onto one of the seats, so he pulls his legs closer to his side of the car, so that we're no longer touching or so squashed up together.

'What are you fucking smiling about?' I ask, angrily.

'You, sailor mouth.' He laughs. 'You're swearing like a motherfucker. We broke you. Well, I suspect we didn't break you, I think we just broke down whatever wall you'd put up to stop the "fucks" and the "arses" slipping out.'

'It isn't funny,' I snap, wincing in pain now that I'm sitting on my bum. 'Will you have a look for me, see what I've done?'

'Yes,' Danny replies in an instant, clearly not about to waste his one and only opportunity to see a part of my body that I would normally keep hidden from acquaintances.

I flip over onto all fours, so that my bum is pointing in Danny's direction, pulling my pants down slowly enough so that I only have to show him as much as is absolutely necessary. I can't believe I'm doing this, but I've clearly injured myself somehow, and it needs checking out. Oh, God, what if I need to go A&E? I feel my cheeks (my face, that is) flush with embarrassment.

'I don't know how to tell you this,' Danny says cautiously. 'I think you must have met Mr Right last night.'

'W-what? What do you mean?' I stutter.

'You have a tattoo on your arse that says "Mr Right".'

'No!' I gasp.

'Yep,' Danny says, stifling a laugh.

I don't believe him, so as I spot my phone on the floor of the car I grab it and ask him to take a photo. As Danny obliges, there's a knock on the window.

'You can't do that here,' the hotel car park attendant advises us as he stares at us both in the back seat, Danny taking pictures of my arse.

'No, we're not – ' I call after him, but he's already gone.

Danny is laughing uncontrollably now as he hands me my phone. Sure enough, in a pretty swirly, girly font and surrounded by hearts is my new tattoo: 'Mr Wright'.

When I asked the universe for a Mr Right, I feel like it wasn't really listening. That'll teach me to take the piss out of cosmic ordering.

I delete the picture as quickly as possible, not only to get it out of my sight, but because, somehow, if the picture no longer exists, maybe my mistake won't either. As I shift in my seat and feel the stinging pain, I am reminded of how real this is, and how there's no way I can put what I've done to my behind, behind me.

'Why do I have Snapchat?' I ask Danny, noticing it on my phone's home screen.

'Oh yeah,' he starts. 'Caz told us to download it, remember?'

I shake my head.

'Yeah, she said the nights get pretty wild, so everyone adds everyone on Snapchat, they keep their stories updated all night and then the next day, everyone can see what everyone got up to before the images and videos self-destruct. Then they all pretend it never happened.' He laughs.

'How do I check my story?' I ask.

Danny taps my screen a few times.

'You don't have one,' he tells me, and I exhale with relief. 'But you see all these bubbles? These are the stories from the people we were with last night.'

I glance down the long list of usernames, not a single one of them sounding even remotely familiar to me.

'Oh God,' I whine.

'Come on,' Danny insists, excited to see the video evidence of the wild night out that neither of us remembers. 'It's like taking off a plaster. Grip it and rip it.'

The first few photos and videos aren't so bad, just lots of general silly, drunken antics in a variety of different bars. To be honest, I'm yet to spot myself or Danny in any of them, which relaxes me a little. Then I spot us, a photo of Danny and me, Dowdy stood between us with an arm wrapped around us both, and a huge grin on his face. We're standing outside a place called The North West Pole, which I easily deduce from the neon pink lit sign behind us. Then, as we watch more pieces of the puzzle, I realise that we're in a strip club. Danny sniggers to himself quietly as we watch, but I can't believe what I'm seeing. Were the videos not playing out in front of my eyes, I never would've believed it.

'Oh my God, look at you,' I squeak when a video of Danny starts playing. I laugh at him, up on the stage dancing to Nelly Furtado's 'Maneater' with one of the dancers. He's wearing a white suit shirt and a black tie that I don't remember him starting the night in, while his lady friend keeps it simple in nothing but her bra, a skirt and a short blue wig. It's safe to say that Danny has no rhythm, but neither does the dancer who clearly made poor choices at some point in her life, and who is clumsily grinding against him.

After suffering so much already today, I allow myself a moment to enjoy Danny's shame – not that he seems at all ashamed by his antics, he's actually amused, but that won't stop me rubbing it in.

'I thought you weren't allowed to touch the girls, you dirty old man,' I tease him. 'I'm surprised they didn't throw you out.'

But then, as we see more video footage of the same moment from a different angle, I realise that the blue-wig-wearing girl in the video – the one who clearly made poor life choices at some point – is *me*. Danny notices this too and erupts with laughter like I have never heard before.

'I broke you,' he laughs. 'I did it. I got you absolutely fucking mortal and I broke your good-girl act. And on the first night. Yes!'

I am speechless. Motionless. I want to tell him to go fuck himself; I want to punch him for leading me astray like this. Instead, I just watch. I just gaze in amazement at the sight of this person who looks just like me dirty dancing, alternating dancing on the pole with dancing all over Danny – *twerking*!

'We look like a budget version of Miley Cyrus and Robin Thicke,' I say softly. 'Only equally as embarrassing.'

Danny's laughter slowly calms down. 'Speak for yourself,' he chuckles. 'I look awesome.'

I take a break from piecing together the puzzle that is last night.

'More, more,' Danny insists.

'Just give me a minute,' I insist, moving to get comfortable, my arse killing me. My body is still aching from head to toe, but the burning feeling Mr Wright left me with is by far the worst. I massage my temples as Danny stares at me expectantly, excited to learn more.

I resume watching the stories. There isn't a video, but there's a photograph that makes it look like we were subsequently removed from the club, possibly due to mine and Danny's commandeering of the stage.

Suddenly, a small group of us are in the tattoo parlour. With several people having things done, I realise why so many of the Manx employees have so many tattoos, because they have wild nights like this. It's like they don't realise that tattoos are for ever! Then again, I can't say anything, not with my new butt ink. As I judge these human colouring books for their tattoos, the harsh reality of what I have done is hit home when I see a photo of me, bending over, showing off my 'Mr Wright' ink before turning to face the camera with tears in my eyes to announce that I 'love it'.

'Look at you crying.' Danny laughs. 'You big baby.'

Then we cut to a video of Danny getting inked on his finger, the buzzing of the needle completely drowned out by his howls of pain.

'Says you, tough guy.'

Danny examines his hand in front of his face, removing the cling film from his right index finger to reveal a moustache tattoo.

'Wow, you basic bitch.' I laugh at him. Well, there's no sense in reserving my swearing for my inner monologue now. This little mortifying archive of information has almost turned into a competition now, Danny and I getting off on watching the other doing increasingly stupid things.

'OK, bro, I'd say we're pretty even with the stupid shit.' He laughs.

'I guess we are,' I reply. 'And you say these self-destruct?'

'They most certainly do,' he tells me. 'Twenty-four hours after they are posted, they will be gone forever, so rest assured.'

'Just one more to go,' I tell him. It's interesting, to watch different people's stories from the same night. It's like solving a murder mystery. Sometimes you just get the same version of events, but from a different angle – an angle that can often be far more revealing. Other times you see an entirely different version of events from a different part of the room. I have to admit, this is a pretty genius idea for remembering the events of a night out, although not something I would practise. It's a good way to fill in a few blanks, but I could've lived a much happier life without the knowledge that I twerked on a lubricated pole while wearing a blue wig.

'That's my username,' Danny says excitedly, noting the last name on the list.

We watch as the night evolves, playing out pretty much the same as it did in all the other stories, except thankfully this one doesn't include our little performance because Danny was too busy dancing to try and capture any Kodak moments. Then we get to the part of the night where we visit the tattoo parlour. Danny has caught the moment Caz dragged me up to the front desk, to explain to the man what I 'want' done.

'She's been through a lot,' I hear Caz explain. 'She wants something strong and powerful.'

That's how we landed on 'Mr Wright'? – that doesn't make any sense.

'Rihanna has this huge goddess across her ribcage. She wants that,' Caz says, showing the tattooist her phone.

I nod, like a drunken fool, before backtracking a little. Good girl, Candice. Be smart. 'Maybe just the name,' I chirp. 'And not on my ribs, like, on my wrist.'

Suddenly, the story is towards the end of the night. It's daylight, and Danny and I are in the back of his car, singing 'Love Shack' together.

'I didn't realise I knew all the words to "Love Shack",' I say, puzzled.

'You clearly don't.' Danny laughs.

The last thing the video shows is Danny presenting me with an ugly, chunky, gold bangle, telling me that he found it, and that I'd need it. Then the video ends.

'Well, it could've been worse,' Danny muses. 'Much, much worse.'

Danny flips the driver's seat and climbs out of the car. I follow him. As I grab the side of the car to steady my achy body, I notice the disgusting second-hand bangle still on my wrist. Finally out of the car, it is only as I go to remove it that I spy the telling cling film underneath it. Danny notices me notice it.

'That'll be your Rihanna goddess tattoo,' he tells me as he stretches his arms in the air, stiff from a night of dancing and a morning of sleeping in the car. 'Which goddess was it, anyway?'

'I'm not a huge Rihanna fan, surprisingly,' I snap. 'And I can't remember a fucking thing.'

That's not strictly true; little bits are coming back to me. Especially since watching the video, just seeing the occasional trigger causes memories – that I would rather suppress – to come flooding back. That said, I don't remember the tattoo, but I'm glad that I went for the name in a small size on my wrist, rather than the goddess herself emblazoned across my body.

I remove the bangle before slowly peeling off the cling film, and that's when the true horror of my poor choices hits me like a ton of bricks.

'You OK?' Danny asks, clearly having seen the look on my face.

'I…I have an Isis tattoo,' I tell him.

Danny's eyes light up, and he looks like he might burst with joy. If this is a competition, and the winner is the person who finishes the night significantly less mortified than the other, then I am certainly the loser.

'I have an Isis tattoo!'

'Isis is the goddess of fertility and motherhood,' he says as he chuckles, to try and make me feel better.

'It's also the name of a militant group who aren't exactly getting the best press right now,' I tell him, as though there is a chance he might not know. 'Not everyone has heard of the goddess, Isis. *Everyone* has heard of the other Isis.'

Unable to hold back a second longer, Danny erupts with laugher, throwing his head back. He calms, but only a little, his laughter steadily continuing. He literally slaps his thigh as he chuckles, his eyes red and so bloodshot they look like they might burst.

It's amazing how different Danny and I are. What I see as a series of terrible mistakes during a difficult time of my life that have left me absolutely mortified, Danny sees as a great night out. A victory. Both a good time and the successful demolition of my good reputation. Everything he could've hoped for.

As I watch him laugh, relishing in my misery, I feel an anger growing inside me. This is all his doing. He goaded me into this night out, into drinking too much, into doing all of this stupid stuff.

'This is all your fault,' I say angrily.

'I told you to get an Isis tattoo?' He chuckles, wiping tears from his eyes.

'No, the bigger picture. This was supposed to be a business trip and you've turned it into a fucking stag do.'

OK, so it wasn't supposed to be a business trip, it was supposed to be a romantic getaway. I can't say as much to Danny, but it's all the same. He's turned this into *The Hangover-fucking-4*, creating the perfect storm scenario to ensure my downfall, and all for his amusement.

'It was fun,' he insists. '*You* had fun. The videos prove it – watch them again.'

'I never want to see them again,' I insist, deleting the app. Interacting with my phone only serves as a reminder that Will hasn't texted me back, which only angers me further.

'It's done, don't worry about it,' he says, talking to me like the hysterical woman I most likely am being. 'Chill out.'

'You're so cluelessly aloof,' I tell him as I pace back and forth in front of his car.

'No, you're too much of a stress head.' He laughs. 'Just calm down.'

'Stop telling me to calm down,' I say through gritted teeth. I am absolutely distraught about everything that has happened and my behaviour last night has only made me feel worse. The fact he's enjoying my suffering is really starting to get to me, but

I can't let it. 'You know what, I'm not speaking to you for the rest of the trip,' I tell him childishly. 'You're nothing but trouble.'

'It's going to be a boring trip if you carry on like that,' he warns me.

'Good,' I reply. 'I'd rather have a boring trip than endure the "fun" of speaking to you.'

'Fine,' he replies. 'I don't want to speak to you either.'

He's putting on this stupid, childish tone – at least I think he's putting it on.

'Fine,' I repeat, determined to have the last word. Danny is happy to leave it at that, climbing back into his car and shutting the door.

I walk towards the hotel. I just need to grab my stuff and then we can go for the ferry – which I'm dreading, but with a hangover like this, I'm not sure I could feel any worse.

Chapter 17

Liverpool is in our sights. Pretty soon I will be back on dry land, safe in the knowledge I never need set foot on a boat again. I haven't spoken a word to Danny since our argument and, like he threatened, he hasn't said a thing to me either.

I've had a lot of time to sit and think, and while I was tempted to call the whole trip off and have Danny take me home, I don't want to give Will the satisfaction. He still hasn't texted me back – I just checked again – but he's bound to be thinking about me and about what I'm getting up to with Danny. If I go home now, I'll just prove to him what a sad cow I am. At least while I'm away, he can think I'm having fun without him – even if that isn't true.

Thankfully my seasickness isn't as bad this time. I'm not sure if this is because my current hangover is so much worse than anything I was feeling on the way over here, or whether it's because I've been following the advice Danny gave me before. Either way, I'm just grateful to not be feeling so dreadful.

I stroll along the deck of the boat towards Danny. I have no intention of speaking to him, but we're about to dock so I can at least follow him to his car in silence. I can see that he's surrounded by a gang of teenage boys with skateboards, but as I get closer I realise they don't appear to be getting along.

'Your mum is so fat, her belly button has an echo,' a kid with long greasy hair poking out from under a beanie hat says to Danny. The kid has a skateboard in one hand, his other is met with a high five from one of his friends, for that zinger he just delivered.

'I can't believe you're making mum jokes.' Danny laughs. 'I like you, kid. You remind me of me when I was a teen – an absolute twat.'

The skater frowns. 'Fuck, I hope I don't grow into you,' he replies, looking Danny up and down. 'You sad bastard, look at your hair. You look like a fucking joystick.'

'Yeah, I've been called that before,' Danny says. 'By your mum! *That's* how you do a mum joke.'

I stifle a laugh, amused but not about to let Danny see as much.

A quick count of heads tells me that there are eight members of this particular gang of skaters. I'm pretty sure they're still school age, but it's the weekend, so they're free to heckle strangers on public transport. They're like robots, each moving around on their wheels, all with the same blank, emotionless, gormless look on their faces, with their greasy hair, beanie hats, baggy jeans and sharp, spiked wristbands that looks like they would guarantee them a little YouTube fame if they came off their boards while wearing them, most likely puncturing whichever organ landed on one the wrong way.

'Topknot wanker,' the kid snaps, but Danny just stares at him, narrowing his eyes. 'What are you looking at, paedo?' the kid asks.

'I'm just imagining what you'd look like with duct tape around your mouth,' Danny tells him calmly. 'Before I throw you overboard. You've got one of those faces that'd look great on a missing poster.'

'Wait, let me get my phone and you can say that again, dude, see what the police have to say about it.'

The kid takes his phone from his pocket and squares up to Danny. What I'm sure most would file under 'bantering' is starting to get heated now, and as sick as I am of Danny, seeing him get arrested for throwing a teenager in the sea (no matter how horrid or greasy said teenager might be) isn't going to help my cause.

'Bring it on, you little cun – '

'Danny,' I interrupt him. 'Time to go.'

'I'm not taking shit from the fucking Lollipop Guild,' he replies.

'Better run along, your mum wants you,' the kid teases Danny. To give Danny his due, as the skaters celebrate victoriously, slapping high fives and bumping chests, Danny does walk away like the bigger man, but not before he reaches forward and grabs something from one of the tatty, black backpacks on the floor while they're not looking. Whatever he's taken, he stuffs into his pocket and we head for the car.

'I'm still not speaking to you,' I tell him.

'I'm still not speaking to you either.' He laughs as we get in the car. Soon enough we'll be able to drive off the ferry and get on our not so merry way to Newcastle, which is the next stop on this road trip to hell. I feel almost at a disadvantage, being on Danny's home turf, but hopefully I'll be able to suggest he goes to see his friends, thus leaving me alone, in peace and unharmed.

We don't get to sit in awkward silence for long before the skater boys are back, and they're circling the car, banging on the windows and yelling. The boy Danny was arguing with is the most vocal.

'Give it back,' he yells, his face pressed up menacingly against the glass.

'Give what back?' Danny asks coyly.

'You know what,' the kid replies, wiping the window clear of his breath. 'Give it back, or you'll be sorry.'

Danny seems unfazed by his threats.

'What are you going to do? Beat me up?'

Before the kid has a chance to reply, a member of staff spies what is going on and calls out, 'Oi! Back up the stairs, you lot.'

'Better yet,' Danny says, mischief in his eyes, 'why don't you tell that bloke what you want back? I'm sure he'll smooth it all out.'

'Son of a bitch,' the kid shouts, before the whole team start beating on Danny's car. When it was just Danny – or even me – that might've been in danger of a violent attack, he didn't seem fussed. Now that the Love Bug is being roughed up, Danny suddenly cares.

'Watch the fucking car, you little pricks,' he yells, but he can't get out to do anything about it. Luckily this reign of terror doesn't get to go on for too long before members of staff come over and put a stop to things, escorting the teens away.

As the doors open for us to drive off I see Danny check his wing mirrors.

'It's clear,' I tell him when he doesn't seem to be making a move.

'I know that,' he replies. 'Just making sure the car is OK.'

'Well, if you will steal dinner money from children,' I snap.

'Have you ever seen teenagers get so upset over a couple of quid?' he asks, wiggling his eyebrows.

'I really don't give a shit,' I reply. 'Still not speaking to you.'

'Still not speaking to you either.' He laughs, finally moving the car.

I shuffle in my seat, my Mr Wright tattoo still causing me discomfort. My Isis tattoo isn't so bad – in terms of pain, that is. In terms of tattoos it's still a fucking Isis tattoo.

I exhale deeply, unable to believe just how badly this trip is going. It was supposed to be this amazing, life-changing holiday from my shitty real life that would ultimately become my real life. Every day would be a holiday, and I would finally be happy. But no, things just had to go tits up, didn't they? At least now I'm down at rock bottom, things can't get any worse. I mean, where else is there to go? Other than Newcastle...

Chapter 18

Remind me never to think anything again – ever. I'm jinxed. Whenever I think things are going to get better, they get worse. Whenever I dare to think things can't possibly get any worse, the universe is hell-bent on proving me oh-so wrong.

Every time Danny utters the term 'YOLO' I fantasise about punching him in the face repeatedly, but I've just learned a valuable lesson. I've spent pretty much every second of this trip thinking about how shit my life is – right up until now, when I realised just how precious my life is.

We were flying along the motorway (well, as fast as the Love Bug would allow) when Danny (who isn't talking to me) told me that the steering felt heavy. I had no sooner mused out loud that this was probably because his car was old enough to be his dad when things got worse. Even I could feel the car pulling to one side – that's when it started violently shuddering, so much my iPad flew out of my hands and disappeared under the seat. As terrifying as it was, it was all over quite quickly. Somehow Danny managed to safely manoeuvre us out of the traffic and to the side of the road. We're in a sort of lay-by, but Danny advises me that it's still dangerous and that we need to get out of the car.

We hop out, Danny first, and then I clamber over the driver's seat as quickly as possible, which I don't imagine looks too graceful. As we make our way to safety, Danny notices what is wrong. One of his tyres is completely flat, and on the car itself, above the wheel, someone has hastily scratched the word 'twat' into the paintwork.

'Those little pricks,' Danny shouts. 'They punctured my tyre. They could've killed us!'

I grab Danny by the arm and pull him as far away from the road as possible, stepping over a little fence into a field. Hopefully we're safe here, but as I hold my phone in the air I realise there's nothing I can do to get any signal.

I glance at the road. It's quite busy but, of course, no one is stopping to help us. I'd accept help from anyone right now, even the Zodiac killer.

'Do you have a spare tyre and a jack or whatever?' I ask.

Danny shakes his head.

'Your car doesn't have a spare tyre?'

'My car doesn't even have a functioning passenger door.' He laughs.

'Can't we drive it now it's deflated?' I ask genuinely.

'They're not run-flat tyres. Classic car, Candy,' he reminds me.

So the fact that this problem cannot be solved is partially because of his old banger of a car, and partly because of his incompetence in not carrying a spare tyre. Not forgetting that this is *all his fault* in the first place.

'This is what happens when you steal from kids,' I tell him, angrily.

'Speaking of which,' Danny says, cheering up a little as he takes something from his pocket. 'If we're stuck here, may as well make it more bearable.'

I watch him fidget around with something for a while, before bringing it up to his mouth and lighting it.

I lean closer, unable to believe my eyes.

'Is that weed?' I ask in a voice so much higher in pitch than it usually is.

'Yep, you want a hit?' he asks as he exhales.

'You're getting high on stolen weed while you're on a business trip? Oh, and with a company-branded lighter, no less.'

'Cool, huh? I got it a couple of days ago. If they didn't want me to smoke, they shouldn't have given me a lighter.'

'It was for lighting Charlie's cake, wasn't it?'

Danny laughs.

I pace back and forth, trying to get some signal for a while. Danny is growing increasingly giggly and it's pissing me off.

'We're stranded at the side of the motorway with no way of getting any help – all your fault, by the way – and all you can do is get high?'

'YOLO!' he yells, annoying me even more.

'You can't just call YOLO every time you do something stupid,' I tell him. 'The clue is in the fucking acronym: you only live *once*. Meaning life is delicate. Meaning don't do stuff that is going to fucking kill you.'

Danny admires what is left of his joint thoughtfully.

'It's better to look back and say: "I can't believe I did that" than it is to look back and say: "I wish I did that".'

'It's better to not die, you high fucking idiot,' I say under my breath. There's no reasoning with him right now.

As I spy a van pull up behind Danny's car, for a split second, a wave of relief washes over me. Why is it that I never think things can get any worse? Because they always do. I take back what I said about accepting help from anyone – I think I'd rather brave being stuck at the side of the road a little longer.

'We're saved,' Danny mumbles, his joint in his mouth, as he waves his arms in the air.

'We're screwed,' I correct him, panic in my voice. 'That's a police van.'

'Oh, fuck,' Danny says, looking around in panic. He takes the joint and the little bag he stole from the teenagers and legs it over to the stream running alongside the field, then throws them in. He runs back over and stands next to me, as though we're the von

Trapp kids reporting for duty. Despite our predicament, Danny cannot suppress his giggles.

'You stay here,' I tell him. 'I'll go talk to them.'

I walk over towards the van as two police officers hop out.

'Car trouble?' the first asks with a friendly smile.

'A flat tyre,' I tell him, smiling back, trying to be cool.

'We'll get you sorted, no worries,' the second policeman tells me. 'Are you the driver?'

'Erm, no, he is,' I say, nodding towards Danny who gives the policemen a big, moronic smile and a wave.

The first policeman beckons him over with a hand gesture before speaking into his radio.

'If you guys are busy, don't worry about us. If we can just use your phone quickly or whatever...'

'It's fine,' the second policeman tells me as he opens the door at the back of the van. 'We needed to stop to let the dog out anyway.'

That's when I realise this is a dog unit van – right as my high colleague rocks up next to me, and as the policeman lets the big, scary-looking Alsatian out of the van. Only a few feet away from us, the dog stares at us for a second. It narrows its eyes, like it knows what we're up to. I give it a friendly smile and make kissy noises at it, almost pleading with it to keep quiet but it's no use. The dog starts making a low, rumbling noise. This can't be good.

Danny stares at the dog in amazement. Still, I try my hardest to get us out of this steadily worsening situation.

'He must be able to smell my cat,' I reason.

Danny falls about laughing at this, right about the time the dog starts barking at him fiercely.

The policeman, now suspicious, walks closer to Danny. His dog gets angrier.

'My dog says you're on drugs,' the policeman says to us. 'What do you have to say to that?'

Now is the time to keep quiet, but this does not occur to Danny the high fucking idiot.

'*I'm* on drugs?' he repeats. '*You're* the one with the talking dog, mate.'

Both policemen are staring at us now, and neither looks amused. Before I know what's going on, the dog is swiftly put back in the van and Danny and I are being apprehended.

As they search us, the policeman searching me notices the cling film poking out of my sleeve.

'What's up your sleeve?' he asks.

'I had a tattoo,' I explain, removing it to prove as much. The plan is to be as forthcoming as possible, because I haven't done anything wrong. Stupid, stupid idea, because the policeman's eyes widen with horror as he checks out my ink.

'You have an Isis tattoo?' he asks in disbelief.

'Yes, but, *Isis* is a goddess – see, it's pronounced differently,' I explain, but it falls on deaf ears. Clearly he thinks he's got a terrorist as well as a pothead.

'I think we need to discuss all this down town, don't you?' he says.

Chapter 19

After leaving the police station with – thankfully – no more than a slap on the wrist, Danny and I catch a taxi to the hotel in perfect silence.

The car drops us at the side of the road outside the hotel, and we stand there with our luggage for a moment. I stare at a spot on the pavement, thinking about everything that just happened.

'You OK?' Danny asks, cautiously. 'No one tried to make you their bitch, did they?'

A joke? Seriously? He thinks a joke might be what I need to feel better about being bundled into the back of a van and taken to a police station?

I shoot him a death stare. 'This is not funny, Danny,' I yell. 'We could've been in big trouble.'

'For cheeking a copper and being a bit high? No one gets a criminal record for that. Chill out.'

I puff air out of my cheeks furiously. 'Let's just get inside,' I say. 'I'm exhausted and I feel dirty – I just want to get a bath and have a lie-down.'

'Do we have to check in at the office?' he asks.

'Fuck that,' I reply. 'After the day I've had and all that time wasted at the police station?'

'Rebel,' he chuckles.

'Let's just go inside.'

From the outside, The Tyne Towers is simply breathtaking. Despite its location in the city centre, the castle-looking, red-brick building is like something fresh out of a utopian novel with all the rich, leafy ivy growing up the sides and creeping in around the windows. Inside, the place is just as stunning, with shiny marble floors and big pillars supporting the weight of the rooms above – that I have no doubt will be beautiful too.

As we try to check in, surprise surprise, there's a problem.

'Sorry, we don't appear to have any reservations under that name,' the receptionist politely tells us.

I stare at her, both in puzzlement and disbelief that this trip can possibly get worse.

'Are you certain you're at the right hotel?' she asks. 'It's just that, just a ten-minute walk down the road, you'll find Tyne Tower. It's a guest house. You'd be surprised how often people confuse the two thanks to their similar names.'

She smiles sweetly.

'I guess that's us then,' Danny says with a shrug. 'Cheers.'

The lady gives us directions and it sounds close so we decide to walk, reverting back to our awkward, angry silence until we come face to face with where we are actually staying. Tyne Tower is also a detached building, except its walls are not home to beautiful leaves, they are coated in grime and blackened with dirt. The window frames are all mouldy, the glass is so filthy it looks frosted and the door looks so old, it might not open. I hope it doesn't.

Inside the building is just as run-down, and the furnishings look older than Danny and I put together. A short, bald man in a string vest is reading a newspaper behind the desk. Upon our entry he doesn't even look up, not until Danny catches his attention.

'All right, mate,' Danny says, waving his hand.

'All right, lad, what can I do for you?' he says, glancing up briefly before looking back at his copy of *The Sun*.

'We're here to check in. Reservation under the name Starr,' Danny says.

'Oh aye, we've got you in room 13. En-suite, that one. You and the Mrs will love it.'

The man moves papers around on his desk until he finds a key, which he tosses to Danny.

'I'll call the porter; he'll help you with your bags.'

I don't know why I was expecting him to use the phone, instead he calls out 'Dragan' at the top of his voice, his Geordie accent so much stronger than Danny's, causing me to jump out of my skin.

Dragan promptly arrives and takes my luggage, leaving Danny to carry his own.

'Wait, sorry, did you say one room or two?' Danny asks.

'One room, lad.'

'OK, just making sure,' Danny replies, saying nothing else. We swap a look for a second, but I don't try and explain it. I don't even know where to begin making a second excuse. I mean, what are the chances of it happening twice?

We step into the rickety old lift with Dragan.

'Are you here for the festival?' he asks us in what I think is an eastern European accent.

Danny and I swap another glance, neither of us having the faintest idea what festival he is referring to.

'No, we're on a business trip,' Danny tells him.

'All work and no play,' Dragan muses. 'If you change your mind about the festival, you let me know, OK?'

We both nod, reluctant to show too much interest in this mysterious festival.

We step out of the lift and Dragan shows us to our room.

'You will settle yourselves in, OK? Call reception if you need anything.'

Again, we both nod.

As Danny opens the door, I'd be lying if I said I had high hopes for the room, if the dirty lobby, the old lift and the creepy corridors are anything to go by. I'm not sure it's possible, but the room is even worse than the other areas of the hotel. We both step inside – leaving our bags outside, like there's an unspoken agreement that we will *not* be staying here.

'I've never seen anything so rank in my life,' Danny says as he slowly spins around in the centre of the room.

I pull my sleeve down over my hand and open the bathroom door with as little force as possible before flicking on the light. It's not a particularly bright light, which makes the tiny, windowless room seem seriously creepy. The bath is brown (although I don't imagine it was when it was installed) and no matter how much I need to pee, there's no way I'm lifting the toilet lid up.

Danny stands behind me and peers inside.

'You gonna have that bath?' he asks jokily – knowing the answer, of course.

'Yeah, if I want to get hepatitis,' I reply. 'Is that blood?'

Danny pulls a disgusted face.

'This place…' I start. 'It's like a haunted Disneyland attraction. I mean…it looks like bodies have been chopped up in that bath. Everything is filthy…'

My voice trails off. I don't need to tell Danny this because he has eyes that can see it and a nose that can smell it.

I feel a tear escape my eye, which I quickly wipe away, but Danny doesn't miss a thing.

'Oi, come here,' he demands, wrapping an arm around me. 'Look, I know it's awkward and we're not exactly best buddies right now, but we could always stay with my family for the night. It's actually my dad's birthday, so he'd love to see me. They're always inviting me back. They keep my bedroom ready for me – you can have that; I'll kip on the sofa. What do you think?'

I consider it for a moment. Do I really want to go and meet a whole family full of Dannys? I mean, I'm struggling to put up with just one Danny. I also know that I'll struggle to wash, sleep and just generally make it through the night in this shithole. All I can think about is how I am exhausted, hung-over and in desperate need of a wash.

'It'll be fun,' he says to entice me, as if that might convince me. 'We always do something fun on birthdays. We can have something to eat, chill out, get a good night's sleep and hit the road tomorrow. My car will be fixed by morning.'

'OK, sure. Thank you,' I reply. As much as I'm dreading meeting Danny's family, anything has to be better than *this*.

Chapter 20

The taxi drops us outside a semi-detached house, right in the centre of a housing estate. There are kids playing outside, kicking a football around, and a couple of dogs are running around without leashes. It looks like a fairly typical street, not too dissimilar to the one I grew up on. So far, so normal.

'Both cars are here, so they're both home,' Danny says. 'They're going to be so surprised!'

I follow him up the driveway and through the front door. He gestures at me with some kind of military hand signal to follow him through the door into the living room. When he said he wanted to surprise them he didn't just mean by showing up unannounced, it seems.

As we enter the room as quietly as possible, we find ourselves staring down at Danny's parents, who are having sex on the living room floor. The worst thing of all is that they haven't realised we're here and they're really going at it. Danny is rendered dumbstruck, but only for a second.

'Oh shit!' Danny yells as he recoils in horror, actually sounding like he's in physical pain.

I glance down at my feet, the temptation to look up near non-existent.

'Shit, lad,' Danny's dad says as he grabs a cushion from the sofa, placing it on top of his wife in a way that attempts to protect whatever modesty they have left.

'Daniel!' his mother beams, before being reminded of their predicament.

'Candy, don't look,' Danny instructs me.

'Already not looking,' I say softly, still staring at my shoes.

'Shit, lad,' his dad says again, clearly struggling to finds the right words to make this OK. 'If we'd known you were coming we'd have baked a cake. Or, you know, we'd not been having sex on the living room floor.'

'Candy, is it?' I hear his mum ask.

Without moving my head, I look at her with my peripheral vision.

'Yes, nice to meet you,' I reply, praying she won't want to shake my hand right now. I don't bat an eyelid at her calling me Candy. Well, now hardly seems like the time or the place to get technical over what I like to be called. 'Both of you.'

'It's my birthday,' Danny's dad tells me, by way of an explanation.

'Happy birthday,' I add, with a half smile, half wince.

Despite her warm, mumsy tone, Danny's mum is young and slim – I imagine she was quite young when she had him. His dad looks older, having lost his hair (something I can't imagine going down well with Danny should he go the same route), but he's a handsome man. I could imagine Bruce Willis playing him in a film of his life, should anyone ever think his story needed telling.

'Oh my God, this is so weird,' Danny practically cries, his usually manly voice the highest I have ever heard it. 'We're staying the night. I'm going to show Candy to my room while you guys put some clothes on.'

'If that's OK,' I add politely, as Danny drags me from the living room and up the stairs. He drags me at such a speed, I don't even have time to take in my surroundings. Next thing, we're in Danny's old bedroom. He closes the door behind himself before leaning back on it and exhaling deeply. His distressed look quickly melts into an amused one – thank God. Things were starting to feel even more awkward.

'I could have done without seeing that.' He laughs.

'Me too,' I reply with a giggle, but then we fall silent, like we've just remembered that we don't like each other very much.

'Well, I'll go make sure my grandparents aren't screwing in the bathroom before you go for your bath,' he jokes. 'Might grab a quick shower. Make yourself at home.'

As Danny leaves, closing the door behind him, I take a seat on his bed and take in my surroundings. As far as I can tell, Danny hasn't lived here since he was a teenager, so it makes sense that I am currently sitting in a teenage boy's bedroom. Like Danny's bizarre personality, his room is neither nerdy nor sporty, it's that healthy mixture of the two he seems to have going on that's rare to find – like, he's the kind of man who could explain the offside rule to you, and reformat your hard drive while he was at it. No, I don't know what either of those things are.

I stroll over to the large chest of drawers, skimming my fingers across the top as I take stock of my surroundings. Everything is so neat and tidy. He was right when he said his mum kept his room ready for him in case he wanted to visit, which it doesn't sound like he does very often.

There's a mirror hanging above his chest of drawers, which only serves to remind me what a mess I'm looking today. The edges of the mirror are covered in stickers, photographs and little mementos like gig tickets. I only run my eyes over them briefly, but a photograph of Danny with a girl sitting on his lap catches my eye. She's a skinny brunette, wearing leather-look leggings, a bright purple halter neck top, and her face is forced into a very severe looking pout/stare combination. She is posing for the camera, but Danny is just staring at her with pure adoration. I take it down to get a closer look, just as Danny walks back into the room.

'The bathroom is free of fornicators, so...' His voice trails off as he notices what's in my hand. He pauses for a second. 'That's Emma, my ex.'

For a moment, I am captivated by the sight of Danny in just a towel. I'm staring at his hard body as droplets of water roll down his torso. I blurt out the first thing that pops into my head.

'Looks like you really liked her,' I say without thinking. Wait, am I jealous? Because there's *so* much wrong with that.

'Yeah, I fell hard for Emma. But she cheated on me, so…'

'Ah,' I reply awkwardly. 'Not cool.'

'Nope. Cheaters are despicable creatures.'

And then he gives me this look, this knowing glance, and it hits me hard and it hurts. It's like he just knows about Will.

'I'm going for a bath,' I tell him, squeezing past him through his bedroom doorway, forcing myself not to look at his body because, as hot as he is, he's annoying. I might be attracted to him physically, but his personality just puts an end to any kind of crush developing.

'I might get my head down for ten, then,' he tells me.

'Fine,' I call back, and I'm not sure who I'm more annoyed at now, Danny or myself.

Chapter 21

While tattoos have never been for me, I have never been one of those people to actively dislike them. You know the type, the ones who bang on about how bad they'll look when you're older, the type to pointlessly start a Facebook 'like' page for people who don't 'like' tattoos.

I can understand why people have them done. It's a huge commitment, and a transformation that is palpable. I understand this. The way I see it, my efforts to lose weight and get in better shape is a similar thing, just without the instant gratification. It's taking charge of your body, changing it in a way that you want, truly making it your own. While I think that's cool, a tattoo is too much of a commitment for me; a tattoo would be like telling me I could only wear one pair of shoes for the rest of my life, which I just could not do. I'm not brave enough to pick one thing and just go for it. That's why I have always known I would never plump for the needle when it comes to style, even though I have always kind of wanted to. Of course, I never bargained on getting drunk with a gang of Manx truckers and a YOLO monger like Danny, and now I have two of them. Not something beautiful or personal, nothing even remotely meaningful, just an Isis tattoo on my wrist and a stranger's name on my arse.

I admire my naked body in the bathroom mirror, the body I spent months trying to make perfect, only to ruin over the course of one evening. I grab the bangle Danny gave me and slip it back on, successfully covering my Isis ink. Then I slip on a pair of white lace French knickers, but as I twist my hips to look at my arse in the mirror, my 'Mr Wright' tattoo is still clearly visible, both through the lace and peeping out below the fabric – there goes my career as an underwear model.

I hurry on my clothes because out of sight, out of mind, apply my make-up and go to pull my hair into my usual side plait, but I pause for a second. As per Danny's request, I literally let my hair down last night, and I've spent today so far with my long locks loose and free – not unlike my stupid drunk personality. Maybe I'll leave it down today. I don't know why; I just feel like it.

I head for Danny's room to find him thankfully dressed, but fast asleep on his previously neatly made bed. I give him a prod with a finger, as though I were a child trying to poke a slug off their slide with a stick.

'Oi,' I say as I prod him.

'Hey,' he smiles, his face falling as he remembers the tension between us. 'Good bath?'

'Marvellous,' I reply sarcastically.

'Least you're speaking to me now, huh?' he teases.

'Danny, don't,' I snap. 'None of this is funny.'

Danny, for once, knows to stop pushing me.

'Let's head downstairs.'

I follow his lead. I'm not looking forward to seeing his parents again, even if they're not connected at the crotch this time, but at least there will be other people I can talk to – people who I don't want to kill for getting me drunk and permanently defacing my body.

'Hello.' Danny's mum beams brightly as we enter the kitchen. 'So this is a surprise. I know it's your dad's birthday, but I never expected you to show up for it. I thought you'd be busy with work. Do you know how long it's been since he visited?' she asks me rhetorically. 'Months – years maybe.'

'All right, Mam, don't exaggerate,' Danny says sheepishly.

'Sorry if we seem rude cooking when we should be getting to know you, Candy,' Danny's dad says as he prepares a salad. 'We're just running a bit late for the barbeque.'

As I watch his dad chopping tomatoes and his mum peeling potatoes, it amuses me that they think I might consider this rude, especially after walking in on them having sex in the living room. It also occurs to me that I hope they've washed their hands.

'It's fine,' I tell him sincerely. 'Can I do anything to help?'

'We're on top of things,' Danny's dad says, a moment's awkwardness following his choice of words. 'I'm Paul; this is Andrea.'

'Nice to meet you both.'

'So, who have we got coming?' Danny asks his mum as he munches a tomato he pinched from the kitchen table.

'Your sister and the kids are coming – Tim can't come, he's working. That's our Clare's fella,' Andrea explains to me. 'Christopher is coming – he's practically replaced you in this family.'

Danny laughs. 'Chris has been my best friend my entire life,' he explains to me. 'He's always been one of the family – so when I left home, that didn't change.'

'That's lovely,' I say.

'Is it?' Paul laughs. 'He's a colourful character is our Chris.'

Danny pulls out a chair at the table and gestures for me to sit down. I sit, and he plonks himself down next to me.

'They diagnosed Chris with Tourette's when he was six,' he continues.

'That must have been challenging,' I reply.

'It took them two years to realise he just swore too much – he still does, just to warn you.' Danny laughs. 'He isn't the smartest person I know, but he's got a heart of gold. He's like a brother to me. Always been there for me,' Danny continues, showing me a side to him that I hadn't witnessed until now.

'Tell her about his science GCSE paper, tell her,' Paul says excitedly, like he's heard this story a thousand times before but still finds it as hilarious as he did the first time it was told to him.

'He didn't get a single question right,' Danny tells me. 'Only his name.' He pauses for a moment, for comedic effect. 'Actually, that's not true. He wrote "Christoper".'

For a moment, I forget that I am mad at Danny and I cackle with laughter at his story. It's been so long since I spent time around an actual family, I'd forgotten how nice it was.

There's a knock on the door.

'All right, motherfuckers,' a loud, male Geordie accent booms as a tall bloke with a shaved head walks in through the back door. I do not need anyone to tell me that this is Chris. He claps eyes on Danny and lights up at the sight of his best friend, but then his expression changes. He looks worried. Danny is just so pleased to see him that he doesn't notice this and he jumps up and pulls his friend in for a hug.

Danny releases him. 'How's it going, mate?' he asks.

'Aye, good,' Chris replies sheepishly.

'Great, actually, Dan,' a female voice says as a short, slim brunette girl steps out from behind Chris. I recognise her from her photo immediately. It's Emma, Danny's ex.

'Wha-what are you doing here?' he asks her, stunned.

Emma slides her arm around Chris's waist, slowly like a slithering snake. She smiles widely as she announces with pride: 'I'm Chris's girlfriend.'

I watch the colour drain from Danny's face. I can tell from the look of anguish on his face that this has not only blindsided him, but it's hurting him too, seeing this is the girl who broke his heart with his best friend, and no one thought to tell him – probably because it would hurt him. The look on his parents' faces confirms this.

As mad as I am at Danny right now, as much as he infuriates me and as much as I wish I wasn't on this trip with him, something kicks in. I know what it feels like to hurt, to be betrayed. I feel weirdly loyal to him. If you'd told me that this was going to happen around the time I discovered my tattoos or got taken to the police station, I would have anticipated enjoying watching Danny suffer like this, but I'm not. I don't like it, and I certainly don't like the smug look on her face.

I jump up from my seat, unable to allow my colleague to suffer a second longer.

'So nice to meet you both,' I say. Danny is standing in front of them awkwardly with his hands in his pockets, so I hook my arm through his and rest my head on his bicep.

'And who are you?' Emma asks me, rudely.

'I'm Candy,' I tell her brightly. 'Danny's girlfriend.'

'You're his *girlfriend*? I thought you were just colleagues,' Danny's mum squeaks, elated. 'He's never brought a girlfriend home before. This must be serious.'

Danny does his best not to let his relief show, and falls into the role of my boyfriend effortlessly, kissing me on the forehead.

'She's the first girl I've wanted to bring home,' he tells his mum, smiling at me.

'You brought me home,' Emma interrupts.

'Yeah, only because you lived next door,' Chris chimes in, his loyalty to his friend creeping back in. Too little too late, of course. Knocking off the ex who broke his heart behind his back probably quashed that loyalty a little.

I hear my phone vibrating on the table behind me so I let go of Danny's arm and go to grab it.

'I'd better take this,' I say, before I even know who it is. I wonder if it's Will, and the thought of what I'll say to him fills me with panic. I step out of the room, pulling the door to behind me.

It's the office, but it isn't Will. It's Caroline, so I decide not to answer it. I definitely cannot face Sweet Caroline right now. Anyway, it's Saturday, and only the first proper day of the trip. I don't need her checking up on me already.

I'm just about to walk back into kitchen when I realise that I'm the topic of conversation, so I hang back.

'*You're* never going out with *her*,' his dad says in disbelief.

'What are you trying to say?' Danny asks.

'Well…you know…'

'That I'm an ugly twat?' Danny laughs.

'Something like that,' Chris jokes.

'No, no,' his mum says hurriedly. 'You're my handsome lad – of course. It's just…you're a little rough around the edges, and she's a very beautiful young lady.'

'Cheers, Mam – I think.' Danny laughs. 'Princesses do kiss frogs sometimes,' he reminds them. 'Speaking of frogs, when did you two start seeing each other?'

'Oi, my baby is not a frog,' Emma says, stretching up on her tiptoes to kiss Chris.

'I wasn't talking about Chris,' Danny replies. This is my cue to go back in there, to stop him showing how hurt he's feeling.

'Just work, checking up on us,' I tell Danny. 'Making sure we're getting *some* work done.'

Everyone is sitting around the table now. All five chairs are occupied, so I sit myself on Danny's lap, hooking my arm around his neck.

Everyone stares at us for a second.

'So…' Danny starts. 'What time is our Clare getting here?'

'Speak of the devil,' she says, bursting into the room, dragging two small children by the hands. 'Danny!' she gasps, surprised to see her brother, before moving her gaze to me. 'Holy shit! How much are you charging him per hour?' she asks me.

I blink at her in disbelief.

'Oh, I'm not saying you look like a prostitute,' she backtracks. 'Just that you're way out of my brother's league.'

I laugh politely, kissing Danny on the cheek.

'How the fuck did you end up with my brother?' she asks, jumping up on the worktop, ready to hear the story.

Danny looks at me, like maybe I had thought this through. My hesitation must tell him that I haven't. Well, I'm making this up as I go along, aren't I?

'Well, we work together. We met at work,' Danny tells them, but everyone looks disappointed, like maybe we might have had a better story for them, to explain how such a supposedly odd couple wound up together.

'We actually didn't get on very well to start with,' I tell them honestly. 'He annoyed the hell out of me.'

'That I can believe.' His sister laughs.

'I actually asked her out during my first day on the job,' he tells them as he gazes into my eyes.

'Your first hour,' I correct him.

'Well who could resist you?' he gushes.

'I'm gonna throw up,' Emma says, and we both shoot her a glance in unison before getting back to our story. The key is to make it believable, so it's probably best I use as much truth as possible.

'So he kept asking and I kept saying no. You see this?' I ask, holding my wrist up.

'That ugly bracelet?' Emma asks, scrunching up her face.

I ignore her bitchy comments and tell my story.

'One night we were on this work's night out, and they can get pretty messy,' I explain. I see a few eyebrows shoot up, like they can't quite believe I am capable of messy nights out. 'Long story short, there was a bit of a misunderstanding at the tattoo parlour that we all somehow ended up in, and I wound up with the most stupid tattoo on my wrist – I was mortified. The first thing Danny did was get me this bracelet, to cover up my mistake so that no one could see. So long as I've got this bracelet, no one will ever see it, and as long as I've got Danny, I know that I've got someone looking after me, cleaning up after me, fixing my mistakes.'

I lean forward and hug him, burying my face in his neck so I can smile to myself, proud of my Oscar-worthy performance. I don't mention that this was less than twenty-four hours ago, that it was Danny who got me so 'mortal' I did such a stupid thing, and that I'm so mad at him right now I want to strangle him. In fact, I don't even know why I'm doing this for him. Perhaps if I do, he'll go easy on me for the rest of the trip, you never know. Protecting him just feels right, and even if he was instrumental in my stupid tattoo, he *did* get me the bracelet to hide it.

As his mum makes delighted noises over how cute we are, Danny and I look at each other, neither of us saying a word, but I can read his mind. He didn't know I had this in me – both my acting skills and my kindness.

'Well, enough mush,' Paul says, clapping his hands as he springs to his feet. 'Time to fire up the barbeque. Give me a hand, lads.'

Chris jumps to his feet like an excitable puppy. Danny places his face close to my neck, as though he was going to kiss it, but he doesn't. Instead he whispers into my ear, 'Thank you.'

I smile at him, to let him know that he's welcome. I guess I just know what it's like to feel hurt and betrayed by the person you care about. It doesn't matter what they do to you – even if they cheat on you – you can't just switch the feelings off. Had Will not betrayed me, I probably wouldn't have done this for Danny. Then again, had Will not betrayed me, I wouldn't even be here in the first place.

I grab my phone and check it – just in case Will decided to text me in the last ten minutes – but no such luck. I decide to text him again, so I'm not just the kind of crazy person who double-texts, I'm triple-texting, but I just need to hear from him. My missed call from Caroline is my in – I'll text him and ask if he needed me for something work-related. It's a desperate move, but I suppose I'm a desperate girl right now. I think for a second. No, I need to be smarter than this. I'll leave it until later.

'It's just so weird that Danny has brought a girl home,' his sister Clare thinks out loud now that it's just us girls.

'I wouldn't have thought you were his type,' Emma adds.

'Well, types change,' I say, reminding myself not to act like a bitch in front of Danny's mum.

'I'm just so pleased he's found someone,' Andrea says as she potters around the kitchen. 'He's not one for staying still.'

'Well, I don't plan on letting him go,' I lie, smiling sweetly.

'But do you not think he's a huge geek?' Clare continues.

I suppose, being his sister, she'll never realise just how attractive her brother is. To her he'll just seem like a big IT dork.

'We have our differences, but we accept them,' I say. Another lie, considering I never have a clue what he's talking about and he thinks I'm the most boring girl on the planet.

Thank God we're not a real couple, huh?

Chapter 22

I'm just going to come right out and say it, spending time with Danny's family has been so much fun. We've spent the evening eating, drinking and being merry. Well, I haven't really been eating. The food looks absolutely incredible, and as much as I would love to shovel it in now that I don't have Will trying to dictate my diet to me, I'm being silly and stubborn. After insisting to Danny that I have been healthy eating for myself and for no other reason, I don't want to give him the satisfaction of seeing me pig out, so I'm stupidly keeping up the charade.

Danny walks over to me and holds out a glass of red wine.

'No, no,' I insist. 'I can't.'

'Why not?' He laughs.

'You know I don't drink well and I'm tipsy already.' I laugh too.

It's weird, but pretending to be friendly and happy with Danny has sort of tricked my brain into being that way. I'm still mad about the previous night, but right now I couldn't care less. I'm just happy being happy.

'Says who?' he persists.

'There's a voice in my head telling me to stop drinking,' I tell him.

Danny takes a step closer to me, our faces just inches apart.

'Don't listen to it,' he says softly. 'It's drunk.'

Before I have a chance to cave into peer pressure, I feel Danny bump into me, spilling the glass of red right down the front of my cream top.

'Oh, whoops,' Emma says, without a hint of sincerity. 'Clumsy me bumping into you like that, Dan.'

'Candy, your top,' Danny says, frozen in position because he knows what to do about as much as I do.

Andrea comes rushing over.

'No drama, Candy, nip into the loo and take that off. Danny, come with me, I'll get you something to help with the stain,' she instructs.

I glance back at Emma as I head for the bathroom, feeling myself growing increasingly angry at her smug look. She's clearly jealous. Well, I'll give her something to feel jealous about.

I close the door of the downstairs bathroom behind me, quickly taking off my top. As I sit on the bathroom counter in my bra, in my drunken state, I finally realise how I'll get Will's attention: I'll send him that dirty picture he asked for. There's no way he'll be able to resist that.

I hold my phone at a flattering angle, pull the biggest most over-the-top pout I can contort my face into and push my boobs together with my elbows. I'm drunk, but not so drunk that taking my bra off seems like a good idea. Instead, I pull one strap down, allowing one of the cups to slip aside just enough to show a hint of nipple. I've never done this before, but less is more, right?

I snap what I think is a good one, just as Danny starts knocking on the door.

'Can I come in?' he calls from the other side.

'Hang on,' I call back, a little snappy, as I fidget with my phone to try and get this sent before I let him in.

'But I miss you,' he calls back. Someone must be there.

'Just a sec, honey,' I say sweetly.

I try to hurry up, rushing my way through the motions of attaching a photo and...sent.

'Right, come in, dear,' I chirp, having made sure my bra is back in place. Then I grab the nearest towel and wrap it around my upper body.

As Danny walks through the door, his phone makes a noise. He takes it from his pocket and glances at the screen.

'Did you just send me a text?' he asks.

'Me? No,' I reply, glancing down at my own phone in my hand. That's when I realise that I have drunkenly, absentmindedly sent my sexy selfie to Danny instead of Will. I snatch his phone from his hand.

'Listen, I need you to just trust me: type your passcode in on your phone and let me delete it. I didn't mean to send it to you and it's embarrassing.'

'Embarrassing? Well normally I'd be all over that, but you did me a huge favour today. Go on then.'

Danny does as he is asked and I quickly delete the photo. Crisis averted.

'I know you're pissed off at me, so it must have taken a lot for you to do what you did for me today.'

'No worries,' I reply.

'Well, I want to return the favour. I remember your friend saying something about you not having a date for her wedding – and I think I overheard the two of you talking about maybe seeing if I'd go with you out of pity. Well, here's the pity. You showed me mercy; I'll do the same for you. I'll go with you.'

'Really?' I ask in disbelief.

'Yeah. Why not?'

I suppose I'm just surprised because I know how hard it was going to be to get Will to go, even before everything that happened.

'Well, thank you,' I tell him. 'I'm going to hold you to that. Speaking of holding you…'

I notice Emma, peeping into the bathroom from where she is sitting in the living room. She has a perfect view, and as unsubtle as she's being, I pretend not to notice her. Instead, I wrap my legs around Danny's waist and pull him close, gently kissing his neck.

'Emma is watching,' I whisper. 'Play along.'

Danny runs his hands up my back slowly as I kiss my way up his neck and nibble on his earlobe. He makes this cute little noise.

'Very convincing,' I whisper.

I keep my eyes on Emma, who is getting increasingly annoyed at our display. She soon gets up and walks away, so I stop, but Danny doesn't let go.

'Danny, she's gone, you can let go now,' I tell him.

'Hmm?' he says. 'Oh, right.'

He releases me, but he looks a bit awkward.

'You OK?' I laugh.

'Yeah, I'm good. Give me your top. My mam says she'll clean it. I brought you this to shove on while it dries.'

Danny hands me a T-shirt with the slogan: 'Talk QWERTY to me' emblazoned across the front.

'You truly are a massive nerd.' I laugh.

'Yeah, well, you're welcome,' he replies. 'Hey, I'm glad we're getting on,' he says as he leaves the room, and he sounds sincere.

'As mad at you as I am for last night…I'm glad we're getting on too. You don't know how much I need a friend right now.'

'Maybe we'll talk about it,' he says with a smile.

'Maybe.' I smile back.

Chapter 23

'Well, I'm beat,' I announce as I pull myself to my feet. It's ten p.m., and as much as I'm enjoying spending time with Danny's family, sitting out on this warm summer's night, drinking too much wine, I know that we've got an early start.

'I'm pretty tired too,' Danny agrees – well, neither of us got much sleep last night, did we?

'Oi, oi,' Chris says. 'They're gonna be bucking tonight.'

I feel my cheeks flush.

'Oh, no.' Danny laughs. 'I told Candy she can have my room. I'll kip on the sofa.'

'Don't be daft.' His mum laughs. 'We were young once; we don't mind if you share.'

I shoot Danny a look.

'Honestly, Mam, we don't mind.'

'It's fine, really,' Andrea insists.

'What are you, a prude?' Emma laughs.

'No at all.' I smile. 'Just respectful of my boyfriend's parents.'

'Well, that's lovely,' Paul says with a nod. 'We're not used to that around here.'

'Well, goodnight, pet,' Andrea says. 'Danny, your dad will run you for your car in the morning. You sure you can't stick around for breakfast?'

'Thanks, Mam, but we've got to hit the road early.'

Danny walks me to the kitchen door.

'Your mum just called me pet.' I chuckle, both amused and warmed by her Geordie charm.

'It's a term of endearment. A term of endearment is a *nice* name that you call someone who you *like*,' he teases, stressing certain words for emphasis. 'I realise the concept is alien to you.'

I laugh sarcastically.

'Listen, you go to bed. I'll sit up for a bit and then sleep on the sofa after everyone has gone to bed. Don't worry,' he whispers.

'Are you sure?' I reply.

'I'm sure. Thanks for everything. Sweet dreams.'

I smile at him for a second before heading indoors and upstairs.

I take off all of my clothes except Danny's T-shirt, which I've decided I'll sleep in, scrub off my make-up and climb into Danny's bed. He's got a double bed squashed into the corner of the room, so I climb in and sit with my back against the wall. I glance at my phone – still no word from Will. It's sad, but when I was with Will, life was just bridging the gaps between moments with him. Whether it was being called into his office for no real reason or just receiving an unexpected text from him over the weekend, when he acknowledged my existence, unprompted, it meant everything. It would send me soaring up on a high that I felt like I'd never come down from...until the next quiet period. My mood was all over the place. I suppose now that he's ignoring me, at least my mood is balanced, even if I am permanently in a bad one.

I sit and think for a while, anxiously picking at my manicured nails, but doing so in such a gentle way that the polish doesn't actually come off because I didn't bring anything with me to touch them up. Time is ticking away, but now that I'm in bed I just can't sleep.

I lean over and flick the light off, before lying back and trying to make myself comfortable. As I lie there in the pitch black something catches my eye: a small, glow-in-the-dark star stuck to the ceiling in the corner of the room. It seems strange, the way it's just tucked away in the corner on its own, but it's beautiful. I can't stop staring at it.

There's a knock on the door, snapping me from my thoughts.

'Come in,' I call out.

'Hey,' Danny says as he shuffles in awkwardly. 'So, my mam is insisting I get to bed. Maybe if I can just chill here with you until everyone has gone to bed, then I'll go back down.'

'Sure,' I reply, sitting upright. 'I can't sleep anyway; I'd appreciate the company.'

Danny closes the door behind him, plunging the room into darkness again, before hopping on the bed next to me. He doesn't get under the covers, but he sits by my side, leaning against the wall too.

'Why do you have one glowing star on your ceiling?' I ask curiously.

'I was – no, I *am* a space nerd. You know that.' He laughs.

'No one is in any doubt over your nerd status.' I laugh. 'Just seems weird that you have just one shoved in the corner.'

'My nana used to live here with us,' he tells me, his voice softening. 'When I was little, she stuck them all over the ceiling for me.'

'Aw, that's cute,' I tell him.

'One day when I was a teen – I don't even remember why now – I think I was pissed off because my parents wouldn't let me do something because I was too young. I remember sitting in here, fuming about how I wasn't a baby any more, and the stars just served as a reminder. So I ripped them all down, all but that one, which I couldn't reach because I was a short-arse thirteen-year-old.'

Danny laughs briefly.

'They diagnosed my nana with cancer not long before I went travelling. I was going to cancel my trip, maybe stick around and go to uni, but she insisted I went, telling me she'd be fine.'

'Did you not go to uni then?' I ask, curiously. I would have thought you'd need to in his line of work.

'Nope. Self-taught. Started working on code on MySpace when I was a teenager, and built on it from there. Got a job at some dot-gone company when I left school, earned enough to travel and since then I've managed to alternate travelling around with jobs here and there. I like to keep moving.'

I smile, although I only understood about half of that. When Danny talks, it's like every other word registers and the rest fall on deaf ears with me. I don't think he's being pretentious, I just don't think he realises that some of us have no idea what a 'dot-gone' is.

'Anyway, my nana wasn't fine,' he continues. 'She passed away before I got home. So, the last star stays. It's going to sound lame but, I don't know, it's like she's watching over me, or something. That one star in the sky that she put there.'

'That's not lame at all,' I tell him. 'I wish I had more to remember my parents.'

'It must have been tough for you, losing them both,' Danny says, taking my hand and squeezing it.

'It was, very tough. I lost my mum first, so at least I had my dad to help me through it. We knew my dad was close to the end, and I remember sitting by his hospital bed, knowing that as soon as he left me, that was it, I'd be all alone in the world. I remember it like it was yesterday though. It was the middle of the night – a horrible, cold, windy winter's night. Two of the nurses on duty had come in to check on him, so he was telling them the story of the day I was born. There was a terrible storm going on while my mum was in labour and, at the exact moment I left my mother's body, all the lights in the hospital went out. At least, that's how my dad told it. The same dad who insisted, despite me being born at 03:13 a.m., that the nurse write down 03:14 a.m. Just in case. The storm, the dip in power and the time I decided to make my entrance somehow convinced my selectively religious father into thinking that he needed to do something – anything – to dispel the bad juju.'

'Better safe than sorry.' Danny laughs.

'My mother, who was far more level-headed, couldn't give a toss about the time I was born, and when I heard this story for the first time she assured me that the lights on the maternity ward only flickered for a second, thanks to the epic storm going on outside. She also told me that on the day in question I repaid her by giving her an utterly filthy, unimpressed look the first time I was placed in her arms.'

The reports of my demonic behaviour over the years were greatly exaggerated. My mum would often remind me how lucky she was to still have nipples, because as a baby I made it my life's work to remove them. She explained that, when she was breastfeeding me, I would often get this look in my eye, a look that always preceded the same, brutal attack. She told me how she would gently plead, 'Candice, no!', to this little demon baby attached to her breast, but I paid no attention to her calm pleas, and I would bite her – hard. For the lone fact that she continued to feed me at all, I will be forever grateful.

'Your dad sounds funny,' Danny says, rubbing my hand. He just seems to get how difficult this must be for me to talk about, despite still having both his parents.

'He was hilarious – rarely intentionally.'

'Were they both ill then?'

'Yeah, my gene pool isn't great. Dementia, diabetes – so even if I make it into old age, I'll probably forget I can't have sugar and eat a cake and die.'

'Well, that's why you've got to make the most of life. I keep telling you, YOLO.' He laughs.

'It's fair enough saying you only live once, but if you live recklessly, that once is going to be short.'

'So long as you're happy. Except I don't think you are,' he says.

'Why not?' I squeak, trying a little too hard to protest otherwise.

'Because you're having an affair with Will,' he replies.

'Me? And Will? Don't be…' My voice trails off. He's not stupid. There's no point trying to pretend he's not right. 'How did you know?'

'I can just tell. He gets jealous when I talk to you, this weird little holiday you guys had planned – you were sharing double rooms. It doesn't take Sherlock Holmes. I'm going to guess that's why you keep checking your phone. You fallen out?'

'When I started seeing him, he told me he and his wife were separated, but living together to keep up appearances. Yes, I realise how unbelievable that sounds, but I had no reason to doubt him. I was in a sad, weak, vulnerable place and I believed what he said because it's what I needed to be true, I guess. When I found out she'd had a baby – his baby – I realised he hadn't left her, and that he probably never will.'

'And you don't want to be a mistress, I take it?'

'Nope.'

'And he wouldn't leave his wife for you?'

'Nope. I can't even begin to imagine a scenario where we're a proper couple. Before, when I would try to imagine it, I would see the most beautiful montage of happy, smiley romantic crap that may as well be set to an Ed Sheeran song. It looked wonderful, and I wanted that, but I'm never going to have that with someone who doesn't text me back.'

'It's good that you realise this,' he tells me. 'Seriously. I thought I was going to have to give you some hard truths, but you're a smart girl. We just need to get your life back on track, that's all.'

'You make it sound so simple.' I laugh.

'It *is* simple,' he tells me confidently. 'Leave it to me, OK? I know you've got offices to visit, but I'm sure we can make time for a little self-discovery.'

'Oh, forget work,' I tell him. 'I'm not doing a second of work for that man while we're away. No one is under any illusions now, fuck it. Although I'm not entirely happy putting my life in the hands of a grown man who picks fights with teenagers.'

'OK, look, I wasn't even going to tell you...but they were saying some stuff about us. I was just sticking up for us and it went a bit too far.'

I think for a moment. 'Us? Or me?'

'Us,' he insists. 'Don't worry about it.'

I feel like Danny is trying to spare my feelings, so I don't push it. I wonder what they were saying about me. I know I wasn't looking too fresh this morning, unless it was my outfit. I know Danny calls me a Stepford Wife, but I don't look that out of place, do I?

I think about it for a moment before announcing: 'Fuck 'em.'

'I like the new Candy much more than the old Candy.' Danny laughs.

I rest my head on Danny's shoulder, suddenly feeling very sleepy.

'I think I do too,' I tell him. And it's true. For the first time in a long time, I'm starting to feel more like myself again.

Chapter 24

For the second morning in a row, I woke up cuddled up to Danny. The only difference today is that my arse is much less sore and I feel less like I want to strangle him. Still, it wasn't intentional. The plan was for Danny to sleep on the sofa once his family went to bed, but I guess we fell asleep.

I saw an entirely different side to Danny yesterday. Despite his cheeky charm offensive, he's just a boy who loves his family and feels pain when he is cheated on. Yes, OK, so he's also the kind of guy who steals drugs from teenagers and pisses off policemen, who gets vulnerable young ladies drunk and tattooed, etcetera, etcetera.

When we got up, Danny's mum was still asleep, so Danny insisted we didn't wake her to say goodbye because she needed her rest. I have a sneaking suspicion it's because he didn't want to endure a painful goodbye, but I'd never say as much. After what he told me about his gran last night, it sounds to me like he doesn't like to keep people too close – in case he loses them, I guess.

His dad dropped us off at the garage, and now we're on the road again.

As we zip along in the now fully functioning (well, as much as it ever was) Love Bug, Danny spies a burger van at the side of the road and pulls over.

'I'm starving,' Danny announces. 'You must be too.'

'I'm fine,' I lie.

'No, you're not – don't think I didn't notice that you didn't eat much last night.'

'I just wasn't hungry,' I tell him as I climb over the driver's seat and follow him to the van.

'Well, you must be now, so breakfast is on me,' he tells me.

'Look, it's not a dieting thing, I promise you,' I start, but he interrupts.

'I'm not your dad. You don't have to explain yourself to me.'

'Oh, I know that,' I reply. 'I was just going to say that I don't eat from anywhere that doesn't have a postcode. No offence,' I add, noticing that the girl working there has heard me.

'You have to eat something, Candy,' Danny reasons.

'I'm fine, I have this,' I tell him, pulling a SkinnyKwik bar from my handbag and opening it.

'That?' Danny playfully slaps the bar out of my hand, causing it to hit the ground so I can't eat it now. 'That's not food.'

'It's a meal replacement bar,' I inform him. 'It's just the right number of calories, but thank you for ruining it.'

'You'll just have to have what I'm having now,' he says with a triumphant smile. 'Two cheeseburgers with chips, please.'

'And do you want your burgers in a stottie or in a doughnut?' the girl asks, breaking halfway through to blow a bubble with her chewing gum.

'I'm sorry, what?' Danny asks, his eyes widening with amazement.

'Do you want it in a doughnut instead? It's a glazed doughnut.'

I feel my jaw drop in a combination amazement and disgust.

'I don't see how I can say no to that,' Danny laughs. 'Two of those please.'

'That sounds kind of fattening,' I start.

'It is,' the girl replies. 'We only get fat truckers eating them – no one as fit as you,' she tells Danny, blatantly flirting. 'And you're going to die,' she tells me.

Before I get a chance to say anything, we're interrupted from our impending coronary by a voice. 'Oi, a word,' the man shouts.

I look over and see a policeman walking towards us.

'Oh, shit, not more police,' I whisper to Danny.

It's only as the man approaches us that we realise he's not an actual police officer, he's a community support officer.

'Oh, don't worry, he's not a real policeman,' Danny tells me. 'You're not a real policeman, are you?'

I know that Danny doesn't mean any disrespect by this, but the officer doesn't take it too well. He looks angry, like maybe he gets this a lot, and it's starting to get to him.

'You littered,' he tells me.

'I littered?' I ask in disbelief. 'When?'

The officer nods towards the SkinnyKwik bar on the ground.

'Oh, come on,' I start. Truth be told, I do feel braver because he's not technically a real police officer. 'He knocked that out of my hand – like, thirty seconds ago. I'm going to pick it up.'

'Pick it up then,' the officer insists. 'Or I'll fine you.'

The officer is clearly pissed off, and unleashing the full force of his authority on us because he can, but this just winds Danny up more.

'Don't do it, Candy,' Danny tells me.

'It's fine,' I insist, bending over to pick it up and dropping it in the bin next to me.

'There's a princess,' the officer patronises me. 'Wasn't so hard, was it?'

'Breakfast is up,' the girl calls out, dumping two polystyrene boxes down in front of us. I grab it and open it, taking in the sight of the enormous cheeseburger encased in a glazed doughnut.

'You're eating that?' the officer asks me, and I nod. 'You're going to die.'

'What does everyone keep saying that?' I ask, irritated. As the three of them stare at me, as though I were a condemned woman about to eat her last meal, something in my head just tells me to prove to them that I am perfectly capable of eating this. I don't know if it's misplaced feminism, this girl flirting with Danny, being all cool and into saturated fat and shit, or the fact this non-policeman is standing next to me, making me pick things up off the ground like it's going to be out of my comfort zone… but I'm going to eat it. I'm going to cast aside the fact that I know nothing of its nutritional content (other than the fact it's bad), the fact that this place doesn't have a postcode (AKA someone to be held accountable if it kills me) and the disgusting fact that the girl who made it is fidgeting with her lip ring and I'm going to eat it – this double cheeseburger, in a glazed doughnut, served in a polystyrene tray that is already swimming in grease. I've been known to offset a few high-calorie days with a little dodgy dieting before, but this is going to be ridiculous.

I lift the burger with both hands – because it truly takes both hands – and stare at it for a second before taking a bite, chewing and then swallowing. I open my empty mouth and showcase the insides for all to see, to show them that I am more than capable.

'Yum,' I lie. It's the kind of thing that I imagine if it were done well it would taste delicious, but it's greasy and sloppy, and yet somehow so incredibly dry at the same time. Still, I take a second bite, because I am a strong, independent woman, and I can eat (what I'd guess is) a 1500-calorie burger for breakfast if I want to.

'No more littering,' the officer warns me, before heading back towards his car.

'I fucking hate guys like that,' Danny says. 'Absolutely drunk with power.'

'Do you think maybe you have a problem with authority?' I ask him.

'Fuck off.' He laughs. 'Why do you say that?'

'Well, the run-in with the police yesterday, now this… You don't do well with it.'

Danny pauses for a second, giving my point a moment's thought.

'Nope,' he concludes. 'Those coppers yesterday were fine – I was off my tits.' He laughs. 'I was rude to them too. They were just doing their job. But this guy, oh, this guy... He has no right to be a dick to you. I hate to see men being dicks to women.'

I watch Danny watching the officer getting back in his car, carefully buckling up his seat belt and checking his mirrors before he starts his engine. I can tell from the thoughtful look on Danny's face that the cogs are turning, and this worries me. Danny is a loose cannon who lives in the moment. He doesn't give his actions a second thought; he just does what he does and that's that, the consequences be damned. For his entire adult life, he has done whatever he wanted, with no one to call him out on his bad behaviour. If he makes a mess of things he simply packs his bags and moves on. No big deal – apparently.

I don't have long to worry about what Danny might do before he picks up the enormous burger in one hand, brandishing it ready to throw it. I open my mouth immediately to tell him not to throw it, but it has left his hand before the first word has left my lips. As the burger flies through the air, life feels like it is happening in slow motion. I hold my breath for what feels like the longest time as I watch the burger soar, praying that the car will be just that little bit too far away for a nerd to reach with a throw – of course, most nerds don't have guns like Danny does.

Splat! The burger hits the officer's windscreen, erupting with such a force that grease, cheese and whatever that pinky-coloured sauce is coats the glass, completely obstructing his view. Of course, he's most likely in no doubt over who threw it. From the moment of impact everything speeds up again, and I feel myself exhale hard.

'Run,' Danny shouts, his brain catching up with his actions. We both run for the Love Bug. Danny gets there first – because he isn't doing this in five-inch heels (well, I didn't realise I'd be dashing for a getaway vehicle today) – but he has to wait for me to get in first, because that's the only door that works.

'Come on, come on,' he shouts. 'I have previous.'

'Of course you have fucking previous, you're a menace,' I snap, clambering over the seat.

Thankfully the officer's window is too filthy for him to safely drive after us, and by the time he is out of his car and on his way over to us, Danny is speeding away, flipping him off and beeping his horn as he leaves him in his dust.

As we fly along the road, Danny makes victorious woo-ing noises.

'We showed him, huh?' He cackles.

I roll my eyes as Danny blows his horn and bursts into a lyrically questionable version of 'I Fought the Law'.

I feel a wave of sickness wash over me suddenly.

'Can you slow down, please?' I ask.

'No, he might catch up with us. Just let me turn off so he can't find us. Anyway, I'm hardly speeding.'

'That's because your crappy car hardly can speed,' I snap. 'It's not that. I feel sick.'

I watch the colour drain from Danny's face, but soon realise that it's not out of concern for me.

'Don't be sick in my car,' he panics. 'I'll pull over.'

'It's fine, just get us to safety.'

'I'd rather be arrested than have a car full of vomit,' he says seriously, pulling over and hurrying out of the car so that I can get out.

I bend over the bonnet of the car, resting my head on my forearms.

'I'm going to be sick,' I announce, moments before throwing up all over the Love Bug.

'Not on the…car,' Danny says redundantly.

I feel dreadful as a cold shiver washes over my body, but I know how much Danny loves his car and I feel bad.

'Sorry,' I say quietly, my teeth bizarrely chattering.

'Hey, don't apologise,' Danny says, rubbing my shoulder. 'It's karma, isn't it? I mess up someone else's car; I get my car messed up. Don't worry.'

Whether or not Danny is upset about me throwing up on his car, he does a brilliant job of acting like he doesn't care. I still feel bad though.

'I'll clean it,' I insist, widening my eyes to try and force myself to feel less dopey.

'Don't be daft, get in the car,' he insists. 'Have a nap. We're not that far from York. I'll take it nice and easy and wake you when we get there.'

'Thank you,' I tell him, climbing back into my seat and snuggling up.

'Maybe hold this bag, just in case,' he adds, pushing a plastic bag into my hand. So I imagine being sick on the inside of his car is still a no-no, then.

Chapter 25

I wake up flat on my back, with my hand over my mouth as though I were trying to keep the vomit inside by any means necessary.

For a moment, I breathe as gently as possible, terrified any sudden movements will make me sick again. Then, as I run my hands down my body, I realise that I'm not wearing any clothes. I sit up and take in my surroundings and realise that I'm in a room that I don't recognise, in a bed that I've never seen before, watching *Pointless* on TV – *Pointless*, of all things!

'Hello,' I call out, panicked.

I hear running water shut off before Danny rushes out of the bathroom, wrapping a towel around his waist, moving his laptop off the bed next to me so that he can sit down.

'You! You had me worried,' he insists, feeling my forehead with the back of his hand. 'Good, you're much cooler now.'

'What… How…' I don't even know what questions to ask.

'We're in York,' he tells me. 'At the hotel. You went a bit weird in the car – you burned right up.'

'So, what, you took my clothes off me?' I ask angrily.

'No,' he replies through gritted teeth, resenting the fact I'm making out like he's some sort of opportunistic pervert. 'I was carrying you in and you threw up all over yourself. And me. Anyway, there are easier ways to see you in your underwear.'

I feel bad for a second, until the last part of his sentence registers.

'Wait, what do you mean there are easier ways?'

'Well, for one, you sent me a basically topless photo last night,' he says.

'How... I deleted that. That wasn't meant for you,' I insist.

'Yeah, I guessed as much. But iCloud is a thing, so you didn't just send it to my phone, you sent it to my Mac too.'

'Fuck,' is about all I can say.

'Was it for Will?' he asks, softening a little.

'Yes. I was drunk; I don't know what I was thinking. I wasn't thinking, I suppose.'

'Did he reply?'

'No. Well, I never sent it. I only sent it to you, and then you interrupted me so...'

'So I delete this...' his laptop makes a noise, confirming as much '...and it's gone for ever. No one else has a copy.'

'Thank you,' I say weakly.

'So, how are you feeling?'

'Like I want to kill you, for making me eat that bloody burger,' I tell him.

'Hey, I didn't *make* you. I'm just glad I didn't eat mine.'

I shoot him a filthy glance. 'My stomach is killing me,' I tell him. 'And I feel like I'm going to be sick again.'

'Bathroom is that way,' he tells me.

I dash for the bathroom as fast as my dizziness will allow, sit on the floor and hover my head above the toilet.

'Your phone is ringing,' Danny calls from the bedroom.

'They can wait,' I call back.

'It's Will,' Danny adds, appearing in the doorway.

Just brilliant. When I want to hear from Will, I don't hear a word. Now, when I neither want nor feel up to talking to him, here he is.

Danny hands me my phone, so I answer.

I am about to speak when a crippling stomach cramp grips me, and that wave of sickness washes over me again. I let out an involuntary moan before saying hello.

'Are you having sex?' is the first thing Will asks, angrily.
'What? No!'
'Candy, do you have my boxers?' Danny calls out.
I spot them on the floor next to me and toss them out to him.
'Sounds like you two are having fun,' he says sarcastically.
'Will, I've been texting you – you haven't replied to me. You caused all this. I didn't ask for any of this.'

Hearing his voice is so bittersweet. I miss him like crazy, but I can't get past his betrayal, or him making me an accessory to his adultery.

'So, what, you just go off with some guy for a filthy week in hotels?' he asks – the hypocrite. Because it was fine when I was doing it with him, even though he was married.

'Because that's what's happening,' I say sarcastically.

'Well, I called the first hotel and they said you didn't sleep there. You didn't sleep in the second, either. I've got you visiting the first office and then nothing. So you're doing *something*, and you're sleeping *somewhere*...'

'I really don't think it's any of your business,' I reply. I mean, the business part is his business, but we both know that's not why this trip is happening, so he can't say anything about it and he certainly can't fire me. 'And just listen to yourself! You have been lying to me – cheating on me for our entire relationship, having a baby with someone else, and you call me up after days but not to apologise, oh no, to be a jealous wanker.'

'Language,' Will reminds me. 'You know how I feel about swearing.'

'What are you, my fucking dad?' I ask angrily.

'Look, you're upset,' Will says calmly. 'But we need to talk about this.'

'Talk to your wife,' I snap, hanging up on him.

I look up from the toilet to see Danny standing in the bathroom doorway with his boxers in his hand. He smiles and gives me a short applause.

'Thanks for looking after me,' I tell him sincerely.

'You're welcome,' he says with a smile. 'Just a bit of food poisoning that I probably caused – it's the least I can do.'

'I don't just mean while I've been unwell today,' I tell him.

'I know,' he replies. 'You know what? I *really* like the new Candy.'

'You know what? Me too,' I tell him honestly.

As the night has gone on, my sickness is fading fast – hopefully the fact I only ate a mouthful of poisoned burger is working in my favour. I felt weirdly hungry when I woke up – probably due to the fact that my system is completely empty – and all I wanted was toast. Toast with butter, which is odd because both bread and butter are foods that I never normally touch.

We're in a four-star hotel, so it's no surprise that toast is not on the dinner menu. Danny offered to pop down to reception and ask if they would make me some because I was unwell and it's all I wanted. Unsurprisingly they said no, but when Danny returned to our room half an hour later, he was brandishing two Asda carrier bags, having bought and successfully smuggled a toaster, bread and butter up to our room. He cooked it up on the desk and served it on the saucers from the teacups. It might actually be the best toast I've ever eaten in my life.

So here we are, sitting in bed in our underwear, eating toast and flicking through the TV channels that the hotel has to offer.

'That really hit the spot,' I tell him. 'Thank you so much.'

'It's just toast.' He laughs.

It might be just toast, but if I were here with Will, there's no way wheat of any kind would be on the menu. The only part of the trip I'd been dreading was visiting all of these amazing hotels with wonderful restaurants, and not being able to indulge in what they had to offer. Well, now I can…and yet here I am, in bed, eating toast.

'Well, now I need another cuppa. Want one?' I ask.

'Sure, but I'll make them,' Danny insists.

'No, you've done enough and I'm feeling loads better,' I say as I climb out of bed, awkwardly transitioning from under the covers to the privacy of a hotel dressing gown.

'I've seen you in your underwear more than I've seen you in clothes these past few days.' Danny laughs. 'Is that really necessary?'

'Yes,' I tell him firmly as I make the tea.

'Well, that's what we'll work on next.'

'What?'

'You getting more comfortable with being undressed around people.'

I laugh. 'You say that like it's normal.'

'It *is*,' he replies. 'But you stiffen up, like you're terrified of your own body.'

'I'm fine with my body, thanks,' I reply, placing his cup down next to him.

'Well, we've got you on solid food; we can get you on better terms with your body. Know that you've got a cracking body.'

'Shut up,' I say, taking the dressing gown back off and climbing in bed.

'No, I'm serious. You're way out of that chubby old wanker Will's league.'

I can't help but smile.

'He tried to contact you again?'

'No, he thinks we're too busy having sex for me to chat to him.'

'Well, if that's what he thinks…' Danny jokes with a wiggle of his eyebrows. I throw one of my discarded crusts at him.

'Oi, didn't your parents teach you to eat your crusts.' He laughs, throwing it back. Danny's face falls seconds after my own does. 'Sorry, I didn't mean…'

'It's OK,' I tell him honestly. Well, it's just one of those things that people say, isn't it? 'It just reminded me of some advice that my dad did give me before he died. It was just me and him, sitting in his room. We'd been quiet for a few minutes and then my dad comes out with: "I know that you're a lesbian, and I love you – know that".'

'Was he confused?' Danny laughs.

'Yes,' I reply. 'But not because he was ill. Because I'd confused him with my lack of a love life. I dressed kind of punky then too, so that and because I'd never brought a bloke home – my dad put two and two together and got lesbian. But he was quite an old-fashioned kind of man, so to hear him say that meant a lot.'

'Yeah, I bet.' Danny laughs.

'Well, I explained to him that a love life just wasn't happening for me. We'd never discussed such things – I'd only ever chatted boy stuff with my mum, but it was like, he knew this was the end. This was the last piece of parental advice I was ever going to get, so he reached out. He told me not to worry about it, and to make sure that I never needed to rely on anyone for anything. He said that while it's nice to have someone to fall back on, when that person is not there you'll come crashing down on your own. He told me to never let a man control my happiness, or my financial stability – well, look at me: miserable, sleeping with the married man who pays my wages, doing all the things he told me not to do.'

'Don't be so hard on yourself,' Danny insists. 'You've just got off track a little, that's all. We all make mistakes but we learn from them and we don't make them again. Hopefully. I can't promise you we won't have any more run-ins with the fuzz.' He laughs. 'Seriously though, I know I annoy you, but I just want what's best for you, and everything I'm doing or pushing you to do is because I think it will make you happy in the long run.'

'You think twerking in a strip club, getting so drunk I get an Isis tattoo, getting driven to the police station in the back of a police van and winding up with food poisoning is going to make me happy?'

'Yes,' he replies confidently. 'Because it's keeping you amused, entertained, on your toes and distracted from your problems.'

'This is true,' I reply. 'But I'm not sure how I feel about you being on a little mission to sort my life out.'

'I'm not going to sort out your life – you are. Will you let me help, though?'

'Yes,' I reply, slowly and cautiously. The truth is that, as messy as things are and as furious as Danny can make me, getting some distance from Will has shown me that the way I used to tiptoe around him, and try and change myself for him, wasn't good for me. Living life has given me this clarity, the knowledge that I can't and won't be happy with Will, so there's no point in trying to fix it. Best to just pick up the pieces and walk away.

'So you want to put him completely behind you?' Danny asks. 'Because if you do, I'll help you, but you've got to go all-in. I'm happy to help you change, but I'm not going to be your girlfriend, taking your phone off you so you can't drunk dial, wailing "he's not worth it" at you as I drunkenly swill you with Lambrini.'

I laugh. The truth is that I have had enough of Will, and the more I think about it, the more I feel like we were just a source of warmth for each other during a cold time. He was unhappy in his marriage; I was unhappy generally. We just sort of paired off, and we shouldn't have. It sounds like Danny needs some convincing, so it's time for a little embarrassing honesty.

'I thought he was going to propose.'

'What?' Danny asks.

'Will. I thought he was going to propose while we were away. I found a ring in his pocket last week, this beautiful, silver band with a huge, gleaming rock on it. I actually thought it was an engagement ring, and I was terrified because over the last couple of days I cut my left hand four times on four separate occasions. At first I was upset and annoyed, that my hand was going to look ugly in the photos. Then I started worrying that it was a bad omen, or that my body was physically rejecting the idea of marriage. But it turns out it wasn't an engagement ring for me – I suppose it was a yay-we-had-a-baby ring for his wife.'

'That's rough,' Danny admits.

'Yep,' I reply. 'But the thought of marrying him now makes me want to cut my left hand off. How can I feel anything for a liar and a cheat? Maybe things would be good to start with, but what's to say he won't trade me in down the line too? I'd never relax. I'd be trying to keep up my Little Miss Perfect act for ever and I'm just so tired.'

'Do you trust me?' he asks.

Again, I'm cautious, but open to ideas. 'Yes,' I reply.

'Then all I ask is that you do as I suggest, OK?'

I think for a moment, excited by the idea, but worried. 'OK, but we need ground rules.'

'State your terms,' he says, clicking the TV off.

'Right, you can't make me eat anything that might make me ill. No more body modifications. No getting me arrested.'

'Deal,' Danny says, holding out a hand for me to shake. 'And this isn't me backing down, it's just that I feel like we've done all that now. Time for new stuff.' He flashes me a cheeky smile.

'You're trouble, mister.'

'*I'm* trouble?' He laughs. 'Look, I'll take responsibility for almost everything, but don't act like you're sweetness and light. I hear you swear, I saw how much you could drink before you got drunk. I saw you twerking at the strip club – well, videos of it at least. And when you were trying to make Emma jealous, that was all you. And let me tell you this, Candy, you've got moves. Your neck-kissing game is strong.'

I try to bow from my position sitting in bed, keeping the covers up high. Danny notices me being awkwardly undressed again, and he looks as though he's going to suggest I flash as part of my life rehabilitation, according to him.

'Don't worry,' he says eventually. 'We've got to let it happen naturally. I throw you in the deep end, you'll drown.'

'Illness aside, today is the first day since the shit hit the fan that I actually don't feel like I'm drowning. I suppose I have you to thank for that,' I say reluctantly.

'No way,' Danny says modestly. 'You might have been drowning, but you were in the shallow end of the kids' pool. You just needed someone to tell you to stand up.'

I laugh a little too hard, causing that sick feeling to come back a little.

'Shit, don't start throwing up again. Never seen anything like it.' He laughs.

'Was it bad?'

'I've seen some things…and I've never seen anyone projectile vomit like that before. You hit the ceiling.'

'I was angry?'

'No, you literally vomited on the ceiling.'

I throw my head in my hands.

'Oh God, I'm so embarrassed. Where?'

'The corridor on the way to the room.'

'Oh, shit! No wonder they wouldn't make me toast.'

Danny laughs, ruffling my hair. 'Right, think we need sleep,' he says, climbing out of bed and stretching out, flexing his muscles in a way that makes me wonder whether he's doing it for my benefit, not unlike a peacock spreading its beautiful feathers to impress the birds. 'Want me to sleep in the bath?'

'Don't be daft,' I reply. 'We can sleep in the same bed. I think we're way past what's appropriate, don't you?' I laugh.

'You're learning well, Padawan,' he says as he hops back in. 'I'm proud of you.'

'What did you call me?' I ask.

'Padawan… Don't tell me you don't get *Star Wars* references?'

'I had a boyfriend, remember?' I tease.

'Yeah, well, with respect, he wasn't exactly a catch.'

'And you are?' I ask.

'I am,' he replies confidently. 'I'm a regular Han Solo.'

'I have no idea what that means,' I reply as I roll over to face away from him, making myself comfortable.

I close my eyes, ready for my first decent night's sleep of the trip, but it isn't to be. Just as I feel myself drifting off, the sound of two people having sex in the room above is quietly audible. At first it's just the creaking of the bed and the occasional murmurs of ecstasy, but then, all at once, things get loud. As though the banging sounds and screams weren't bad enough, the light fitting in our room must be loose because it's making a noise and flickering like we're at a rave. I quickly flick it off, but with our sense of sight shut off, our hearing becomes heightened.

'Yes…yes…yes…' the lady upstairs moans repeatedly, slowly but steadily, with just a few seconds separating each word.

'Am I handsome?' I hear Danny ask.

'Yes…' the woman seemingly replies.

'Are Macs better than PCs?'

'Yes…' the woman predictably replies.

'Did Candy secretly enjoy dancing in the strip club with me?'

'Yes…'

I can't help but laugh. Just like that, the awkwardness is gone.

'You have a go,' he tells me.

I wait to get the timing right.

'Is Will a wanker?' I ask.

'Yes…'

'It's a like a Magic Eight Ball.' He laughs. 'Will I ever be a millionaire?'

'Yes…'

'Will I marry Matthew McConaughey?' I chime in.

'Yes...'

'Are you faking it?' Danny asks her, and perfectly timed, the woman lets out one final long, loud 'yes' before it's silent again.

We laugh together before eventually everything is silent again.

'Night, nerd,' I say as I close my eyes.

'Night, bro,' he replies.

Chapter 26

It's Monday morning, and I'm feeling loads better – despite not getting much sleep, because the couple upstairs were at it like rabbits, having these frantic sex sessions, a quick rest period and then getting straight back to it. I do feel loads better though, so much so I just ate four slices of toast that Danny made me. Here's the thing: I don't care. I don't just feel well, I feel alive. I'm ready for whatever Danny has to throw at me today.

Our next stop is Birmingham, and today the weather today is absolutely sweltering. You know how we have crappy weather all year round, except for that one day in summer where we get three months' worth of heat over twenty-four intense hours? Well that day is today, and the Love Bug is like an oven. I really need to convince Danny to get a better car. It's not that his car isn't cool and it's not like he hasn't spent money doing it up, but there's just so much stuff that cars have now that I realise I've been taking for granted. Things like air conditioning, electric windows, more than one door that opens – you know, standard stuff.

But Danny refuses to trade it in, which is sort of sweet, I guess. Will is the kind of guy who moves on to other women when he's bored of his current one, and Danny is the kind of guy who is loyal even to his car, and even when it's letting him down.

I feel like Danny is someone I could be really good friends with. Yes, he's got me in some bother, but he's taken care of me. Even back on the first day when I was throwing my guts up over the side of the boat, he went out of his way to make me feel better, and that corny bangle story I sold to his family – I might have made it sound mushier than it was for effect, but it was essentially true. I fucked up; he was there to pick up the pieces. That's exactly the sort of friends I need in my life, especially now I'm going to lose a bit of Amy to wedded bliss.

'So we're not visiting the office today?' Danny asks as he drives through Birmingham.

'Nope,' I reply. 'We're not visiting any more offices, full stop.'

'Badass.' He laughs. 'Well, we can do whatever we want then. What do you fancy?'

'I don't know,' I reply. 'I've never been here before.'

'I worked here for a few months; I can show you the sights.' Danny thinks for a moment. 'Well, I'd take you to Cadbury World, but I don't want you to get overwhelmed,' he teases.

I laugh sarcastically. I don't know what Cadbury World is like, but I imagine it to be like Willy Wonka's chocolate factory, and the mood I'm in today I'd be like Augustus Gloop, drinking from the chocolate river. Of course, we all know what happens to him, so maybe that's not such a great idea.

'I noticed that the circus is in town…but you don't strike me as the kind of girl who has much time for clowns. I know what we'll do,' Danny announces.

'Why am I worried?' I ask.

'Let's just go get checked in and then you'll see,' he tells me mysteriously.

Chapter 27

Danny has his hands over my eyes as he steers me into a building. Two days ago, this would have felt like a suicide mission and there's no way I would have let him do this. Today, I'm actually quite excited.

'Ta-da,' he announces, removing his hands from my eyes so I can take in my surroundings.

The large room is alive with screens of various sizes – more than I have ever seen in one place in my life – and flashing, colourful lights are everywhere. There's an elaborate-looking bar in the corner, made up of Tetris blocks, which looks pretty cool. The place is busy with people, all engaging in different video games. Upon closer inspection some of the people aren't real at all, they're life-size statues of what I'd imagine are video game characters – a few of them look familiar – but it's hard to tell who is real and who is a statue because some of the people appear to be in fancy dress, I think, unless it's a geeky style thing.

'What is this place?' I ask, amazed.

'It's a gaming bar,' Danny informs me, although I suppose I'd guessed as much. 'I told you, we need to expand your geeky knowledge.'

'Oh, you mean you're going to make me play video games with you and get my arse handed to me.' I laugh. 'Well this may surprise you, mister, because I might be out of touch with gaming these days, but I was quite the Sega Mega Drive player when I was a kid.'

'You had a Mega Drive?' he asks, clearly amazed I did anything for fun other than stare at my Barbie dolls and wonder how I too could get a waist as thin as my neck.

'I did. You may not know this, but it wasn't a particularly cool thing for little girls to be into, so I didn't pursue gaming as a hobby.'

'What was your favourite game then?' he asks.

'Streets of Rage,' I reply confidently. 'Specifically, Streets of Rage 2.'

Streets of Rage is a side-scrolling beat-'em-up game, very typical of its time. It was simple: fight your way through levels of bad guys before battling the final boss. Just because it was clear to follow, doesn't mean it was easy though, and I lost hours to it as a kid.

'Did you complete it?' he asks.

I shake my head.

'Nope. Only child, none of my friends were into it – I feel like if I'd had someone to play co-op with me, I would have nailed it, but I always had to go it alone.'

'Well they have a Mega Drive here,' he informs me. 'So you might be in luck. Fancy a game?'

I nod my head excitedly.

Soon enough we're plonked down in front of a big screen, sitting on a boxy-shaped sofa that Danny informs me is inspired by something called Minecraft. As I examine the wired, tatty-looking controller in my hands, the familiarity of the directional arrows and the A B C buttons comes back to me. It feels right in my hands, and it reminds me of when I was a kid. In an instant, all my happy childhood memories with my parents rush through my veins and leave me with this warm, joyful feeling all over.

'Ready to kick some arse?' Danny asks.

I give him a serious nod. 'Let's do this.'

It takes us a while, but we do it. We beat the game, and I feel like I have resolved some unfinished business that has been hanging over me my entire life, without me ever realising it. We slap each other a double high five, much to the amusement of the people around us. As we were playing, a little crowd gathered around us, cheering us on as we progressed through the levels.

'They have a café here too,' Danny tells me. 'Want to grab something to eat?'

'Sure,' I reply. 'I'm starving.'

We stroll into the futuristic-looking café and take a seat at one of the tables. A waitress places two menus down in front of us.

'Can I order for you?' Danny asks excitedly.

'OK, sure,' I reply. 'But go easy on me. I'm still recovering from my heart-attack burger.'

The waitress comes over, and Danny tells her what we'll be having. I'm excited to see what he chooses, but at the same time still a little nervous.

'Any drinks?' she asks.

'Can we get two Resident Evils, please,' he says, smiling at me.

'And to eat?'

'Two Mario Mushrooms, please.'

'Sure thing,' she replies, dashing off.

'Oh God, go on...' I say, prompting him to tell me what I've got myself into.

'You look worried.' He laughs. 'Don't be. Resident Evils are cranberry juice, lime and sparkling water. A Mario Mushroom is an omelette.'

I stare him, surprised by his healthy choices.

'What? You think all gamers eat is crap?' He laughs. 'I eat clean.'

Thinking about it, I suppose he would have to eat relatively clean to maintain a body like his.

'OK, what's the deal with that?' I ask.

'What?' He laughs.

'I don't mean to stereotype,' I start, lowering my voice just in case I offend anyone, 'but your typical nerd doesn't have muscles like Max from Streets of Rage.'

'So?' He laughs again.

'So you didn't get like that playing Wii Fit,' I tell him.

The waitress places our drinks down in front of us. Danny lifts his glass, looking at me thoughtfully as he drinks through the straw.

'You said earlier that it wasn't cool for girls to play Mega Drive when you were a kid – well it wasn't that cool for lads either,' he tells me. 'I was a chubby, gaming nerd and that made me an easy target for bullying. So as I hit my teens and I started leaning-out, I started going to the gym. I built up some muscle and even though it stopped me getting my arse kicked, I've always been that chubby nerd on the inside.'

'That worked?' I ask.

'It did. By year 11, when I was tall and with decent muscle mass, I was breezing through life as a nerd. I remember the last World Book Day I dressed up for at school, I was Frodo from *Lord of the Rings*.'

I shrug my shoulders.

'Have you seen the films?' he asks.

I give him a look intended to convey: 'Of course I fucking haven't.'

'Have you ever seen any images of Elijah Wood's character in the films?'

'Yes,' I reply.

'Well that's Frodo.'

'Makes sense with the hair.' I laugh.

'Well, who is going tell a tough-looking kid he can't be Frodo if he wants to be Frodo?'

'Good point.' I smile.

The waitress places two delicious-looking omelettes down in front of us.

'Enjoy,' she says, and we both thank her.

'So all this...' I gesture at his body '...is to scare off predators?'

'Well, it turn out the chicks dig it, so I stuck with it.' He laughs with his mouth full. 'But originally, yes, I puffed myself up like a blowfish.'

'Who messes with a blowfish, Jesse?' I ask rhetorically, doing my best Walter White impression without thinking.

'Was that *Breaking Bad*?' Danny asks, surprised. 'Did you just quote *Breaking Bad*?'

'Erm, yes,' I reply. 'I love it.'

'This surprises me,' he admits. 'Never had you down as a *Breaking Bad* kind of girl.'

'Well, Netflix is bae – what else am I going to do with my time?' I laugh.

'I just had you down as more of a *TOWIE*, *Made in Chelsea*, *Geordie Shore* kind of girl.'

'Oh, cheers,' I reply. 'Nope, never watched an episode of them. *Geordie Shore* is your turf, not mine.'

'I met a girl from *Geordie Shore* once,' he tells me. 'Gemma or Jenna or something.'

I think that's supposed to mean something to me, but it doesn't.

'It wasn't long after the show started, and I was living back in the hometown for a short job, sharing a flat with this lad called Rocky – never found out his real name. Anyway, he would bring different women back all the time. I'm not sure I ever witnessed him spend more than a couple of nights alone. One night he brings back this woman from *Geordie Shore* and they were at it all night, and I mean all night. They were so loud, you'd think cameras were on them. The next day I get up and she's sitting at the table in her underwear, eating cereal. I awkwardly drank my coffee as she got through two bowls, assuring me Rocky had told her she could see herself out. I was out late that night, and when I got home I could hear Rocky at it with someone. Next morning I get up and Rocky has gone to work, but this same lass is sitting there, eating cereal. Five days she stuck around. Every day I would get up and there she'd be, eating breakfast. After one day

Rocky wants her gone, but she just wasn't going anywhere. It was hilarious.'

I laugh. 'You've got some stories,' I tell him.

'A few. But you must have some too.'

I shrug my shoulders.

'Come on,' he reasons, but as hard as I try, I don't have anything.

'I have a few after this week.' I laugh. 'But no, nothing.'

'No awkward moments? No holiday romances? No awkward one-nighters with Z-list celebrities?'

'Nope. I never had any wild teenage years because I was looking after my parents, then I got with Will not too long after that. Oh, actually...' My voice trails off.

'Go on,' Danny prompts as he eats.

I push the food around on my plate a little.

'No, it's not a nice story,' I insist.

'Come on, try me.'

'I had a one-night stand – my one and only one-night stand,' I quickly add.

'You dark horse.' Danny laughs. 'What happened?'

'It was sort of while I was seeing Will, actually. We had this night in a hotel planned after a work party, but then his wife turned up and he not only ignored me all night, but he told me I'd have to leave. I was upset – and that was when I was thinking it was because they were pretending to still be together, not because they were actually still together. He wasn't very nice to me that night, so by the time I'd got a few drinks in me I told him I wasn't going to do this any more, to which he said "fine" – although he later told me he was calling my bluff, but at the time I thought he meant it, that I meant so little to him. That's why it was so easy for me to go over and flirt with Liam after our argument, one of the young drivers. Will looked furious – I think that's why he got so upset when he would see me talking to you.'

'Yeah, that explains a lot.' Danny laughs. 'So what happened?'

'Long story short, Liam took me back to his flat. It was awful. A disgusting, dirty place in the attic above a Chinese takeaway. After you climbed all the stairs you walked into his grubby kitchen. He poured me a vodka and Coke in a pint glass and it was so strong it made me feel sick. I remember setting it down to one side with no intention of drinking it and hoping I didn't offend him. Then he showed me into the other room and it turns out he didn't even have a bed, just a tatty old sofa with an old duvet on top. It was a single duvet, with Thunderbirds bedding on it, but it was all faded like maybe he'd had it since he was a kid or he'd picked it up from a charity shop.'

'Oh, nice,' Danny says sarcastically. 'So you…'

'Yep,' I admit. 'On the floor. It lasted all of five minutes before he – honest to God – announced: "I'm spent" and rolled off me. It was gross and horrible. He had the worst carpet burn on his knees to show for his efforts, and for a moment he sat and picked at his skin. I just lay there, on the floor, almost shell-shocked and most definitely not in the least bit satisfied. There's no way in hell I wanted to stick around, but it didn't matter. He asked me to leave, like he was done with me, so I needed to get out. He slapped me a high five as I left. So, that was that.'

'That's not a nice story at all; that's horrible,' Danny gasps.

'I warned you,' I tell him, setting my fork down because I've lost my appetite suddenly.

'Does he still work there?'

'Nope. I was wracked with guilt and all it did was push me back towards Will. I told him the next morning. He was furious with me – and even more so with Liam. He transferred him to a different branch of the company.'

'Which one?'

'Birmingham.' I laugh.

'Shit, no wonder you don't want to go there,' Danny says. 'So, note to self, help Candy have more anecdotes that won't make the person listening to them want to kill themself when they hear it. Can we go there so I can punch him in the face, please?'

I laugh. 'He's not worth it.'

The waitress wanders over when she notices that Danny's plate is clean and that I am not eating.

'Everything OK?' she asks.

'Great thanks,' Danny replies.

'Great,' I echo. 'Just full.'

'Any desserts?' she asks, nodding towards the dessert board on the wall.

'Two Rainbow Rocky Roads, please,' Danny says.

'That doesn't sound like clean eating,' I say once the waitress is gone.

'Yeah, but pudding is pudding. If it were clean, it wouldn't be worth it. Plus, I think we both need cheering up after that story.'

'Yeah. Sorry,' I say weakly.

'Don't apologise,' he insists. 'Just promise me you won't ever let another man treat you like crap again, because you're an awesome lass. Naive, maybe. A little bit of a fuddy-duddy at times, yes. Borderline stuck up, perhaps – '

'OK, I get it,' I interrupt him, sufficiently offended.

'But you're sweet and you're funny and you're a top lass. Any man would be lucky to have you.'

I am temporarily taken aback by such a sweet and sincere compliment. I don't really know what to say, but it doesn't matter because the waitress puts our desserts down in front of us.

It's a delicious-looking, chocolaty rocky road, except its insides are all kinds of different colours, making it brighter and more beautiful-looking than your average slice. Just looking at it causes my mouth to fill with saliva in anticipation.

'Okay, this looks amazing,' I announce excitedly, grabbing my fork.

Danny smiles. 'It's just nice to see you eat,' he says, quickly adding, 'without you throwing up on my car afterwards.'

'I know I've said it a billion times,' I start, placing my fork down for a second, but instantly wanting to pick it back up and eat, 'but I am sorry about that.'

'It's fine,' he assures me. 'Some people are worth swilling bodily fluids off your car for.'

'Ew! Yes, I bet it's seen worse,' I say, grossed-out but amused.

'Actually, I don't think it's ever seen better,' he replies.

Chapter 28

Running through the street, dodging the pedestrians speed-walking in the opposite direction not unlike something from a video game, with nothing but a copy of the *Birmingham Post* to protect me from the elements, I couldn't feel happier. Today has been so much fun, despite it being the hottest day of the year fast turning into the wettest day of the year with the loudest thunderstorm of the year.

When we decided to walk from the hotel to wherever it was Danny was taking me today, my concern was that it was too warm. Turns out what I really needed to worry about was having to walk back in the heavy rain. Every time the thunder claps I can't help but squeak, but a particularly loud rumble really makes me jump, causing me to drop my newspaper umbrella on the ground. I go to pick it up but it's already soggy, so Danny pulls me underneath the shelter of a fire escape between two buildings.

'God, you're so high maintenance I want to push you in front of traffic,' he jokes. 'We're nearly there now. I can actually see the hotel.'

'Can we just rest for a minute?' I ask. 'My feet are killing me.'

'That's because your shoes are basically a weapon,' he tells me.

I laugh, shivering a little because the rain is surprisingly cold.

'Come here, kid,' Danny insists, wrapping his arms around me, rubbing his hands on my back to try and warm me up.

A droplet of water drips from the staircase above us and lands right on my nose, so Danny pushes me back against the wall out of the way, bringing a hand forward to gently wipe my face with the backs of his fingers before embracing me with both arms again. With his body pressed up against mine, his arms wrapped around me and his face just inches from my own, the noise of the city and the storm slowly fade out, until it's just us. All I can see is Danny, all I can hear is his heavy breathing from running, all I can smell is his aftershave. We stare at each other for a moment and I get that feeling I always get when he looks into my eyes, like he knows exactly what I am thinking and how I'm feeling. Today, I don't mind, but that bothers me even more.

I wriggle free from his grasp. 'Look, the rain has stopped,' I say awkwardly, stepping out onto the pavement. Whether the rain had stopped or not, I needed to move to get out of that situation.

'Candy, look out,' Danny warns, but it's too late. A car drives past at such a speed, ploughing through the puddle next to me, spraying me with water. All that effort to try and keep dry and I'm soaked. As I stand there, dripping wet, Danny joins me on the pavement…just as the sun comes back out.

Danny lets out a little laugh at my expense, but it's awkward now. Whatever kind of moment we were having, I ruined. But I can't have moments with Danny, for all kinds of reasons.

We walk back the rest of the way to the hotel in silence, before heading up to the room. I unlock the door and step to one side so that Danny can walk in first, but he doesn't.

'I might go and chill in the bar for a bit,' he says, nodding down the corridor towards where the bar is.

'Yeah? Well, I'm just going to have a bath so…'

'OK, cool,' he replies.

We pause for a second, before we both open our mouths to speak at the same time. I'm not even sure what I was going to say, because as soon as we realise the other is about to say something we pause again.

'OK,' I say, eventually. 'Well, see you.'

'Yep,' he replies, strolling off slowly. He glances back a couple of times, before meaningfully walking the rest of the way.

I head inside and close the door behind me, looking at my soggy reflection in the mirror.

'What the hell are you doing?' I ask myself. Before my reflection has a chance to reply, there's a knock on the door. My first thought is that it's Danny, that he's come back to say whatever it is that he was going to say before. As I open the door and see that no one is there, it occurs to me that if it were Danny, he would've just used his key. With no one there, I close the door and head back in. As I slowly peel off my wet clothes, there's a knock at the door again. I hurry my top back on and open it, but there's no one there again.

'Hilarious,' I call down the corridor, confident someone is messing with me.

I take off my clothes and run my bath before climbing in and overanalysing what just happened with Danny. If I didn't know better, I'd think we were about to kiss down that alleyway. OK, so he *is* gorgeous, but he's been more like a big brother to me this trip – apart from when we were pretending to be a couple, obviously. That, plus the fact I'm still in a mess over Will, are two very good reasons why we shouldn't go there. Plus, I clearly annoy him as much as he annoys me. At this stage, an awkward kiss would be a terrible idea, especially considering we've still got a few days left before we head back home.

I am distracted from my thoughts by that familiar knock on the door. I know it's the same one, because it follows that same rhythm, but I'm not playing.

'Fuck off,' I yell, not that they'll hear me. They'll have run off down the corridor and hidden by now.

I mean, no one could ever start anything with Danny anyway, because he doesn't stay in the same place for long enough. Will even offered him a full-time position, but he didn't want it, and he made it clear that nothing would change his mind, so that's that I guess.

Another knock at the door. So much for my nice relaxing bath.

I climb out, grabbing a fluffy white towel and wrapping it around my body.

I shuffle over to the door and look through the peephole, but there's no one there. I pick up the phone next to me and call reception.

'Hello,' a man chirps.

'Hey, someone keeps knocking on my door and running away,' I tell him.

'Ah,' he replies, sounding unsurprised. 'We've got a school trip staying with us – spirits are high.'

'Well, if you could…lower their spirits,' I request. 'It's driving me crazy.'

'Of course,' he replies. 'I'll have a word.'

I have no sooner put the phone down when there's that knock at the door again. As I'm standing right behind it, I take this as my cue to catch out whoever is doing this, so I fling the door open and step out into the corridor.

It all happens so quickly that I'm not even sure how it happens. I only make it out quick enough to see the backs of three teenagers' heads as they leg it away, but as I made my dash through the door my towel must have got caught on something in the room, ripping it from my body. I realise this in the same second that the door to my room closes behind me. For a moment, I freeze. Unsure what to do. I mean, I'm butt naked, locked outside my room. What *can* I do? I think for what feels like a very long time, but it's probably only a few seconds.

If I can get along the corridor towards the bar, I can get Danny's attention and he can let me back into the room. Oh God, but he's going to see me naked! But what choice do I have?

Thankfully, the door to each room is recessed, so I can dash quickly from one to another, ducking in whenever I think I hear voices. I make it halfway along the corridor when I notice a shining beacon of light – well, a lit-up stand with tourist information booklets on it. I grab one and open it up, before using it to protect my modesty. I cover my boobs with my free hand, and I'm careful to keep my back to the wall as I sneak along the corridor. When I finally reach the door to the bar, I have no idea what to do next. I can't go in there. I notice the fire alarm on the wall next to me. No, I can't do that. Not only is it against the law, but all that would do is bring everyone out, not just Danny.

I slowly push the door open and poke my head around, glancing around the room for Danny. I spot him nursing a drink, looking down at the table deep in thought.

'Danny,' I call in a loud whisper, but he doesn't hear me. 'Danny,' I say again, a little louder. This time he hears me and looks up. 'Can you come here, please?'

I wait until he is making his way across the room before stepping into the doorway of the nearest room.

'Where have you gone?' he asks once he's out in the corridor.

'I'm here,' I say, stepping out.

'What the fuck?' he asks, his face lighting up like I've never seen before. 'Nice Bullring.'

Danny nods towards my crotch. I look down and see that the tourist brochure I'm using as underwear has a big picture of the Bullring on the front.

'Look, I got locked out of the room. You need to let me back in before someone sees,' I say quickly.

'OK, sure.' Danny, as amused as he is, snaps into action, hurrying along the corridor and unlocking the door. As soon as it is open, I hurry after him. As I step inside I grab my towel from the floor, and in one swift moment I ditch my brochure and wrap it around my body.

'What the hell happened?' Danny asks.

'These fucking kids kept knocking on the door and running away and – '

Right on cue, there's a knock on the door. Danny opens it and growls like a pissed-off Shrek in an attempt to scare the kids off, but it isn't kids at all, it's a hotel employee and he looks terrified.

'I just…I, erm… The kids are under the supervision of their teacher now, so it won't, erm…it won't be happening again,' the employee stutters.

'OK, cheers,' Danny says. As the employee shuffles off, that terrified look still on his face, Danny calls after him: 'Sorry mate.'

Danny closes the door, whips off his soggy T-shirt and hops onto the bed.

'Did you see that?' he asks me, amused. 'He shit himself.'

I sit at the desk and throw my head into my hands. 'I am mortified,' I mumble, my voice muffled by my face being covered.

'Ah, it's no big deal,' he replies.

'At least no one else saw me but you. I should be thankful for that.'

'I don't know,' Danny chimes in. 'They're bound to have CCTV, so…there's that. Even if they're not watching it live, if they ever look over it – Christmas,' he concludes.

'Fuck off,' I snap.

'What?' He laughs. 'You've got an amazing body; you should show it off more.'

'Danny, there's showing it off and then there's being a crazy naked-in-public lady angrily chasing children. You can get put on a list for that.'

He laughs. 'Look, we said we needed to make you more comfortable with nudity – well there you go. You were naked in public and you didn't die. That's got to make you feel better, right?'

'Surprisingly, Danny, no, that doesn't make me feel even a little bit better.'

'Just when I think you're chilling out and being fun, you get all uptight again,' he sighs.

'Uptight?' I squeak angrily. 'Uptight? Just because I don't want to beave children/hotel security/*you*?'

Danny hops to his feet, grabbing a dry T-shirt and running his hand through his damp hair as he looks in the mirror, before tying it up in a topknot again.

'I'm going back to the bar,' he says. 'I'll leave you to get dressed.'

'Fine,' I call after him.

'Fine,' he replies, slamming the door behind him. And just like that, we're frenemies again.

Chapter 29

Waking up in bed, the first thing I see is Danny. He's just inches away from me, and he's already awake. When I got in bed last night he was still at the bar.

'And what time did you get in last night?' I ask, moving a little further away from him.

'What are you, my wife?' He laughs.

'I bloody feel like it, having to wake up next to you every day,' I reply.

He smiles. 'You don't have to,' he reminds me. 'And yet you somehow always do.'

'You're like herpes, mister. Once you get under the skin, that's it. Riddled for life.'

'I remember when you were a lady.' He laughs. 'So, was that our first marital tiff last night?'

'Something like that,' I reply. 'Let's forget about it.'

'Sure,' he replies. 'And it was only eleven p.m. when I got back. You were flat out. I didn't want to wake you.'

'No worries,' I reply.

We lie there for a moment until my phone starts vibrating.

'It's been doing that on and off for about twenty minutes,' Danny tells me. 'I had a peep to see if it was worth waking you, but I saw that it was Will.'

'Yeah, I wouldn't have wanted waking up just to ignore him anyway,' I tell him.

'Just to make it clear, that was not me intervening. Like I said, I'll never do that. You're a big girl.'

I pull open the curtains and let the sunlight beam in, squinting my eyes that aren't quite adjusted to the fact that it's morning yet.

Danny stretches out in bed, filling the space I was occupying as well as his own.

'I'm not used to sharing.'

'Yeah, tell me about it,' I reply. 'Never shared a bed with anyone before.'

'You're good at it,' he tells me. 'You keep to your side – don't lash out. Sometimes you move in for a snuggle, but that's OK. Anyone would think you were an old pro.'

'You're killing me with kindness this morning,' I reply, shooting him a filthy look as I search for something to wear. 'Shall we just head back home?'

'What? But we're having so much fun.' He laughs.

I shoot him a look.

'OK, it's on and off…but we could be having even more fun. We're getting there. Just give it another day?'

'Fine.' I give in. My emotions are all over the place and I've no idea what's going on, or what's going to happen, but I suppose delaying the inevitable for a little longer won't hurt. I might as well make the most of it.

I hold up two pencil skirts, near identical except for the fact that one is black and one is grey. I examine them for a second before deciding I'll wear the black one with the white shirt I have picked out.

'Hmm, decisions, decisions,' Danny teases, trying to mimic my Mancunian accent. 'Which middle-aged woman skirt will I wear today? I know, the one with the least colour.'

'Fuck off,' I snap – something I seem to do often with Danny, sometimes joking, sometimes serious.

'You need a new wardrobe,' he tells me. 'One that is more you, that you have chosen.'

'I *needed* to be naked, is basically what you told me last night.'

'Yeah, well naked is done now. Now we need to get you some clothes that you feel sexy in. You look like you're going for a job interview. At a bank. For old people. In the 1950s.'

'Finished?'

'For the blind,' he adds, so I flash him my middle finger. 'Well, baby steps,' he tells me. 'We might be moving slowly, but at least we're moving forward.'

'We sure are, fridge magnet,' I call back as I head into the bathroom.

I close the door behind me and sit down on the toilet. I have my phone in my hand, and I stare at the screen, just glaring at the missed calls from Will until my tired eyes ache and I have to look away. I've spent months just hoping and praying he would cause my phone to spring to life. Even when I knew he was in a meeting or out for the evening and there was no chance he'd call me, I'd still check my phone longingly, constantly. Now that I don't want to hear from him, he just keeps calling and, do you know what? It makes me cross. It proves that he could have called me more often than he did. Well, fuck him. I open up my contacts on my phone and find Will's name, clicking block so that he can't contact me any more. There. I can't be clearer than that.

I wash my face and brush my teeth before slipping on my 'job interview' outfit and heading back into the room. Danny is still stretched out on the bed, watching TV with the covers kicked off and his arms behind his head. I feel myself bite my lip, quickly raising my hand to my mouth so that Danny can't see.

'You OK?' he asks, noting my sudden movement.

'I'm fine,' I tell him coolly.

Danny hops to his feet with that puppy dog energy he always seems to boast. 'Quick shower and we can go,' he tells me. 'Cardiff today.'

'Awesome,' I call after him.

As soon as he closes the bathroom door behind him, I plonk

myself down on the bed. I'm glad we're back on good terms, but I don't really understand why we were even nearly on bad terms. I don't have feelings for Danny, do I? I know I look at his body, but I'm only human. That doesn't mean anything. We're just good mates, that's all. I've never had a good male friend before, and I think I'm just getting my wires crossed. I'm on the rebound. I need to remember that. But if that's true, then why did I feel like shit last night when we were apart? And why did I lie there, wide awake, just waiting for him to come back, only to pretend I was asleep when he did get in?

No, I can't think like this. I just need to enjoy the rest of the trip and, if I'm going to worry about anything, it should be what I'm going to do when it's time to go home. Danny won't be around for much longer, but I'm going to be stuck working for Will, having to see his stupid face every day. There's no way I can continue working there, is there? But I can't exactly afford to just walk out. I suppose I'll have to start looking for something else and hope I find something fast.

The thing is though, if I don't have feelings for Danny, then why do I care less about having to see Will every day than I do about the thought of no longer seeing Danny every day? Let alone not sharing a bed with him…

Chapter 30

It's another hot, sunny day as we park up in Cardiff.

'Another day, another four-star hotel,' Danny muses.

As we unload our luggage in the hotel car park, I struggle, the sun making me feel sluggish. Danny laughs at me, pushing his way in front of me, lifting my bags out for me.

As I wipe sweat from my forehead with the back of my hand, something small catches my eye. It's a pug, sitting on the ground next to us, just watching us.

'Danny, look,' I whisper.

Danny turns around and looks down at the pug.

'Jesus.' He jumps. 'I thought it was a rat or something.'

'Aww,' I coo, crouching down on the floor and beckoning it over. 'What a little cutie. Come here.'

The pug waddles over to me, rolling onto its back so that I can tickle his tummy. He's wearing a collar, but there's no ID on there.

'Is he OK?' Danny asks.

'He feels warm,' I tell him. 'It's too hot for him to be out here.'

Danny looks around to see if there's anyone about looking for him, but there's no one.

'There's a shop across the road,' Danny points out. 'I'll go get him some water.'

'Thanks,' I call after him, before addressing my new friend. 'Well, aren't you handsome, huh? Yes you are.'

The pug rolls around gleefully as I continue to tickle his tummy.

My arm is getting tired, but I keep going. I don't want him to wander off – he needs water.

'Here we are,' Danny says. 'Cup your hands.'

I do as he asks and he pours a little water into them. The pug drinks it up, so Danny pours some more.

'I got these too,' he says, shaking a box of dog biscuits, causing the dog's tiny tail to wag frantically. Danny pops the box open and gives him one. 'I'm going to call him Kevin, because he's all alone and fending for himself,' Danny says, putting on one of those cute voices people reserve for talking to babies and small animals.

'Hello, Kevin,' I say in a similar tone, tickling his tummy again because he seems to like it. 'He feels warm,' I tell Danny. 'We need to get him out of the sun.'

'Do you think they'll let him inside the hotel?' he asks.

'I don't know. Call them,' I suggest.

Danny takes out his phone and, after a quick google to find the number for the hotel, he calls and asks about their policy on pets.

'Yeah, it's a no,' he tells me, scratching his head as he wonders what to do. 'We'll have to sneak him in. Just until he cools down, and we get on to the RSPCA or something.'

'We can't sneak him in!'

'You didn't mind sneaking things in when we were in York,' he replies, like I'm being unreasonable.

'Yeah, a toaster and a few slices of bread, not a fucking pug. You can't smuggle a dog into a four-star hotel!'

'Not even a dog as cute as Kevin?' Danny asks as he hooks his fingers into the corners of Kevin's mouth, making it look like he's smiling. As my heart melts, all common sense goes out of the window.

'OK, how do we do this?' I ask.

'Right.' Danny claps his hands together. 'You go and check us in, then come back out here and help me with the bags. I'll figure it out.'

I nod in recognition of the plan before dashing inside to check in, hurrying back out as soon as I have the key. When I get back outside, Kevin is gone.

'Where'd he go?' I ask.

Danny gently raises my holdall. It isn't zipped closed, but he opens it more so I can see inside. Kevin is in there, snuggled up inside one of my bras. He's so cute, I can't handle it.

'Grab something light, so it looks like we've got our stuff. I'll carry this one carefully.'

We walk into the hotel lobby, trying our hardest to look casual. As we step into the lift, I'm aware of the man behind the front desk who checked me in staring at us. I give him a wave, as though to confirm that this is the other person staying in the room and he nods. Just as the lift door closes, Kevin tries to make himself more comfortable, causing the bag to move.

'Do you think he saw?' I ask.

'He can't have,' Danny concludes.

Once we're in the safety of our room, Danny lets out Kevin, who immediately tries to take a few run-ups at the bed, but fails to jump even close to high enough.

'Come here,' Danny says, scooping him up and plonking him down.

Kevin makes himself comfortable, so Danny gives him another biscuit.

Danny and I both sit down, searching on our phones to figure out what we can do to try and get Kevin home again.

'I've got the number for a local dogs' charity,' Danny tells me. 'But the line is engaged.'

'Well, keep trying,' I tell him. 'I'll keep looking into other options.'

After thirty minutes of trying, the line is still engaged.

'Right, I don't think it's far – I'll pop over there and see what's what,' Danny says as he hops to his feet.

'Are you taking Kevin with you?' I ask.

'I'll leave him here,' he tells me. 'Just in case they won't take him and we have to smuggle him back in.'

'OK, well, hurry back,' I tell him.

'Will do,' he replies as he rushes out.

'Well, it's just me and you, Kevin,' I say to him when we're finally alone.

I shuffle around the room, looking for something to do to amuse myself, deciding that I'll give Amy a call and let her know how things are going.

'Hello,' she answers almost immediately.

'Hey, how are you?'

'Stressed with wedding shit, but nothing I can't handle,' she replies. 'How are you?'

'Fucking marvellous.' I laugh.

'You must be!' she gasps. 'You swore! Why are you swearing?'

'Life,' I muse.

'So, how's it going?' she asks. 'Is it as boring as you thought it would be without lover boy?'

'I got blind drunk with truckers, I took my clothes off and danced in a strip club, I pretended to be Danny's girlfriend to make his ex jealous, got taken to the police station in the back of a van, nearly had a second run-in with the fuzz while I was eating a double cheeseburger that was served inside a doughnut – which gave me food poisoning – and I'm breaking all the rules at the hotels. Streaking down the corridors, smuggling things in – toasters, pugs, the usual kind of thing. So yeah, pretty boring really.'

Amy doesn't say anything.

'Hello?' I say, to check she's still there.

'Is that all true?' she asks.

'Yep,' I reply. 'Oh, and I got two tattoos. "Isis" on my wrist, and "Mr Wright" on my arse. That's Wright with a W – that cosmic ordering is fucked up. It doesn't listen.'

Amy laughs loudly down the phone. 'Candice, I'm just… I'm so happy for you.'

'You're happy for me?' I laugh.

'Yes! You're having fun! Proper fun, the kind your life has been severely lacking. It sounds like Danny is a good laugh?'

'He is,' I reply, but my lack of detail gets my friend wondering. 'Anything, you know, between the two of you?'

'We're just friends,' I tell her. 'Although we are sharing a bed every night, and he has seen me naked way more than I'd intended on – which was ideally never,' I quickly add.

'You like him,' she sings. 'You like him and you want him and you want his babies.'

'Shut up,' I reply.

'Has something happened between you?' she asks again.

'No. Well…we had a sort of moment.'

'So, what did you do?'

'I freaked out and caused an argument with him,' I admit. My friend tuts. 'What? I'm out of practice.'

'You need to seduce him,' Amy concludes. 'You can do this. Just… OK, maybe one evening when you're undressed, because your clothes don't exactly scream "seduction", you know?'

'Says you, cheesecloth,' I laugh and it catches my friend by surprise.

'You're cheekier now. I feel like I'm getting the real you back now that you're shot of Will.'

I glance over at the bed and notice that the dog has gone. 'Shit, Aims, I'd better go, Kevin has vanished.'

'Kevin?' she asks, confused.

'Kevin the pug,' I half explain.

'So *everything* you said was true?' she asks.

'Yep.'

'Isis though?'

'It's a long story,' I tell her. 'Anyway, speak soon.'

'Have fun,' she sings.

I hang up the phone and start looking for Kevin. I soon find him in the bathroom, trying to drink from the toilet, so I grab a teacup and fill it with water. Kevin then waddles over to the biscuit box and yaps for one. I quickly take one and throw it to him to keep him quiet, but he immediately wants another one. I glance at the box and read that small dogs are only allowed two to three per day, so I'd better not give him another one. Plus, he's not exactly the slimmest dog I've ever seen.

Kevin barks, except he doesn't sound much like a dog, he sounds more like a tiny boar.

'Listen, you can't have another, it will make you poorly,' I explain, stupidly thinking that maybe I can reason with a hungry dog.

Kevin barks, giving no shits.

I shush him, praying he keeps his mouth shut. He would if he knew what was good for him. If he's found in here we'll all be thrown out.

Still, Kevin barks. I grab the TV remote and switch it on, skipping through the channels to find something that will mask his little yap. One of the channels I flick past has an advert for dog food on, and as the dog on the screen yaps, Kevin breaks into a howl. I quickly switch the TV off, and grab Kevin another biscuit, hoping one over the recommended daily amount won't harm him. This appeases him for a second, but just when I think we're out of the woods, there's a knock at the door.

'Fuck, fuck, fuck,' I rant as I usher him into the bathroom. I use a biscuit to get him to follow me, but I don't give it to him. I shut the door on him, praying he keeps his little doggy mouth shut before going to answer the door. It's the guy who checked me in. I look at his name badge. Phillip. It's nice to know who I'm going to be pleading with.

'Hello,' I say brightly.

'Mr Starr?' he says.

'Do I look like Mr Starr?' I ask, pulling a face.

'One must never assume,' he tells me. 'This is Mr Starr's room. Was that Mr Starr who left shortly after you arrived?'

'No,' I admit. 'That's my guest though. We both work for Mr Starr. This is a business trip.'

'What business, might I ask?'

'Haulage and warehousing and distribution – oh my,' I joke with a little giggle, but Phillip is immune to my charm.

'Do you have a dog in here?' he asks, cutting to the chase.

'A dog?' I ask, feigning shock. 'Of course not!'

'I think you have a dog in here,' Phillip continues.

'One must never assume,' I remind him. 'When you assume you make an ass out of U and ME.'

My sense of humour does nothing for Phillip. I fidget nervously with whatever I am holding and he notices. I follow his gaze to my hands and realise I'm clutching a dog biscuit.

'Is that a dog biscuit?' he asks firmly.

'No. Well, yes,' I babble, unable to explain its bone shape. 'But it's mine. They're made from charcoal. They're great for weight loss. I love them.'

Phillip stares at me for a moment, as though he's waiting for me to take a bite to prove a point. Luckily before I have to, he continues with the evidence to support the claim there is a dog in my room.

'Guests in neighbouring rooms have reported howling,' he informs me.

'Well, yeah, that was me,' I tell him in a hushed tone, raising my eyebrows.

'But you're in here alone,' he immediately replies.

'Yes,' I reply as flirtatiously as possible. 'A girl gets lonely.'

Phillip just walks away, clearly unfazed by my flirtatious tone, the image of me touching myself until I howl and chomping on dog biscuits to try and keep my figure, bizarrely, not doing it for him.

I close the door behind me and breathe a sigh of relief, but it's short-lived because I open the bathroom door to find Kevin chewing up a towel. Before I have a chance to react, Danny walks back in.

'Good news,' he announces. 'They'll take him in and find his owner.'

'Good,' I reply, kicking pieces of chewed-up towel with my foot. 'Because I don't think we're cut out to be parents.'

Chapter 31

So it turns out we were on some kind of red alert at the hotel in Cardiff, and as such they were looking out for us behaving suspiciously. Fair enough, we *were* acting suspiciously, but this made it even harder for us to try and sneak Kevin out of the hotel. When we were sneaking him in it was hard enough, but we couldn't risk getting caught sneaking him out either, or they might have thrown us out of the hotel. One night sleeping in Danny's car is more than enough for one lifetime, so we were careful to be discreet – well, as discreet as you can be when you've got a hyperactive pug in a Louis Vuitton holdall. It was tough, but we managed it, lurking around near the lifts, just waiting for a moment when Phillip disappeared into the office. Then we made a mad dash for the door and soon enough we were saying our goodbyes to Kevin, having the good sense to pose for selfies with him before we left, because we didn't ever want to forget him.

Had I taken this trip with Will, I'm not certain how it would have played out. Sure, we could've got it on all day and all night without worrying about who might walk in on us, but would that have been it? The whole extent of our fun? Thinking about it, just because sex is the only kind of fun we ever got to enjoy together, it doesn't mean that if we were to spend normal time together like a normal couple that we would instantly have a blast. I mean, what do we have in common? If everyone says I was being a more boring version of myself to try and be more like Will, then there's no way we would've had fun. We didn't chat on the phone much because we couldn't, but what if we had been able to? I try to imagine doing these long journeys in the car, just Will and me, and I can't imagine what we would talk about, or what we would listen to. How Julie the cleaner isn't doing her job properly with a Classical FM backdrop? No thank you.

With Danny, car journeys are a blast. Hour-long treks feel like no time at all when we're chatting about everything from TV shows we watched when we were kids, to what we'd call a pug if we had a pug of our own. When we're not chatting, Danny will be telling me funny one-liners and lip-syncing to songs on the radio to try and make me laugh, which he always does. There's just something about seeing this big, buff nerd grooving to Wilson Phillips's 'Hold On' that could make even the most serious person smile.

It may have been a hasty decision born of an emotional reaction to a rough day, but I am so glad that I have taken this trip with Danny. For all the epic fuck-ups, scrapes with the law, mortifying situations and so on, I cannot deny that I am having the time of my life. I don't think I've ever had this much fun, and even though, at times, I am the most stressed out I have ever been, I don't think I've ever felt so chilled out. So chilled out, in fact, that this afternoon we're in Brighton and I've done a potentially silly thing… I've agreed to let Danny give me a makeover. Well, not him personally making me over, but he is facilitating me getting one.

The shopping stage was fine. Terrifying, and I feel sick with nerves at wearing any of these outfits in public, but fine. I can wear one of the, frankly, intimidating outfits the shop's stylist picked out for me tonight (based on my brief of wanting to dress more confidently, and enhance my natural features), but then I can take it off, safe in the knowledge I gave it a go, and I'll never have to wear it again. The same goes for the OTT make-up I've bought, that can come off in a few wipes. But here, now, sitting in this chair at the hairdresser's, I am terrified. It's a really funky place and I don't think anyone working here has a hair do that would see them succeed in a job interview for any other professions, except perhaps the circus.

I twirl my longish ash-blonde locks nervously. This is my natural colour, and I've never dyed it before. I've never really had more than a trim, so I'm dreading the 'expert advice' I'm waiting on. Unlike the clothes, the hair won't be so easy to rectify. Not without another sitting in the chair, and I'm not exactly flush with money right now. I can't even really afford this, but I figured I could use my wages from this week, seeing as though I haven't actually done a second of work, and pretend it was a holiday.

If I'm being honest, as nervous as I am, I'm a little excited too. Part of me just wants to go for it.

A guy with a blue reverse mohawk (at least that's what I imagine it is) comes over and introduces himself as Zane.

'So, I hear you're after something completely different,' Zane says as he ruffles my hair.

'Yes,' I reply confidently. 'A different colour, for sure. Maybe a different shade of blonde...'

'Is that really what you want?' Danny chimes in. 'You can have anything, anything at all, you could go for something really different if you wanted to.'

I appreciate him trying to give me the confidence to go for it. I'm just so scared.

'You have a great base for whatever you want,' Zane says excitedly.

'Well, okay, I do fancy a different colour, I'm just not sure what, maybe you could say what you thought might suit me, although I don't think I want it any shorter,' I say.

'I'm thinking we dye you lilac,' Zane says with a nod. 'It will really suit your skintone. Then we'll put in a few extensions to give you a bit more length and a bit more volume – boom! You'll look a million dollars.'

Wow. Lilac does sound cool but... can I really pull it off?

I glance back and forth between them in the mirror for a few seconds, taking one last look at my blonde hair. Say goodbye to the old Candice.

'Fuck it,' I blurt out. 'Do it.'

As soon as the words leave my lips it occurs to me to immediately change my mind. I know it's only hair, and that technically it could be fixed if I didn't like it, but there's no way I could afford all the work it would take to have the lilac completely removed.

You know what? I need to take a few risks. Do a few things that can't be easily undone. Well, now that Zane is slopping the dye on my hair, there really is no turning back.

I smile to myself as I watch all traces of the old me being covered up. The boring, stuffy, Candice I had morphed myself into to please Will is being plastered over, ready for me to start my life again.

Since we arrived, they've been playing booming, clubbing music here in the salon, but the mood changes suddenly when Jack Duff's new track comes on. He's a singer/songwriter, not unlike Ed Sheeran or James Bay, with his poetic lyrics and beautiful acoustic sound making him sure to be the next big thing, picking up the Mercury Prize, going multiplatinum and then recording a cover for the John Lewis Christmas advert over the course of the year.

'I love this song,' I say with a sigh, to no one in particular.

Danny is sitting next to me, twirling in an unoccupied chair as he thumbs through a copy of *Tatler*.

'This romantic junk?' He laughs.

'Yep,' I admit. 'I don't usually like this kind of music, and it's not because I'm heartless, although that is up for debate,' I joke. 'It's just... I don't know. I usually opt for the strong chicks, like Beyoncé or Kelly Clarkson. But I like this. I like Jack. He makes me feel a rush of something in my chest, like maybe my cold heart might be thawing, just a little, and he writes the kind of lyrics that make you feel like it might be quite nice to have someone who gives a fuck about you.'

Danny smiles. 'You know, despite being self-depreciating and littered with expletives, that might be the sweetest thing I've ever heard you say,' he tells me. 'Perhaps you're not the cold robot you make yourself out to be.'

'Perhaps I'm not.' I smile.

'Rinse time,' Zane chirps, interrupting our conversation.

After my hair is rinsed, Zane escorts me back to my seat.

'Wait, don't let her look in the mirror,' Danny insists. 'Face her away from the mirror while you dry her. It'll be a surprise.'

'I'll do your make-up if you like,' one of the girls sweeping the floor offers. 'Then the change will seem more drastic, extreme makeover style.'

'Fab idea,' Zane replies.

'Okay, sure,' I say as sit down in the chair. This is exciting.

So, as it stands, I have the makings of a new wardrobe, I've had my hair dyed a drastically different colour, I've had some hair cut off, some added in, and a young woman has spent the better part of the past hour covering me in make-up. Finally, I am twirled around to look in the mirror, and I hardly recognise myself.

'That is not me,' I squeak, waving my hands to see if the movements of the girl looking back at me correspond with my own. They do. That's definitely me.

With different hair and make-up, I look like an entirely different person. It's not just that though, I feel different. I feel confident. I feel like I look good, and I think that is making more of a difference to the way I look than any external makeover ever could. I want to stand tall, throw my shoulders back and let people see me, rather than skulking around in my Stepford gear, keeping my head down.

'I don't know what to say,' are about the only words I can eloquently force out.

'Say you like it,' Zane insists.

'I love it!' I exclaim. 'I really love it.'

'You look incredible, Candy,' Danny says as he rubs my shoulders. 'Oh, God, she's going to start blubbing.'

I laugh as I check my eyes. It is actually taking a lot of willpower to prevent a few happy tears escaping, but tearing up with all this slap on would take me from zero to Alice Cooper in a matter of seconds.

'So, are you taking her out to show her off?' Zane asks Danny.

'Yes,' he replies. 'I've got it all planned out.'

'Oh really?' I ask.

'Really,' he replies. 'Brace yourself.'

Chapter 32

As I get ready in the bathroom at the hotel, Danny tells me about his plans for our big night out.

It turns out, the hotel we are staying at has its own nightclub called Eros, and Danny has got us on the guest list.

I take one of my new dresses from out of the bag. It's a red micro minidress, covered in glitter – so much so, my body and the bathroom are both coated in loads of glitter now too.

I slip the dress on, and I don't know how it's possible, but it seems to boast even less fabric than it did before when I tried it on.

'Well, what do you think?' Danny calls from the bedroom – I must be taking too long.

I slip it on and examine myself in the mirror. There's no way I can go out in this, it's about as low-cut as it is short, and the only thing it leaves to the imagination is what I'd look like wearing clothes.

'I'm not so sure,' I call back.

'Whoa, you look hot,' Danny exclaims as he enters the bathroom unprompted. 'Don't forget these,' he adds, tossing me a pair of sky-high black heels. I slip them on, but the fact they make me so much taller than my usual five foot six only makes my dress seem even shorter.

'Yowza,' he yells.

I laugh self-consciously. 'Are you sure I look OK?' I ask nervously, my newfound confidence fading fast.

'Bro, you look incredible,' he says sincerely.

'You're really trying to make this bro nickname stick, aren't you?' I laugh.

'Well, guys probably call you nice names all the time. I like to be different. Anyway, you get mad when I call you Candy.'

Thinking about it, I haven't told him off for calling me Candy for a while now.

'You know what, I feel more like a Candy now,' I admit. It must be my new look.

'Well now that you like it, I'm definitely going to stop calling you that.' He laughs. 'Seriously though, you look amazing. You look: this emoji.'

Danny does the 'OK' gesture with his hand.

'Thanks, nerd.'

I take one last long hard look in the mirror at the new me. So this is Candy Hart, and I think I like her. I bite my lip nervously as I stare at myself, yanking the dress down over my thighs, only for it to ping back up.

'OK, let's go…before I change my mind.'

Chapter 33

Eros is as sexy as its name suggests. As soon as you walk through the door you are greeted by an overly-bronzed, buff bloke wearing a pair of wings and the tiniest pair of pants I have ever seen on a man – scrap that, on any adult human. He carries a bow and arrow, just like Eros, but it only seems to prevent him from doing his hosting job properly.

'So, what's the plan now?' I ask Danny over the loud music.

'I know it's early days, but perhaps you need to start moving on. Maybe we just need to get you flirting with someone to start with, see if you've still got it in you.'

'Yesterday I told a perfect stranger that I howl when I masturbate,' I reply. 'Clearly, my flirting game is weak.'

Danny laughs. 'With the right person, I think you'll be fine,' he assures me, squeezing my hand, and if I didn't know better, I'd think Danny was flirting with me. Of course, he isn't. This is Danny and he flirts with everyone – I need to keep reminding myself that. 'Unless, you're too scared to go for it.'

'I'm not scared,' I insist. 'My flirting might be rusty, but I'm just as game as the next girl. What, do you think I can't pull the trigger?'

'Not until you prove it,' he replies.

We've had quite a few drinks but, although I can feel my confidence growing thanks to being slightly drunk, I am not sure this is going to make me suddenly suave enough to bag me a boy.

'I'll be right back,' I tell him before wandering over to the bar.

As if it isn't hard enough walking in these ridiculous heels, Eros is quite dark, and the areas surrounding the dance floor are scattered with beanbags that looks like clouds, as well as tables and chairs, and booths that all seem to be packed with people. I pull my dress down awkwardly, trying to keep my arse covered as I walk. It's very tight-fitting, but thankfully shows off my curves in all the right places. Teamed with my new lilac locks and my heavy make-up that the girl at the salon did for me, I do look completely different, and I'm not quite there with the confidence yet. Still, we're in a dark nightclub, so it's fine.

'I'll have a strawberry Bellini, please,' I tell the barman, raising my voice a little to make sure he can hear me.

He hands me my yummy-looking drink – they really go all-out with their cocktails here – but as I reach in my bag to grab my purse I accidentally elbow the person next to me.

'My gosh, I am so sorry...' I babble, but my voice trails off as I finally make eye contact with the man next to me. For a second we just look at each other and smile.

'Hey,' he says. 'I'm Jackson.'

'Hello,' I reply, immediately intrigued by his accent. 'I'm Candy.'

I shake Jackson's hand and we share a few more seconds of just staring at each other and smiling. Jackson is tall and muscular, he has quite short, dirty blonde hair that is effortlessly but intentionally messy, and a pair of eyes so blue, I feel like I could dive into them. I can see his black shirt buttons struggling to do their job of containing his muscular body, and I can't say I'd be that upset if they failed.

I glance over at Danny, who is watching me like a hawk, probably just making sure I'm OK. I think about what he said, about how I need to put Will behind me and at least take the first steps of moving on, even if it's just flirting with this dude in this bar.

I take a long sip of my drink before attempting to turn on the charm. I just need to channel Blair from *Gossip Girl*. She'd know what to do in this situation.

'You're not from around here,' I observe.

'Neither are you,' he replies. 'Northerner, right?'

I nod my head.

'Cute accent. My grandma is from Huddersfield, but I grew up in Australia,' he tells me. 'Melbourne.'

That explains that delicious accent.

'What on earth are you doing here?' I can't help but ask.

'I'm a pro rugby player,' he tells me. 'I'm here with a few of my teammates – over there.' Jackson points over at one of the booths. I glance across the dark room and see a few waves from his friends. I politely wave back.

'So you're Australian and a professional rugby player? It's like you're just listing all the sexy things you can think of. My brain can't even process this. Next you'll be telling me you taste like chocolate – you don't, do you?' I ask. Hmm, the confidence is coming back a little too quickly. Perhaps I should have gone a little easier on the Dutch courage.

Jackson laughs. 'So, are you working?' he asks.

'I am,' I reply, impressed at his good guess, because I doubt I look like I'm on a business trip.

'That's cool,' he replies. 'You're very sexy, you know.'

For a moment, I just gaze into his gorgeous blue eyes. He smiles back at me and about the time I notice how perfectly chiselled his strong jaw is, is about the time I do something completely out of character from me. I lean forwards, place my hands on either side of his face and kiss him. It's a frantic, fast-paced red-hot kiss. Jackson is into it too, his tongue creeping in and out of my mouth as he grabs a fistful of my new, big hair. I move back slowly, trying to disguise my delight at making such a bold move. I didn't know I had it in me. Neither did Danny, it seems, because I peep over at him and he looks dumbstruck.

'Shall we take this to my room?' Jackson asks.

I pause for a split second before I answer, battling the gut feeling that is telling me – no, demanding me to say no. But then

I think about Danny, and this weird little crush on him that I feel sneaking up on me. It's manageable now, but I worry it could get out of hand if I don't nip it in the bud. He doesn't think I'll do it. He was pretty much goading me before, talking me into it…

Jackson stares at me expectantly.

'Let's go,' I reply confidently.

Jackson takes me by the hand and leads me across the room. As we pass Danny, I give him a subtle thumbs up, like, there, I did it, I pulled the trigger, or I'm about to at least.

Jackson's room is on a much higher floor than ours and, as such, is about three times the size of ours. In fact, I think his bed might be as big as our bathroom. I take a seat on the edge of it as I watch Jackson unbutton his shirt. He pushes me back onto the bed before slowly peeling off my tiny dress – like it was ever going to get in the way anyway. Jackson presses down on top of me, his rugby player's body weighing heavy on my tiny-by-comparison frame. We kiss passionately again, with way more steam that I'd ever shared with Will, but it's not as sexy as it looks in the movies. Our teeth are banging together, I can feel his chin wet with a mixture of our saliva, and I just know that my big curls are going to be crushed from rubbing against the pillow – and there's no way I'll ever be able to recreate my new do myself.

Jackson runs his tongue across my lips before slowly flicking it all the way down my body, stopping when he gets to the tiny red thong I bought, so that it didn't show under my tiny red dress. But as Jackson seductively takes my underwear in his mouth, beginning to pull it from my body with his teeth, I have nothing but Danny on my mind.

'Wait,' I insist, stopping Jackson in his tracks.

'Oh, right, sorry,' Jackson says, rummaging around in his pocket. He pulls out a black leather wallet and removes a large wad of notes before folding them in half and stuffing them between my boobs. 'That should cover it,' he says with a smile, like he's being overly generous. 'If I throw in a little more, will you pee on me?'

For a moment I can do nothing but blink at him. The fact he is paying me and the fact he wants me to pee on him both battling for space at the forefront of my mind, but I can't process either. Finally one thought is victorious, and I manage to speak.

'You're paying me?' I ask.

'Yes,' he replies. 'Wait, are you not a prostitute?'

'No,' I reply slowly, cautiously, paralysed with shame.

'Oh shit,' Jackson replies, looking about as mortified as I feel. 'It's just I thought with you saying you were working and, you know, the dress…' His voice trails off.

I use the back of my hand to wipe away what is left of our kisses from my mouth before anxiously nibbling my thumbnail. Sure, I could get mad at Jackson. I could get upset and burst into tears. Me last week would have done all of these things, but the new me… I just laugh. I erupt with laughter and it's not the cute little giggle I use to acknowledge jokes, it's my honest-to-God laugh, the kind that makes you look ugly but you don't even care.

With Jackson still hovering between my legs, I scooch away from him and retrieve my dress from the floor, slipping it back on, still laughing to myself. I grab my shoes and head for the door.

'You can keep the money,' Jackson calls after me. 'Just, please, don't tell anyone.'

I grab the money from my cleavage, having forgotten it was even there, and toss it on the floor.

'Don't worry,' I call back. 'I won't be telling anyone about this.'

I close the door behind me. Well, I won't be telling anyone except Danny. He will find this hilarious and he said I didn't have enough stories so here's another one: the time a professional sportsman mistook me for a prostitute and asked if he could pee on me. Or if I would pee on him – I forget. Either way, I'm fairly certain I couldn't have gone through with it, not even for a famous Australian with massive muscles who, FYI, did not taste like chocolate, just beer and cigarettes.

I slip my shoes back on as I head down the corridor, with

the intention of heading back to Eros to find Danny. I stumble a little as I slip on the second one, pretty much falling into the lift where a porter catches me, so I thank him. When Will broke my heart, I couldn't imagine ever feeling happy again, but I have been through a lot since then. I have mutilated my body – poisoned it too. I've shattered my good reputation, breaking rules left, right and centre. I have been offended in about thirty different ways. I feel exhausted, I feel dirty and, possibly scariest of all, I feel like I have no idea how my life is going to play out. Not the next few years, but even just the next few weeks. But do you know what? I feel alive. I feel more alive than I have ever felt in my life. I am not just existing, I am living and I realise that Danny is a big part of that.

I glance around the club for him but he's nowhere to be seen, so I ask the barman who was serving us earlier.

'The guy I came in with...' I start.

'Left about ten minutes ago with a gaggle of girls,' he replies.

'Oh, OK, thanks.'

That pang of jealously slaps me across the face again. Would Danny really go off with a group of girls? Then again, would *I* really go off with a random guy? Stranger things have happened.

I decide to head up to our room, to see if he's there. He isn't and I don't know why I'm surprised. He's Danny, and all the ladies love Danny. Messy-haired, dimple-faced, geek-chic Danny.

I slip off my dress, wind my hair up into a bun on top of my head and take off my make-up. For a second, I examine my body in the mirror. My feet are aching from wearing such high heels, my body is covered in red marks from wearing tight underwear and tight clothing and my head is a little itchy, probably from the dye earlier. Why do we women do this to ourselves? Danny almost exclusively dresses for comfort, and still manages to look stylish, but for girls, beauty really is pain.

I slip on the T-shirt Danny gave me when I stayed at his house, because I've been sleeping in it, because it's comfortable and, if truth be told, I like the way it smells. I grab my phone, find Danny in my phone book and hover my thumb over his name, wondering whether or not I should call him. I want him to come back to me, so I can tell him my funny story and we can cuddle up like we always do. Thinking of him out somewhere having fun with girls – multiple people who will undoubtedly be charmed by him, that he could potentially get off with, and all of them not me. Shit. I don't like these odds, but worst of all, I don't like this feeling. This dizzying, sick-to-my-stomach, punch-to-the-gut feeling, except this time I can't blame it on food poisoning. I've done what I never wanted to do – what I never thought I'd do in a million years – I've fallen for Danny.

I tap my phone to call him, only to hear his phone vibrating on the bedside table at his side of the bed. Brilliant. So not only is he out having fun, but he's also going to know I was just sitting here, pining for him. I can't have that. I grab Danny's phone to try and delete the missed call, but he has a passcode on so I can't – crap. Before I have a chance to wonder if I can get around this, Danny's notifications catch my eye and there's a text from his mum. I can only see the snippet of the conversation, but her reply says: 'It sounds like you've got it bad for this girl. I'm so happy for you. x'

Are they talking about me? And even if they are, does he mean it, or is this all part of the act? Maybe he's just hoping she'll relay this information to his ex…

With all traces of Candy Hart removed, washed off and tied back, I climb into bed, just plain old Candice, alone in the world, life still as messed up as ever.

Chapter 34

It happened again. It happened the first few days after I split from Will, but as the focus shifted from my impending spinsterhood to just having fun with Danny it stopped… Well it's back. I have sweet dreams, but not so vivid I can recall them in the morning, and I wake up feeling great, but only for a second, only until reality hits and it causes my body to jolt like I'm waking up from a nightmare – except I'm not waking from a nightmare, I'm waking up in a living nightmare.

'Sorry, did I make you jump?' Danny says, rubbing my shoulder gently. I roll onto my back and see that he's climbed in bed next to me. It's the middle of the night. I lift my weary head to make myself more comfortable so Danny places an arm behind me, pulling me close so my head is resting on his chest. He locks his strong arm around me, not so tightly it's uncomfortable, but in a way that makes me feel safe.

'It's OK,' I reply, sleepily.

'So, good night with that bloke?' he asks.

'Yeah,' I lie. 'Where did you get off to?'

'This hen party invited me into town, right lively bunch of Irish lasses,' he explains, and I feel my brow tighten with tension. 'So we were in this club in town and two of them take me to one side,' he starts in that familiar storytelling tone he always adopts to tell me one of his famous stories, but his animated manner quickly dissolves. 'Anyway, I couldn't do it,' he tells me honestly. 'Not *it*, I mean I couldn't even entertain them. I went for a walk and then I came back here. Didn't expect to find you here, actually.'

I stroke his chest lightly with my fingertips. 'I was in Jackson's room all of five minutes,' I tell him. 'I couldn't go through with *it* either. You were right; I'm just not the kind of girl who can do this like that.'

Well, it's true that I couldn't go through with it, and I realised that before any money changed hands. I decide not to tell Danny that Jackson thought I was a prostitute, because I don't want him to think I was going to go through with it, when I *really* wasn't.

With his free hand, Danny swipes a piece of hair from my face that must have fallen loose while I was sleeping.

'How is it you look so beautiful when you've just woken up?' he asks.

I slap his chest playfully, a little harder than I intended to but I'm still half asleep, in my defence.

'You're such a piss-taker,' I tell him.

'I am, but I mean it,' he insists. 'Most beautiful girl I've ever laid eyes on. Why do you think I asked you out the second I saw you?'

'Because you're a cocky twat?' I reply.

'Well, that's probably what gave me the confidence.' He laughs. 'But, no, it's because despite your granny outfit and the grumpy look you had plastered across your face, something just shone through. Something that I liked. And just so you know, you didn't need this makeover to look good. Right now, half asleep, with your hair in a bun, no make-up on your face apart from that smudge of eyeliner that you missed when you washed your face, in that T-shirt that I got at a convention where I was easily the coolest person there, and that's saying something…you're flawless.'

I open my eyes again and tip my head back to look up at Danny, suddenly feeling very awake.

'It wasn't that I didn't like you,' I tell him. 'It's never been that I didn't like you – despite your moments of arrogance, your overly easy-going attitude and that stupid topknot that I want to chop off with scissors every time I look at it,' I tease, mirroring his criticism. 'It was just…Will stuff. For an entire year every aspect of my life has been dictated by Will stuff. You know, when I left Jackson I came looking for you, I wanted to tell you how happy you're making me.'

'You make me happy too,' he tells me.

Danny reaches forward and gently takes my chin between his thumb and his index finger. He tips my head back a little before leaning in and kissing me. It isn't the frantic kiss I shared with Jackson, but it's just as passionate – if not more so. It's the kind of kiss that feels so good, I know that I'll wake up and wonder if I dreamt it or not.

Something kicks in, some kind of autopilot that makes me act without really thinking, and I pull myself up, climbing on top of Danny, whipping off my T-shirt before leaning forward to continue our kiss. Danny runs his hands down my sides, resting them gently on my hips. When I kissed Jackson I felt like I was misbehaving, like I was breaking all the rules and acting out of character, but this just feels right. I don't feel like I'm trying to be sexy or bold, I'm just enjoying the moment and that's all that matters sometimes.

Chapter 35

I wake up slowly as the smell of toast fills my nostrils, hunger striking me the second it registers.

'Morning, bro,' Danny says brightly. As nicknames and terms of endearment go, I should take issue with this one more than any of the others, but this one feels special, personal...ours. 'Sleep well?'

'Like a baby,' I reply, stretching out, unfazed by the fact I'm completely naked.

'Funny, I didn't hear you wake up to cry every hour,' he jokes and I laugh sarcastically. 'Breakfast in bed is served.'

Danny places a plate of toast in front of me before hopping in bed next to me with his own plate. He clicks the TV on and starts eating.

'Don't worry about the calories; you burned plenty last night,' he jokes. 'So when you key what you're eating into your weird little app, factor that in.'

I laugh. Actually, I haven't keyed anything I've eaten into my app in days. It just didn't seem important now I'm not trying to be what Will wants me to be.

I swallow my first mouthful.

'This is lovely, thank you,' I say, sipping the cup of tea that I've just noticed sitting next to me.

'You're welcome,' he replies. 'I wanted to get up before you and go out and get bread so I could surprise you. I even bought jam.'

'I noticed.'

'Well, I didn't buy it, technically I stole it from someone's room service tray on my way back to the room, but it's the thought that counts, right?'

'Right.' I laugh.

We finish our breakfast as we watch TV. Checkout is in an hour, but neither of us is rushing. Today we're headed for London for our last night before it's back home and back to reality.

'Last night happened, right?' he asks, his eyes fixed on the TV.

'It did,' I reply.

'So, what now?'

'Now, nothing,' I reply. 'Don't worry about it. It was good, but I get it.'

'OK,' he replies with a smile. 'Let's just have fun today and figure things out as we go along.'

'Sure,' I reply.

'Have you decided what you're wearing today?' he asks, changing the subject.

'Life was easier when I wore the same, dull outfits all the time,' I joke. 'This is a whole thing.'

'All that matters is that you dress for you,' he says with a shrug. 'Don't over think it.'

'You're right,' I reply, climbing out of bed, grabbing a few things and taking them into the bathroom with me. My bun must have fallen out over the course of the night, and I look in the mirror and observe that my hair looks awful, but I don't care. It's 'bed hair', and that's a look, right? Mine is just very legitimate bed hair. There's no time for a shower now. I'll just have to wait until I get to London to smarten myself up. I hop into my outfit and admire myself in the mirror. My messy hair seems to work with my shorts and my off-the-shoulder top, so at least people might think I've done this on purpose. I put on some make-up – more than I used to, because I liked the way it looked last night, although I'm not sure I apply it as well as the girl at the salon did.

Still, when I walk back into the bedroom, Danny takes a break from blindly flinging things into our suitcases to wolf whistle.

'Look at you,' he says, pulling me close.

'I look rough,' I tell him.

'You look perfect.'

'I think I'm a few plastic surgery procedures off perfect, but thank you.' I laugh.

Danny moves his face towards mine, but I wiggle free from his grasp.

'No, no. We need to get a move on.' I laugh. 'If we miss checkout, they'll bill Will for another night.'

'Stop trying so hard for people who don't give a fuck about you,' he tells me. 'Let him get fined. Let's be honest, bloke's got a shitload of bad karma heading his way – what's paying out a 150-pound fine, or whatever?'

I shoot Danny a look.

'OK, fine, fine.' He laughs. 'To the Bug-mobile!'

As we head for the door with our bags, and only minutes to spare, Danny notices that he's forgotten to pack the toaster.

'Just leave it,' I insist, safe in the knowledge it was cheap, and that we probably won't *need* it.

'What?' he asks, shocked. 'Where's your sentimental value? That's not just any toaster, it's *our* toaster. It's the one that got you through food poisoning, the one we used to celebrate easing the sexual tension we'd spent weeks building up. This toaster is special.'

I laugh. 'OK, fine, just…where are we going to put it? My new clothes are taking up all the spare room we had.'

'I'll just carry it,' he insists.

'Danny, you can't just carry a toaster.'

'Why not?'

'What will people think?'

'Who cares what people think?' he laughs, picking it up. 'Come on.'

As I follow Danny through the hotel with his toaster under his arm, I am in awe of just how few fucks he gives, and it occurs to me that maybe that's why he's such a happy person. Perhaps happiness is synonymous with not worrying about what people think of you, because you're free to do whatever brings you joy without the burden of how being judged will make you feel.

'Good morning,' he says to an elderly lady who is staring at him with her mouth open. 'Toast?'

'Oi, keep walking,' I tick him off, suppressing my laughter.

We load our stuff into the car before getting in ourselves, Danny laughing as I climb over the driver's seat first like it's a perfectly normal thing to do now.

'We've clocked some miles this week,' Danny says. 'It's funny, I never would have thought it possible to cover so much ground and fit everything in, but thanks to Will's anal itinerary, it's all gone according to plan.'

'Planning, lying, being a wanker – he's a man of many talents,' I say bitchily.

Danny sucks air through his teeth playfully. 'I'm still not bored of hearing you swear.' He laughs. 'Anyway, my phone says we'll be there in a couple of hours.' Danny places it on the dash-mount. 'Kensington,' he observes. 'Old Will was pushing the boat out, huh?'

'I guess he was,' I reply.

'Right, well, to London,' he bellows. 'And today's musical accompaniment: the soundtrack from *The Good, The Bad and The Ugly*.'

'Nerd,' I say to myself. 'Such a huge, huge nerd.'

'Hey, there are two kinds of people in the world,' he starts, adopting what I imagine is a cowboy voice. 'Those who think *The Good, The Bad and The Ugly* is the greatest film ever made, and those who are wrong.'

I stare at him blankly.

'OK, let's go.' He gives in. 'Let's go see what kind of damage we can do to the capital.'

Chapter 36

'Congratulations to you both,' the hotel porter says as he unlocks the door to our room.

'Congratulations?' I ask, following him inside.

'On your wedding, of course.' He laughs.

'Of course,' Danny replies. 'Wifey, you forgotten already?'

'Silly me,' I reply, puzzled, but going along with it.

It's a big room, but it's only once we're all inside that I notice the place is cluttered with romantic crap.

'So, this is the honeymoon suite,' the porter starts. Ah, so that explains the rose-tinted glow coming from all the extras. There are rose petals all over the bed, leading up to the bath, and beyond. Candles are lit, dotted around the room, and the lights are dimmed. The place looks beautiful, but it's too beautiful, and it smell so good it stinks. 'Your dinner reservation is tonight at eight p.m. I guess I'll leave you two to it.'

With a knowing wink, the porter leaves.

'He booked the honeymoon suite for you,' Danny says, amazed, when we're finally alone.

'Yep,' I reply, equally as dumbstruck.

'Don't you find that really gross?'

'Yep.'

'Not so gross I won't drink this champagne though.' Danny laughs, pouring two glasses and placing one in my hand. 'To us,' he jokes.

I clink my glass with his and knock it back.

'You're quiet,' Danny observes.

'Yeah, I feel weird, I guess. This is so weird.'

'Well, I'll drink his booze, but we're not eating his dinner. I'll sort something, OK?'

I nod my head.

'Would you rather not sleep here?' Danny asks me.

I glance around the room, at all the roses, the gigantic teddy bear holding the 'I love you' plaque, the plate of heart-shaped chocolates... It's just so weird. It's smoke and mirrors. I probably would have been blown away by it all if things had gone to plan, but now I know the truth... It's just the sickest kind of deceit shit that no amount of rose petals can cover.

'It's fine,' I tell him. 'No one has ever done anything special for me, and this is certainly that...but it's not.'

Danny smiles and gives my shoulder a reassuring squeeze. 'Right, bro, go run yourself a nice bath and get yourself dolled up. I'm taking you out tonight. I want you to sit in this hotel bath so long you get out looking like that woman from *The Shining*.' He laughs.

'I get that one,' I reply to his movie reference excitedly, before remembering just what she looked like. 'Maybe not that long though.'

'Do as you're told, Candy. I've got plans to make.'

'Sir, yes, sir,' I reply, giving him a little salute.

After a long soak, as instructed, I head back into the bedroom to find that Danny has returned. He's sitting on the bed, eating chocolates, sipping a cup of tea, and throwing potpourri at the teddy bear, punching the air victoriously whenever a piece sticks to its head.

I tighten my fluffy robe before sitting down on the bed next to him.

'Want a sip?' he asks, offering me his cup.

I glance inside it and turn my nose up at the contents.

'No thanks,' I reply. 'I didn't know you drank herbal tea.'

'I fucking don't,' he scoffs. 'But it's all they've got in here.'

I run my fingers through my wet hair, trying to free a few of the knots, wincing as I do so.

'I'm not looking forward to attempting to curl my hair with my straighteners,' I admit. 'Zane made it look effortless.'

'If you can't do it, I'll have a go,' Danny says, but I widen my eyes with horror.

'Like I'm going to let you touch my hair, man-bun.' I laugh. 'Anyway, I'm a girl; you're a boy. I'm just supposed to be better at this stuff.'

'Hashtag: everyday sexism,' Danny jokes. 'OK, well, I'll leave you to dry your hair off and I'll have a shower. Everything is in place for tonight.'

'Why am I so worried?' I ask – worried.

'Don't be,' he instructs, leaning over and kissing me on the cheek before disappearing into the bathroom.

I briefly touch my face where he kissed me before setting up the hairdryer and the straighteners at the dressing table.

I remember what Zane told me about leaning forward while I blow-dry my hair to give it more volume, and I nail it, but then it's time to curl. I section my hair off and take a small piece, placing it between the hot plates before attempting the manoeuvre Zane showed me. As I let the piece of hair fall I can't help but notice that it's not curly at all, in fact, it's just straightened it. Crap.

I take the same piece of hair and then try again, this time only managing to put a bend in it halfway down. Wow, I didn't realise you could put a right angle in your hair.

I put down the straighteners and fold my arms angrily. This is impossible. How do girls do this every day?

Danny walks out of the bathroom with a towel wrapped around his waist. He grabs the hairdryer and begins blowing his hair.

'Having trouble?' he asks, raising his voice so that I can hear him over the dryer.

'Just taking a break,' I lie.

'A break from folding your hair?' he asks, laughing at my attempt.

I frown at him, so he clicks the dryer off.

'Come here,' he insists, picking up the straighteners. 'Look, you've got to angle the straighteners downwards,' he explains. 'And the slower you do it, the tighter the curl, see?'

Danny lets the piece of hair drop, and it's curled beautifully, like a corkscrew. He does another two before handing me the straighteners back.

'You try,' he insists.

I follow his instructions and finally manage to get a piece to curl. It's not as good as Danny's, but I get better at it as I go along.

'Thank you,' I say, mildly irritated that he's better at this stuff than I am, but grateful for his help.

'Let me know if you need help with your make-up too,' he shouts as he continues to dry his hair. 'Or your bra – but I'm better at taking those off.'

I laugh and shake my head. 'So what are we doing tonight?' I ask.

'It's a surprise,' he tells me, sweeping his hair back from his face.

'I hate surprises,' I tell him. 'The honeymoon suite was a surprise, and look how that went.'

'Yeah, but I'm not banging you behind my wife's back, am I? I'm good at surprises. My surprises don't involve me fathering children. Not if I execute them well.' He laughs as he slips on his clothes. 'The surprises, that is. Not the children.'

'Hey, where's your topknot tonight?' I ask.

'No topknot tonight,' he replies, buttoning up his shirt. It's only as I realise that he's got his hair down and blown back that I realise just how smart he's looking this evening in his black trousers and his white shirt. He blows his glasses clean before putting them on. 'Nothing I can do about these though,' he laughs. 'Not if you want me to see.'

'I always liked Clark Kent more than Superman anyway.' I smile.

'That's good,' he replies, 'because I've always preferred shirts to Lycra.'

'Speaking of Lycra,' I start, grabbing my dress for the evening. 'Are you sure about this?'

'I'm sure I'm sure,' he replies. 'Why?'

I glance at the white, sparkly bodycon dress.

'Erm, I have like fifty reasons.' I laugh. 'It's tight – very tight. It's white and I'm clumsy and I spill things.'

'It's supposed to be tight,' he points out. 'And you'll look amazing in it – you need to feel comfortable though. And we can always get you a bib.'

I laugh and thank him.

'Right, I need to go get set up,' he tells me, instantly arousing my curiosity.

'Set up?' I ask.

'Yes, you'll see,' he replies. 'Get ready. I'll send someone for you when I'm ready, OK?'

'OK,' I reply, nervously. As Danny leaves the room, I can't help but think about how lucky I am to have him in my life right now and whatever my surprise is, at least I know it's not the honeymoon suite.

Chapter 37

'You're so lucky,' a female hotel employee tells me as she escorts me into the lift. 'Your hubby has pulled out all the stops.'

'He's certainly something,' I reply, noticing that the lift is going up and not down.

'I mean, wow. I'd kill for a bloke to do this for me,' she continues, visibly swooning from her encounter with my fictional husband.

I smile and nod.

The lift doors open and the girl leads me along a bare corridor in what looks like an area of the hotel only usually used by staff. We walk up a short staircase before stepping out onto the roof. It's dark, but there are fairy lights everywhere. Over in the corner Danny is sitting at a candlelit table, set for two. On the floor next to him there's an air mattress covered in a variety of cushions in different shapes and sizes, that looks so cosy I would dive into it were it not for my super-tight dress and my sky-high heels making even walking feel like a challenge.

The girl leaves the two of us alone and Danny comes over to greet me.

'Well, this is very romantic for a nerd,' I tease. 'Is that a Jack Duff album playing?'

'What can I say? They didn't have the *Guardians of the Galaxy* soundtrack. And I *can* do romance when I want to.'

'It seems you can.'

'Dinner is coming to us. And if you really don't want to sleep in the forced romance zone, we can sleep under the stars – for the story,' he quickly adds.

I smile widely. I'm impressed and I can't hide my gratitude. In fact, a wave of emotion washes over me and I feel a happy tear escape one eye.

'No, no crying. You know I can't handle women crying.' He laughs. 'I just wanted to do something nice for you. You said no one has ever done anything big for you, well, here you go.'

'Thank you,' I reply sincerely.

'Shall we sit down?'

I nod, making my way over to the table.

As we approach the edge of the building, I take in the breathtaking view.

'Wow,' is about all I can say. From up here, you can see across London for miles, with a perfect view of the park right in front of us.

'Amazing, isn't it?' he sighs. 'And London is tiny compared to some of the places I've visited. You'll have to let me take you to a few places, show you what there is to see there.'

'I'd like that,' I reply as I manage to drag myself away from the scenery and sit down. I pick up my menu and glance over it, struggling with what to order because it all sounds so good.

'This is me wooing you, in case you can't tell,' Danny explains. 'Just like I was last night when you went off with that Aussie.'

'Easy mistake to make. Also, if you think you have to woo me because we slept together last night, you're wasting your money.' I laugh.

'Why do you keep insisting that last night was just a one-off?' he asks.

'Because…you only do one-offs?'

'I do people as many times as I want to do them, but there aren't too many people I want to do more than once,' he replies, before realising his wording. 'You know what I mean.'

'I do. But…I just didn't think you did relationships.'

'I don't *not* do them.' He laughs. 'Just never met anyone worth doing one with.'

'But plenty worth banging on your car?' I reply, raising an eyebrow.

'The number of women I have banged on my car has been greatly exaggerated,' he replies, sipping his champagne.

We pause our conversation while we order our food, but the second the waiter has gone I am straight back to it.

'So...'

'So, what?' He laughs.

'So, what happens when we get back?' I ask.

'Candy, nothing needs to happen. No one has to promise anyone anything. I just know I'd like to spend more time with you. I want to spend my days annoying you and getting you in trouble and making you watch *Star Wars*. And I want you to spend yours driving me mad, keeping me out of trouble and pretending to enjoy *Star Wars*, because that's what you do when you like someone, OK?'

'I don't know if it's all the romantic stuff surrounding us that made that seem like the least romantic thing I have ever heard, but OK.' I laugh.

'I can tell you I've got a wife if that sweetens the deal at all?' he teases.

'Oi, not funny,' I reply, trying to keep my face straight.

'Too soon?' he asks.

'Too real,' I reply.

Danny smiles. 'So we're a bit of a double act,' Danny muses. 'The kind you can publicly discuss. The kind who watch their parents having sex on the living room floor together.'

'Fond memories of that,' I reply sarcastically, although I notice he referred to us as a double act and not a couple, so I'm still none the wiser. All I know is that I'm happier, and that's fine by me.

'Here's to many more,' he says, raising his glass. 'Well, more fond memories, not more old people banging. To us!'

'To us,' I reply, clinking my glass with his.

After a delicious dinner and lots of champagne, Danny and I are lying on the air mattress. We're on one of the tallest buildings around, so with the lights off and the sky clear, we've got a perfect view of the stars. It's a warm summer night, but not so hot it's uncomfortable, so we're sleeping on the roof.

'How did you pull this off?' I ask. 'I mean, getting permission to be up here, dinner up here, sleeping up here…'

'Let's just say there's a manager with a teenage son who just got lots of very expensive software for free,' he tells me with a laugh.

'I won't ask,' I reply.

'Why, because it's illegal and you're a square?'

'No, because it sounds boring,' I tease.

I snuggle up closer to Danny, resting my head on his bicep, placing one of my legs on top of his.

'You're worth it,' he tells me. 'At work, you always seemed so sad, and I remember thinking that all I wanted to do was make you happy – even if it was just by stapling an invoice to my foot.'

'I keep meaning to ask, did that leave a scar?'

'I knew you were watching.' He laughs. 'Nope, that's the great thing about the human body – it never ceases to amaze you with how much it's able to recover from without leaving a mark.'

'Like failed relationships,' I tell him.

'Exactly,' he replies. 'Sometimes the people we fall for are not the ones we get to spend the rest of our lives with, and sometimes it hurts, but sometimes we realise it just wasn't meant to be. No matter how hard you try and how carefully you plan it, things just don't work out the way you hoped they would. But it's OK, because life gives you plenty of opportunities to start over – not just every time something goes wrong, or even each morning – every second of life is another shot, another chance to make better choices.'

'You're very wise,' I tell him.

'You say that like you're unsure if it's a good or a bad thing.' He laughs.

'It's good because you're smart, but it's bad because you know it,' I reply.

'Come here, bro,' he says, freeing his arm to wrap it around me.

I snuggle up in his arms, exhaling deeply as I feel myself relax.

'It's funny to think that after all these nights of not being able to sleep, I might actually be able to get some shut-eye tonight, and I had to sleep outside to achieve it.'

'I don't think so.' He laughs, running a hand up my thigh. 'Do you know how many light fittings there are below us that we can make swing?'

'Yes, yes, yes,' I reply.

Chapter 38

'What are you smiling about?' Danny asks me.

It's six a.m., and I've just woken up on the roof after a night of not very much sleep with Danny.

'Oh, not much,' I reply. 'Except I had sex on a roof last night, and I wasn't even that drunk.'

'You're a big, brave girl, huh?' He laughs as he stretches out.

'Oh, totally,' I reply sarcastically. 'But I probably only felt so brave because we're on such a tall building, no one could possibly see.'

'Oh, they definitely have CCTV up here,' he tells me casually.

'No!' I gasp.

'Oh, yeah. I checked. I don't mind an audience; I just like to know it's there, you know?'

'You're winding me up,' I insist.

'I could point the cameras out to you?'

'No thanks,' I reply quickly. 'I'm happy not knowing.'

'I'm starving,' Danny says. 'Reckon they've got somewhere we can plug the toaster in up here?'

I laugh, although I don't think he's joking.

'I'd suggest we go get showered and changed and head out for breakfast, but I don't want to get up. I don't want today to happen.'

'You don't want to go back?' Danny asks.

'Nope,' I reply.

'Well, let's go somewhere else,' he suggests.

'I can't,' I sigh. 'Responsibilities – and it's not just my work, or my flat. I've got Amy's wedding tomorrow.'

'Oh yeah, well, I'm looking forward to it,' he says, reminding me that he said he'd go with me. 'Anyway, you've got me around now. Life won't be like it was before.'

'This is true.' I smile. I kind of feel like I can tackle anything with Danny backing me, as cheesy as it sounds.

'We'll just take it a day at a time, and see what happens,' Danny tells me. 'You don't have to have everything figured out.'

See, this is what I love about Danny. When things are bad you can be the kind of person who has a breakdown, writes about it for all of Facebook to read, and makes sure everyone knows that you're having a tough time, or you can be more like Danny, take things a step at a time, and when things are bad just plant a smile on your face and crack on. It's called getting on with life. Your timer doesn't stop ticking just because you're having a bad day. Every day counts and every day could be your last. With my rubbish family medical history, I am more determined than ever to make every day count.

'OK, let's get up, let's head back…before I change my mind.'

'OK, but after breakfast,' he insists. 'And after this.'

Danny climbs on top of me, pinning my wrists down above my head before kissing my neck slowly.

Cameras be damned. I'm making the most of these last few moments, before it's back up north, back to reality, back to face the music.

Chapter 39

As we checked out of the hotel, the manager gave me a knowing glance and a wink, the kind that confirms there were definitely CCTV cameras up on the roof. I don't care though; I'm just so happy right now.

The trip home was loads of fun, with Danny keeping me amused for the entire journey. He insisted I get some sleep while he drove, but I didn't want to just abandon him. Plus, as much as I trust him, I still like to keep one eye on him.

As fun as the trip was, after four hours in the car I am ready to get a bath, put some comfortable clothes on and get in my own bed. Danny and I can't get enough of each other though, so the plan is to both head home, freshen up and then meet up later for a threesome with Netflix. *House of Cards* is on the agenda, and Danny is determined to catch me up before the new season starts.

Danny pulls up in the taxi bay outside my flat and insists on carrying my bags up for me, much to the annoyance of the actual taxi drivers parked outside. We share a quick kiss before he leaves, but I don't even have a chance to get my shoes off before my phone rings.

'Candice, are you back?' Sweet Caroline asks, without so much as a hello.

'Caroline – just,' I reply. 'What's up?'

'We need you to come in,' she tells me.

I glance at the time. It's nearly the end of the working day and it's Friday.

'Erm, OK,' I reply. 'Right now?'

'Right now,' she replies, hanging up.

I quickly use the bathroom, glancing in the mirror, fluffing up my hair and touching up my make-up before heading back out. In my ripped skinny jeans and my awkwardly low top, I'm not exactly dressed for the office, but I'm not technically supposed to be there, so they'll have to take me as I am.

I grab my handbag, hop into one of the taxis outside and soon enough I'm at Starr Haul HQ, making my way up the banana, heading for the office I share with Caroline.

As I walk through the door I notice her sitting at her desk, but then I glance over at my desk and see that Stephanie – Will's wife – is sitting there.

'Caroline, can you go get us some tea, give us a moment?' Stephanie asks her.

Caroline nods and shuffles towards the door. As she passes me she looks me up and down, uttering something only loud enough for me to hear.

'You look like a prostitute,' she says.

'You're not the first person to say that,' I call after her, giving no shits what she thinks, but Stephanie's presence here has me worried sick. She never really visits the office.

'Sit,' she insists, nodding towards a chair that has been placed in front of my desk that isn't usually there.

As I sit down, I notice the pram in the corner of the room, with their new baby boy fast asleep in there. I'm assuming it's a boy because of all the blue crap surrounding him.

'I'm just going to blurt it out,' she starts anxiously, taking a deep breath, composing herself. 'I found out Will was cheating on me this morning. Pictures on his phone, so there's no lying his way out of this one.'

I stare at her, paralysed by fear, terrified by what she's going to do. Suddenly, I don't feel safe being in a room with her. I imagine trying to explain myself, only for her not to believe me and pour scalding hot tea over me while Caroline holds me down… I give myself a mental pinch and tell myself to calm down. I just need to explain, and maybe – hopefully – she'll believe me.

'Mrs Starr, I am so sorry,' I start, unsure how on earth to make it sound as heartfelt as I mean it.

'It's not your fault,' she says, wiping her tears away with the backs of her hands. 'But obviously there's a lot of fallout for the business, so we're in crisis mode here. Will has gone AWOL, the chicken,' she snaps. 'So it's all hands on deck, if you don't mind.'

'I…I didn't think you'd want me to help,' I stutter.

'Of course I do,' she insists. 'I know it must be hard; I know that Will looked out for you – almost like a dad to you – this must surprise you.'

I stare at her for a moment, confused. As I wrack my brains for any possible reason she could be so cool with me after I have wrecked her marriage, I realise something: I never had my photo taken with Will. Not even once.

'You said you found photos,' I push, inconsiderately.

'Oh, yes,' she says angrily. 'Him with the woman who cleans his office.'

'*Julie*?' I ask.

'That's the one,' she replies. 'Needless to say, I sacked her. I've stepped in while Will is off having his pathetic little meltdown – he's probably with her. I'm on the board of directors and this company is my kids' future. I'm not going to let it go to shit because he can't keep his dick in his pants – again.'

I had never imagined Stephanie to be the kind of lady who swears, but she's only human, I suppose. All this time I was feeling like shit over how Will betrayed me, and here's this poor woman with three kids to him who has been repeatedly cheated on and lied to by him. And not only has he done it before, but he's been cheating on both of us with a third person as well. Julie the fucking cleaner, the one he would always complain about, the one he *needed* to keep having words with about the poor job she was doing… He's a piece of shit. All this time I was worried about being the other woman and I wasn't even that, I was the *other* other woman.

'I am so so sorry,' I tell her. 'If there's anything I can do…'

'Thank you,' she replies, her eyes filling up with tears again. She seems to be alternating between tears and fits of anger, and I don't blame her at all. 'No doubt he'll surface tonight, in time for his fucking party.'

'Party?' I ask.

'Yes, the big company party to celebrate the anniversary of him taking over, the egotistical twat.'

'Oh,' I reply. I'd forgotten about that. All employees are expected to attend. Well, all but Julie, I'd imagine.

'So, Caroline will be back in a moment. She's putting a damage-control plan in place – everyone is talking; it's horrible.'

'I can't even begin to imagine,' I tell her honestly.

'I won't be at the party tonight, but… I doubt she will, but if Julie turns up, will you call me, please?'

'Sure,' I reply, nodding my head as I grab my phone to text Danny, to remind him about the work party tonight.

Danny: See you there. Which dress have you chosen? Xx

Me: The red one. See you soon. Lots to tell you… xx

I stare at Stephanie for a moment and the hurt look on her face makes me feel sick – sick with myself. I may not have been knowingly sleeping with her husband, but I was sleeping with him, and I can't help but feel bad. So technically it wasn't me who ended their marriage, but what does it matter? Their marriage *is* ruined.

As Stephanie rummages around, shuffling the paperwork in front of her, I notice the ring I found in Will's pocket on her finger, confirming that the ring was never intended for me, and proving what a piece of shit Will really is. I feel like I've had a lucky escape, to make it out of such a horrible situation without having my heart broken or my reputation damaged.

I don't know if Julie, his other other woman, knew the real deal or if he lied to her too, but that girl's reputation is trashed. She's the girl who slept with her married boss and ended his marriage, just days after his wife gave birth. I can't even imagine how things would be playing out for me right now if I had been her. I'm just glad I got out when I did. I never wanted to hurt anyone; I just wanted to be happy. Now I realise that I wasn't happy at all, I can move on with my life. One thing I do know for sure is that I can't wait to hang out with Danny tonight.

Chapter 40

We're in the lavish reception room of one of the biggest hotels in Manchester, but despite the beautiful surroundings and the masses of guests dressed in their best, there's an atmosphere. I'm guessing everyone knows, but no one seems to want to talk about it. No one but Danny and me that is.

'That monumental twat,' Danny says a little too loudly, causing the barman serving us to raise an eyebrow. 'So we're all here celebrating a man who we all know is a bastard?'

'Pretty much,' I reply, glancing around the room. There are yellow balloons everywhere, a big banner saying: 'Keep up the good work, Will' and tables of food all around us. Danny was delighted to learn it was a buffet set-up, and not a sit-down meal, and every so often we have to drag our conversation across the room so he can eat more. The food looks delicious, with different tables laid out with a variety of world foods. Everything is a miniature version of what it claims to be, which is why Danny reasons he's eating twice as much. There's canapés, burgers, pies, sandwiches, wraps and lots of Chinese and Indian stuff. There was talk of mini pizzas and, since Danny learned of this, I feel like he has constantly had one eye on the kitchen doors, like a dog keeping an eye out for the neighbour's cat, ready to pounce and devour it the second it rears its head.

Danny takes his fork and stabs the balloon next to him, causing everyone to jump. It happens too quickly and there are too many balloons for anyone to notice where it came from.

'He doesn't deserve balloons,' Danny reasons. 'Oh, fun game, let's see how many we can get rid of as the night goes on. It'll be easy at first, too many to tell, but as they get less we risk getting caught. Deal?'

'You're on,' I tell him, shaking his hand, only to find my own returned with ketchup on it. He's like a big kid, and I love it.

'Watch out, Nurse Ratched is on her way over,' Danny warns me. I watch as Sweet Caroline heads over towards us. She's wearing a big, frilly white dress, and I can see her eyeballing my own choice of attire. I am wearing the red daring dress that I wore to Eros, and if Caroline thought I looked like a hooker in my jeans, then this is really going to upset her. She drops her handbag, then bends over to pick it up.

'Danger pop,' Danny whispers to me, stabbing another balloon, making everyone jump again.

'What was that?' Caroline asks, returning upright.

'Nothing,' I smile, stifling a laugh. 'How are you, Caroline? You look lovely.'

'As do you, dear,' she replies. 'I do hope you're not cold.'

'Well, you know, it is summer and I'm a big girl.'

'You certainly are,' she replies, pursing her lips with disapproval as she glares down at my chest. 'Boss will be along in five minutes, just letting you know. Probably best we don't mention helping Stephanie out after hours yesterday, lest we hurt his feelings.'

'No, we wouldn't want to hurt his feelings,' Danny interrupts. Caroline shoots him a look before wandering off. 'Who invited Miss Havisham?'

'Oh, she goes all-out for parties, our Caroline.'

'I wish she'd go all-outside, and stay there.' He laughs, before his happy look dissolves into a more serious one. 'You worried?'

'I'm fine. It's just weird. But I've got you.' I squeeze his hand. 'Couldn't be happier.'

'Good,' he replies. 'Because... Oh, oh, pizza.'

Danny drops my hand like it's a grenade and follows his nose in the direction of the Italian food.

'Be right back,' he calls. 'I'll bring you some, beautiful.'

I laugh, climbing to my feet and smoothing out my dress. I'll just pop to the bathroom and touch up my make-up because, it turns out, the more you wear, the more you have to keep applying.

I walk through an archway into a large sitting room, where the doors to the toilets are situated either side. There is a line of sofas leading down the centre of the room, with gold-framed mirrors all over the walls reminding me of that horrifying scene with all the heads in *Return To Oz*.

I nip into the loos, quickly but steadily apply more make-up, and head back out to find Danny and my pizza, which, truth be told, I'm actually getting more and more excited about by the second. The few people sitting on the sofas before have vacated the room, making it even creepier than it was before. As I speed-walk towards the main room I literally bump into someone heading for the toilets at an equally speedy pace.

'Will.'

Will looks me up and down and I see a flicker of something in his eyes that makes me think he maybe didn't recognise me at first.

'Wow,' he says, his eyes widening. 'I mean…wow. You look so different.'

'Good different?' I ask, suddenly finding it hard to be angry with him although I'm not sure why, because I should hate his guts right now. And there I go again, seeking his approval.

'Wow different,' he says, staring at me for a moment, looking me up and down, taking in the new me.

Will looks different too – wow different, but not good different. He looks pale and his eyes look dark, like he hasn't been sleeping, like he's been worrying. I always thought of Will as this strong, powerful man. Shut off from his emotions, business-minded – that old cliché. Turns out he's human like the rest of us.

'I'm sorry,' he blurts out, and while he sounds like he means it, it just doesn't feel sincere. If he really was sorry, if I really mattered to him, then he wouldn't have done this. As if lying to me about being separated from his wife wasn't bad enough – you could try to explain it away as cowardice, if maybe he was too scared to leave her but wanted to – but now that I know he was knocking off Julie too! Will just wants to have his cake (cupcakes, pastries, brownies – the whole damn bakery) and eat it.

'It's fine,' I tell him. Not because it's OK, but because I don't care.

'It's good though, because now we can be together.'

'What?'

'Things were messy before,' he explains. 'But now, everything is out in the open. Steph has kicked me out – *we* can be together.'

For a moment, I just stare at this man in front of me, smiling widely at me, waiting for me to agree to ride off into the sunset with him.

'It's too late.'

'It's not too late,' he insists. 'It's not like you've met someone else.'

'I have actually,' I tell him.

'But it's only been a week. Who could you have met?'

I look down at my shoes and twist my heels awkwardly.

'Danny,' I admit.

'The IT guy? No, no. He's not right for you. And he won't treat you right.'

'He won't cheat on me,' I snap.

'No, he'll just leave you to go skiing in the Alps or on safari in Africa. Guys like that don't stick around, Candice.'

'Because you were in your marriage for the long haul.'

'I suppose I deserved that, but everyone deserves a second chance. I gave you a second chance at work. Has he made a proper commitment to you? He hasn't, has he?'

I think for a moment, although about nothing in particular. My brain can't process this right now. Will, sensing I need a little coercing, steps towards me, placing a hand on the small of my back, pulling me closer. With his free hand, he gently strokes my face with the backs of his fingers before pinching my cheek, like he always does. It feels familiar, and at first it feels good, but all it does is remind me of how bad things really were, and how terribly he treated me.

I don't know why, but I hesitate before pulling away. My brain is telling me to recoil in horror, but my body is lagging behind. I catch sight of someone in my peripheral vision and glance to the left, to see Danny watching us. He's got two plates of pizza in his hand, which he places down on the nearest table before walking away.

'Shit,' I say, wiggling free from Will.

'Wait,' he insists, grabbing my arm to stop me from leaving.

'Get off me,' I demand. 'I need to explain to him.'

'We were happy before,' Will says desperately.

'No, we weren't. I thought we were – I thought you were going to propose. How insane is that? I was deluded.'

I snap my arm away from him and chase after Danny, catching up with him as he makes his way towards the exit.

'Danny, wait,' I call after him.

Danny halts immediately, but doesn't turn around.

'What?' he asks, and it breaks my heart to be truly in his bad books.

'That wasn't anything,' I tell him truthfully.

'It looked like something.'

'Yes, the last desperate act of a very desperate man.'

Danny turns around and looks at me, but then I notice his gaze travel to over my shoulder.

'Oh look, it's your shadow,' he says angrily.

I turn around and notice Will behind me.

'Candice, we need to talk. It's important,' Will insists.

'I have something important to talk to you about, actually,' Danny says, marching over to Will. 'I quit.'

'You can't just quit mid-job,' Will insists. 'That's breach of contract.'

'What are you going to do about it, old man?' Danny asks him.

'Look, OK, we all just need to calm down,' I reason, noticing how tense things are getting.

'I might be older than you, but I'm better than you,' Will tells Danny. 'You're just some jumped-up, pumped-up employee who thinks he's "cool" because he's got a stupid hairstyle and he goes to the gym. You have no idea what the real world is like, or what a proper, committed job is like. Most importantly, you can't treat Candice how she deserves to be treated. You're just not good enough, kid.'

Danny doesn't even take a second to absorb Will's words, he just lashes out, punching him in the face so hard Will hits the floor.

'My nose,' Will shrieks, grabbing his face. 'I think he broke my bloody nose.'

Will has his hands to his face, but I can see blood escaping from the sides, dripping all over his white shirt. I grab a cloth from the table next to me and hold it over Will's face for him.

'Candy,' Danny calls my name. 'I don't know where I'm going, but I'm going. Are you coming?'

'Wait,' I insist. 'I can't leave him like this.'

'You really can,' Danny replies, clearly annoyed that I'm helping Will at all.

'You've caved his fucking nose into his fucking face,' I snap. 'I can't just fucking leave him.'

'Language, Candice,' Will manages to tick me off, blood rushing into his mouth as he does so.

'Oh, shut the fuck up, Will,' I bark.

'Going now,' Danny warns me.

'Can't you just stay still for two seconds?' I snap at Danny. 'This is what you do when things get tough – you just piss off. I have a life; I can't just run away because things are messy.'

'He'll never be dependable,' Will chimes in. 'You said as much before, that he hasn't committed to you.'

'You said that?' Danny asks me.

'No, I didn't say that, but he asked me if you had and I just didn't say that you had…and you haven't,' I remind him, because he hasn't, but now probably isn't the time or the place. But I do worry. What if I leave with him now and then he leaves me?

My words leave a look on Danny's face that I don't think I'll ever forget. He looks at me, sad and disappointed, but only for a second before storming off. Danny has proven time and time again that he's there for me, but will he always be? He does just disappear when he feels like it, but can I just quit my job and my life without a second thought? Can I risk everything to just see what happens with Danny, who I know has a reputation for getting bored of real life?

I sit on the floor next to Will, my hand still held securely over his face. I slowly and cautiously remove the cloth and see that the damage isn't as bad as it seemed now that the bleeding is slowing down.

Will spits out a mouthful of blood.

'I *was* going to propose,' he tells me.

'What?'

'I was going to ask you to marry me, while we were away. I booked us the honeymoon suite, I arranged us a special dinner, and I was going to pop the question.'

'Are you fucking high?' I ask in disbelief.

'I love you,' he says with a smile, flashing me his red-stained teeth.

'You're still married, crazy person,' I snap, raising my voice. 'And you're lying – stop lying to me. I saw Stephanie. She had the ring on.'

'OK, so I wasn't going to propose. But we can be together now. Properly. And I did book us the honeymoon suite to make things special.'

'Yes, I was wondering about that. That was so gross.'

'I thought you'd appreciate the surprise – like the dress I bought you. Did you like it?'

I cast my mind back to the floor-length black dinner dress that Will bought me before we went away.

'No,' I tell him honestly. That's when I realise that Will doesn't know me at all. From picking out boring clothes for me, to telling what I should eat, to ticking me off for drinking and swearing. Danny never did any of that. He encouraged me to enjoy myself, to speak freely, and even when we went shopping together, he encouraged me to buy what I wanted, and what I thought I'd look good in. I feel like myself again. I think I love him and I've hurt him.

'And what about Julie?' I ask, but then I realise I don't care. I don't need his excuses. Nothing he can say could fix this.

'She was a stupid mistake. I love you,' Will says again, in case it didn't sink in the first time.

'You love me, you loved your wife, blah, blah, blah. Love isn't done and dusted, Will. Loving someone is a conscious choice that you make every day, not just a phrase you bat around. If you love someone, you don't hurt them.'

'But I didn't mean to hurt you,' he insists.

'But you did. With ease. In a spectacular fashion.'

I climb to my feet and head for the door.

'Candice, don't go,' he calls after me.

'You know what?' I twirl around and flip him off with both hands. 'I quit too.'

Chapter 41

I'm not saying I'm bad at relationships, but I've managed to lose two boyfriends in as many weeks, only cementing my theory that I'm going to die having had more cats than husbands.

Tomorrow morning I have to be up early for Amy's wedding, and yet here I am, at one a.m., sitting in Becky's Diner drinking tea that is far too weak to be even a little palatable. Still, it's the only place that's open 24 hours so here I am.

There's a young couple – about my age – at the table next to me, although it sounds like they've just met. The guy doesn't seem so bad, but the girl is absolutely wasted.

'What's your name again?' she asks him, although it's hard to make out her accent as she slurs her words and shoves chips into her mouth.

'Simon,' he tells her slowly, like he's repeating himself for the millionth time.

'I'm going to just call you Pablo,' she tells him, hitting him on the nose with a chip before putting it in her mouth. 'You just look like a Pablo; I think it's your moustache.'

I glance up at Simon/Pablo and see that he doesn't have a moustache at all, and I laugh to myself.

'You want to get out of here, Pablo?' she asks.

'Sure,' he replies, taking her hand and leading her out, their food hardly touched, just left on the table.

I can't actually think of anything worse than getting drunk and pulling some random dude in a burger bar in the early hours of the morning. In fact, I'd rather have the burger.

I don't want to be single. I don't think I'd be very good at it. I was absolutely crap at it before I met Will, and I don't know how Danny and I ended up together, but it wasn't my allure, that's for sure.

I can't do nights out, flirting, dates! The thought of signing up for something like Tinder, putting my face out there for guys to swipe through, judging me on my hair, the size of my nose, the colour of my eyes. Even something like Plenty of Fish, where you fill out a profile, doesn't inspire me with much confidence. I mean, Danny and I had nothing in common, and yet we were perfect for each other. I fucked that up though, didn't I? I should've just left Will to bleed out.

It's back to nights in, eating my sad little dinners for one, watching Netflix and stroking my cat to stave off the loneliness. No, that's not a euphemism, although give it a few months and I'm sure it will be.

I consider ordering another cup of tea, because this one has gone cold, but then it occurs to me that I'm unemployed now. I don't have any real savings, I already kind of live from cheque to cheque, and I don't see last month's wage lasting me very long at all, not after my little splurge in Brighton. Spending one pound on a cuppa might not seem like much, but I'm not sure how many cuppas I've got left in my account.

My phone buzzes on the table in front of me and I quickly grab it, hoping that it's Danny. I've been trying to call him since earlier, but he isn't answering. It isn't Danny; it's Amy.

> Amy: So nervous. Can't sleep! Xxx

> Me: Don't be nervous, you're going to be so happy together. Xxx

> Amy: Didn't think you'd be up... Are you with a boy? ;) xxx

I glance at the drunk dude next to me, who's decided he'll share my table with me. He's hunched over eating a cheeseburger, the burger grasped so firmly in both hands that he's squashing it to a pulp. He keeps looking from left to right, like one of the other drunk dudes might try pinch it from him.

> Me: Not quite. Sitting in a diner on my own, just thinking about things. Spectacularly fucked up the boy thing. Xxx

> Amy: Which one? Xxx

> Me: Danny. Xxx

> Amy: No, which diner? Xxx

> Me: Oh...haha. Oxford Street. Xxx

The next I hear from Amy, she's standing right in front of me. Her long brown hair is wound up in a bun on top of her head and she isn't wearing a scrap of make-up. The thing I love the most about Amy is that she probably doesn't care either. She's got the kind of self-confidence most girls could only dream of.

'Holy shit,' she gasps. 'Look at you!'

'Oh yeah.'

I'd forgotten about my makeover, and it only reminds me of how happy Danny made me.

'Let me grab a drink. You can tell me all about it.'

'Aims, you're up early tomorrow – you're getting married! You can't sit here with me and the other losers. You should be sleeping,' I insist, causing burger boy next to me to flash me a momentary look of being hurt and offended, before getting over it and getting back to his meal.

Amy looks at him and wrinkles her nose.

Becky's at this time of night is wild. People are coming here after their nights out, and they are animals – something about alcohol just does that to people. They're eating meat, dry humping (at least I hope that's as far as it's going) strangers in the not so dark corners of the room, everyone has their volume turned up to maximum as they squawk at each other and bark their orders and you can forget about any kind of queue – it's every man for himself. I mean, they actually have a bouncer on the door. At a diner. Need I say more?

'It's fine. Two seconds, OK?'

I smile and nod.

While Amy is at the counter, she looks back at me and smiles.

'Here, I brought you another tea,' she says, plonking it down in front of me. 'Shit, Candice. You're hardly recognisable. You look fucking incredible!'

'Oh, thanks,' I say casually.

'Your hair is going to look cracking with your blue bridesmaid dress. I'm even changing my plans,' she says excitedly. 'You rock the big, sexy curls, so I think we'll go with that.'

I smile weakly.

'OK, what happened?' she asks.

'Well, you were right about Danny. He's the most amazing man I have ever met…but then – '

'Oh, let me guess… Will stuff?'

I nod. My friend is used to hearing this phrase.

'Fuck mother-fucking Will,' Amy rants. 'You might not think it's as bad, but he was cheating on you with his wife. End of. You deserve better than that.'

I bite my lip, scared to tell her the full story.

'What?' she asks, reading my mind.

'As up for debate as the wife thing might be, the fact he was knocking off the office cleaner too is pretty clear cut.'

I watch a rush of colour tint my usually pale-skinned friend's complexion.

'So, I'm going to go and punch him in the fucking face,' she says through gritted teeth. 'Where is he?'

'Save your hand,' I tell her. 'Danny already did it.'

'Good for him. So, what's the problem?'

'Me. I'm the problem. I should have left with Danny but I didn't. I stayed to help Will, to hear him out…and when Danny was helping me, one thing he always said was that he wasn't going to be my intervention, the one who had to forcibly stop me interacting with Will. I shouldn't have needed stopping; I shouldn't have given him the time of day.'

'Bit hard when you work for him,' Amy reasons, rubbing my hand.

'Yeah, I quit.'

'*You* quit?'

'Yep.'

'But…you're *you*,' she replies, clearly struggling with a way to get her point across without offending me.

'Yep. Well, now I'm single and soon to be unemployed.'

'Well…at least your hair looks nice.' She laughs, and even I crack a smile. 'Candice, you're going to be fine. Don't worry about any of this tonight. Come back to mine, get some rest and just have fun tomorrow. Don't think about any of this.'

I glance at my phone to check the time (and, if I'm being honest, to see if Danny has texted me) but I only catch a glimpse of the screen before my battery dies.

'OK, sure,' I tell her. 'I don't suppose you have an iPhone charger, do you?'

'You know how I feel about Apple,' she frowns. 'But Ted will, I'm sure.'

I knock back the last of my tea and climb to my feet.

'Damn, girl,' Amy calls. 'Look at you. I can't believe this is you.'

'I might look different, but I'm still the same fuck-up on the inside.'

Amy grabs me and hugs me. 'Yeah, but you're *my* fuck-up.'

Chapter 42

Remember that kids' game show *Finders Keepers*? Well, if you were to cut Amy and Ted's big house down the middle today and peep inside, it would look like that. Rooms busy with people, frantically searching for Amy's something old – a necklace that her gran gave her for her eighteenth birthday.

I'm in Amy's bedroom with her, going through a chest of drawers that is full of various pieces of jewellery, weird little knick-knacks and all kinds of hippy gizmos and gadgets that I couldn't begin to identify.

'What the hell are these?' I ask, examining the tiny wooden dolls I just found in a little yellow box. They're like minute scarecrows, with their rigid bodies and their arms and legs stuck out bolt straight. They have a pained look on their faces, one that I noticed looking back at me in the mirror this morning.

'They're worry dolls. You can borrow them if you like,' Amy says, peeping out from inside her wardrobe before getting back to hunting for her necklace.

'It's fine,' I tell her. 'They look like they've got enough on their plate.'

One of the hairdressers shuffles awkwardly into the room. 'Erm, Amy, I really need to start your hair,' she says softly.

'I need to find my necklace,' Amy says, raising her voice slightly at the poor girl.

'OK, bridezilla,' I say gently, pulling her out of the wardrobe. 'Go get your hair done. I'll find your necklace, I promise.'

'Are you sure?' Amy asks. 'Because I can't get married without it.'

'I'm sure. Go, go.'

Amy reluctantly leaves the room, leaving me alone, surrounded by mess, with the impossible task of finding the silver locket her gran gave her. Her gran passed away not too long ago, so I know how much it means to her to be able to wear this today.

Where is this bloody necklace? Nothing annoys me more than a question that I can't google to find the answer to – not that I could google this anyway. My phone is completely flat and Ted has taken his iPhone charger with him. Do you know what? It's kind of liberating, this forced break from technology and social media. Not that anyone was going to contact me anyway.

OK, universe. I don't ask you for much but this is for Amy. Please, tell me where to look. Just give me a sign or something – ideally a sign that doesn't involve a tattoo that I'll be stuck with for the rest of my life.

As I laugh at myself for being so ridiculous, something catches my eye. The corner of a blue scarf falls from the top shelf of the wardrobe and hangs in the air. That was spooky. I know Amy was just in there a few minutes ago but this just fell, just now. I walk over to it cautiously. Is the universe really offering to help me for a second time? I reach up and tug the scarf, only for it to send a box full of CDs crashing down on me. One CD in particular lands on my bare foot, corner first.

'Fuck, fuck, fuck, fuck,' I rant in pain.

I pick up the offending CD, and it's a compilation of karaoke classics. Of the five tracks it boasts proudly on the front of the box, the first one it lists is 'Love Shack', and it makes me think of Danny.

'Fucking universe. Fuck you!'

I look down at my foot and see that it's bleeding. It might not be as bad as a tattoo, but I'll certainly have a scar to show for my second attempt at cosmic ordering.

I hop to the bathroom, desperately trying not to drip blood on the cream carpet. (I mean, seriously, who has a cream carpet?) Once inside I grab some toilet roll and hold it on the cut until the bleeding stops before examining the nasty gash. This is definitely going to show in the shoe I'm wearing today. Perhaps if I stick a plaster on it, maybe a flesh-coloured one, it might not look so obvious.

I limp towards the sink and open the door on the medicine cabinet in front of me. I spy a box of plasters and grab them, and what else is underneath but the necklace we've been hunting for, just sitting there on the shelf, all alone.

I laugh and shake my head. The universe really needs to work on a more gentle approach.

I prance downstairs victoriously, where I find Amy having her hair curled. Lea, Amy's bitch-bridesmaid that I hate, is sitting next to her. They're flicking through a copy of *The Daily Scoop*.

'I don't think I've ever seen a tabloid in your hands,' I can't help but blurt out. Amy has many causes, opinions and good fights to fight, and I know that reading tabloid news does not fit any of her agendas.

'I'm redirecting my anger,' she tells me. 'Their Bikini Babez feature is the objectification of women.'

She throws the newspaper across the room.

'It's nice to see it's working.' I laugh. 'Anyway, be angry no more, because I found it.'

'You found it?' Amy squeaks, jumping up from her seat mid curl, causing her to have one piece of hair that is very straight. I notice the pained look on the hairdresser's face and can't help but feel sorry for her. Amy is such a chilled person, but this wedding is making her loco. 'Where was it?'

'In the bathroom cabinet.'

'What? That's so weird. Well, thank you. You're a lifesaver.'

I smile and shrug my shoulders, to let her know it was nothing.

'So, we get to meet this mysterious boyfriend today then,' Lea says to me. There's a tone to her voice, like maybe she doesn't believe me. Typical that I really am single now, so no boyfriend is going to be here. I don't want to give her the satisfaction though.

'He has to work,' I lie, but it's a waste of my breath. The look on her face confirms that she doesn't believe me.

'Oh no, does he?' Amy says, continuing the lie, but in a not particularly convincing manner. 'That's a shame.'

'Yeah, well, maybe next time,' I joke, giving my friend a playful push back towards her chair.

'Oi, there won't be a next time.' She laughs, sitting back down.

I head back upstairs, to make a start putting Amy's room back to normal while I'm waiting for my turn to have my hair done. If there's one thing I'm good at, it's tidying. It's just a shame I can't clean up my own mess.

Chapter 43

Amy and Ted tied the knot at the Woodland Park Estate, just outside Manchester. They exchanged their vows down by the lake, in front of their family and their closest friends. They couldn't have hoped for better weather. It was neither too hot nor too cold, without so much as a hint of breeze, and the sun shining brightly in the sky. They have a beautiful wooden altar for wedding ceremonies here, with a stunning archway covered in perfect white roses, and both Amy and Ted looked cool as hell in their alternative outfits: a big, cream floaty dress for Amy and Ted in a white shirt with the sleeves rolled up, with grey trousers and a grey waistcoat. I have to admit, for a hipster, Ted wears the look well. They look great together, like one of those cool couples everyone is jealous of. You just know that they'll be happy together, having so much fun doing super cool, eco-friendly things. Jealous? Moi?

The reception is in full swing now, and compared to the subtle ceremony, the after-party is lavish and huge.

Amy and Ted are having their first dance to REO Speedwagon's 'Keep On Loving You' when the DJ announces that the bride and groom would love it if other couples would join them on the dance floor. It feels like almost everyone gets up to dance – certainly everyone from the top table – everyone but me.

'Aw, it's a shame this elusive fella of yours left you hanging, isn't it?' Lea says smugly as she gets up to dance with her boyfriend.

'I'd never leave her hanging,' a voice from behind me says.

It's that familiar Geordie accent that I've grown to love over the past week.

I turn around and see Danny standing there, suited and booted and looking incredible.

'And you are?' Lea asks.

'Danny Wright,' he introduces himself, offering her his hand to shake. 'Nice to meet you.'

I feel my jaw drop. 'You're my "Mr Wright"?' I ask, much to the confusion of the other guests listening to our conversation.

'I am,' Danny tells me. 'And you're my "Miss Hart".'

Danny begins unbuttoning his trousers.

'What are you doing?' I ask. 'You can't take your pants off at a wedding,' I remind him, just in case he might've missed that life lesson at some point.

Danny lets his trousers fall to the floor before turning around and lowering his boxers just enough to show me that he has 'Miss Hart' tattooed on his arse.

'Fancy a dance?' he asks.

'Go on then,' I reply, a big smile on my face, not only because I'm happy to see him, but also because Lea looks so jealous she might throw up.

Danny leads me to the dance floor and takes hold of me like a pro.

'Hi,' he says softly.

'Hello,' I reply. 'What are you doing here?'

'I promised you I'd be here, didn't I? I owed you one.'

As we move slowly around the dance floor something occurs to me. 'I didn't tell you where the wedding was though.'

'Yeah, and I've spent all day trying to figure it out, but I didn't know anyone who knew you and the bride – it was a nightmare. That's why I'm so late.'

'How did you work it out?' I ask curiously.

'Just when I thought I was out of options, I found your iPad in the Love Bug. Found the info in your calendar.'

'Oh, that was lucky. Wait,' I start as Danny dips me. 'I have a passcode on my iPad.'

'Yeah, let's not dwell on that,' he chuckles, flashing me those dimples that make me melt.

'So, you're my "Mr Wright"?'

'I was scared to tell you at the time,' he explains. 'And I was terrified to tell you about the "Miss Hart" tattoo on my arse – I thought you'd hate that even more than you'd hate having my name on you. It's been hard hiding it from you.' He laughs.

Danny Wright. So Danny is literally my 'Mr Wright', the one whose name will be forever on my arse. I feel like the universe is playing a cruel joke on me for mocking cosmic ordering so much, or maybe it worked exactly as it was supposed to and I've just been too stubborn to accept it all this time.

'No topknot – again,' I observe.

'Well, I wanted to look smart – again. When you were pretending to be my girlfriend, you reined in the Stepford thing. Now, I'm pretending to be your boyfriend, the least I can do is pretend I'm cool.'

My face falls at his use of the word 'pretending', but I try not to let it show.

'You're not that good an actor,' I tease.

I lean forward and rest my head on Danny's chest, just enjoying a moment of being close to him after I was so sure he'd never speak to me again. Even if he is only here out of duty, everything feels OK when I'm in his arms.

'I don't want to pretend,' Danny whispers into my ear.

I look him in the eye, surprised he still wants anything to do with me.

'You make me feel like no one else ever has. Like I might like to stay still.'

'That's funny, because you make me feel like I want to go places.' I laugh.

'So we bring out the best in each other,' he concludes.

'I suppose we do.'

'I never expected to fall for you,' he explains. 'Even after everything that happened in London, I knew I wanted to spend more time with you, but I've never been the kind to lock things down… But seeing Will try to worm his way back in with you – it made my blood boil. Like when that fake copper was having a go at you, or those skaters were asking me if you were my mum – '

'I knew they were making fun of me,' I interrupt.

'I'll never be able to stand by and watch anyone hurt you, and if that means I have to be around you all the time, to keep you out of trouble, then so be it,' he jokes, well aware he's usually the person who lands me in trouble.

I glance over at Amy who is dancing with Ted. Her arms are wrapped around his neck, but she manages to give me a thumbs up.

'You make me feel like that emoji with the hearts for eyes,' he explains.

'You make me feel like this emoji…' I pout my lips and wink my eye.

'There's a constipated emoji?' he asks. I playfully slap his face.

'Well, bro, what next?'

'I quit my job,' I tell him.

'*You* quit your job?' he asks.

'Why is everyone so surprised by this? Yes, I quit my job. About thirty seconds after you left and thirty seconds before I left Will in a bloody mess on the floor. I shouldn't have even given him the chance to explain.'

'Don't worry about it,' he tells me, placing his hands either side of my face. 'It's a new and weird emotion for me, but I felt jealous. I was worried I was going to lose you to that prick.'

'Never,' I tell him. 'I never want to see him again – and now I'm unemployed, I don't have to.'

'Well, where shall we go?' he asks. 'Anywhere you want. We

can travel across America, sunbathe in the Caribbean – we can even climb Everest if you like.'

'Hmm.' I think for a moment. 'To be honest, I'd quite like to go back to the North West Pole and get my twerk on.'

The song finishes and a much faster one comes on.

'Well, you don't need to go to the Isle of Man to do that.' He laughs, twirling me.

As I dance with Danny, it just feels like something has truly fallen into place for me. It's like he just makes me happy without even trying.

As annoying as it is, and as much as I cringe to say it, if Danny has taught me anything, it's just how spot-on his YOLO attitude is. He is absolutely right. You do only live once, and it's important to make the most of it. Life is too short to be anyone's plan B or their dirty little secret. If you love someone, you should tell them and show them every single day, because you never know when your or their time is up.

Time spent worrying about what is going to happen is truly a waste, because as hard as we try, we're not always going to have control over everything. If we can change what's worrying us then we don't need to worry, we just need to change it. If we can't change it, then what's the point worrying? All we can do is live in the moment, drinking up every last drop of life, making the most of it. Because you know what? We really do only live once and it's up to us to make that once count. This is it, right here, right now. This moment.

Teenage years a distant memory? No husband, no house and no kids? Trapped in that middle ground where you no longer feel like a kid, but you're not quite a fully functioning adult either? Looking at the lives of the girls you went to school with on Facebook, it couldn't be easier to monitor just how far off-track your life has gone in comparison. They seem to have their shit all figured out, but who says that's the track you have to take? Wear dresses so short pro sportsmen mistake you for a prostitute if you want to.

Get ridiculous tattoos. Eat whatever you want, so long as you're happy and you're healthy. It's OK to have no idea where your life is leading you. Your best friend might have the next ten years of her life all planned out, and you might not know what you're having for dinner tonight, but it's fine. I have no idea where life with Danny will lead me, but this just excites me more.

Danny pulls me close and kisses me.

'You see everyone staring at us?' he asks.

I glance around and notice that we do have a few pairs of eyes on us.

'What are they looking at?' I ask.

'The Geordie lad, desperately in need of a haircut, dancing with the most beautiful girl in the room.'

I smile, so widely my cheeks ache.

It doesn't matter where you are in life, as long as you're living it.

Truth or Date

Ruby Wood is perfectly happy playing the dating game – until she has a red-hot dream about her *very* attractive flatmate, Nick. He might spend every day saving lives as a junior doctor, but he's absolutely the last man on earth that fun-loving Ruby would ever date.

The solution? Focus on all of Nick's bad points. And if that fails, up her dating antics and find herself a man. So what if she manages to make disapproving, goody two-shoes Nick jealous in the process …

Only, after a series of nightmare first dates, there's still just one man on Ruby's mind. Maybe it's time to admit the truth and dare to ask Nick to be her next date?

Always the Bridesmaid

Rom-com writer Mia Valentina has it all – money, success and a glamorous LA lifestyle. But when a wedding invitation arrives, demanding her presence as chief bridesmaid for her sister Belle, chaos ensues.

Mia's barely been back in England before she accidentally injures the groom, unintentionally 'curses' the wedding, and finds herself in a compromising position with her sister's soon-to-be brother-in-law.

With the wedding of the year spiralling out of control and best man and fireman Leo by her side, will Mia use her rom-com expertise to save the day?

Here Comes the Ex

Luca is used to being 'the single one' – which is partly why she dreaded going to the wedding of an old university friend. Surrounded by faces she hasn't seen in 10 years, Luca can feel herself being sucked back into the immature, decade-old gossip that no one seems to have forgotten.

But when Tom walks in, Luca's heart stops. He was her 'almost boyfriend', and she had been completely swept off her feet by him … but he's currently standing next to the girl he broke her heart with at a party all those years ago.

As the evening draws on and the champagne continues to flow, it's clear that Tom can't take his eyes off her. Will Luca's luck in love finally take a turn?

Acknowledgements

A massive thank you to my editors, Victoria and Charlotte, and to the rest of the HQ Digital UK team for all of their hard work on my books.

A shoutout to my Pink Ink girls, Tay and all the lovely reviewers for all of their support. Thank you to everyone who has bought a copy of any of my books, and thank you for all the lovely feedback - I hope you enjoy this one as much as my others.

Finally, huge thanks to my family and friends for all of their support. And for celebrating every little victory with me with cocktails/coffee.

Dear Reader,

We hope you enjoyed reading this book. If you did, we'd be so appreciative if you left a review. It really helps us and the author to bring more books like this to you.

Here at HQ Digital we are dedicated to publishing fiction that will keep you turning the pages into the early hours. Don't want to miss a thing? To find out more about our books, promotions, discover exclusive content and enter competitions you can keep in touch in the following ways:

JOIN OUR COMMUNITY:

Sign up to our new email newsletter:
http://smarturl.it/SignUpHQ

Read our new blog www.hqstories.co.uk

𝕏 https://twitter.com/HQStories

f www.facebook.com/HQStories

BUDDING WRITER?

We're also looking for authors to join the HQ Digital family!
Find out more here:

https://www.hqstories.co.uk/want-to-write-for-us/

Thanks for reading, from the HQ Digital team

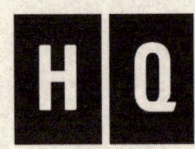